1 (or more) murders

A WINNING RECIPE FOR MYSTERY LOVERS

Don't miss these Hemlock Falls Mysteries . . .

A PUREE OF POISON . . .
While residents celebrate the 133rd anniversary of the Battle of Hemlock Falls, the Quilliam sisters investigate the deaths of three people who dined at the Inn before checking out . . .

FRIED BY JURY . . .
Two rival fried chicken restaurants are about to set up shop in Hemlock Falls—and the Quilliams have to turn up the heat when the competition turns deadly . . .

JUST DESSERTS . . .
There's a meteorologist convention coming to the Inn, and it's up to Quill and Meg to make sure an elusive killer doesn't make murder part of the forecast . . .

MARINADE FOR MURDER . . .
The Quilliams's plans for the future of the Inn may end up on the cutting room floor when a group of TV cartoon writers checks in—and their producer checks out . . .

A STEAK IN MURDER . . .
While trying to sell the locals on the idea of raising their own herds, a visiting Texas cattleman gets sent to that big trail drive in the sky. The Quilliams set out to catch the culprit and reclaim their precious Inn . . . without getting stampeded themselves!

continued . . .

A TOUCH OF THE GRAPE . . .
Five women jewelry makers are a welcome change from the tourist slump the Inn is having—until two of the ladies end up dead, and the Quilliams are on the hunt for a crafty killer.

DEATH DINES OUT . . .
While working for a charity in Palm Beach, the Quilliam sisters uncover a vengeful plot that has a wealthy socialite out to humiliate her husband. Now the sleuths must convince the couple to bury the hatchet—before they bury each other.

MURDER WELL-DONE . . .
When the Inn hosts the wedding rehearsal dinner for an ex-senator, someone begins cutting down the guest list in a most deadly way. And Quill and Meg have to catch a killer before the rehearsal dinner ends up being someone's last meal.

A PINCH OF POISON . . .
Hendrick Conway is a nosy newsman who thinks something funny is going on at a local development project. But when two of his relatives are killed, the Quilliam sisters race against a deadline of their own . . .

A DASH OF DEATH . . .
Quill and Meg are on the trail of the murderer of two local women who won a design contest. Helena Houndswood, a noted expert of stylish living, was furious when she lost. But mad enough to kill?

A TASTE FOR MURDER . . .
The annual History Days festival takes a deadly turn when a reenactment of a seventeenth-century witch trial leads to twentieth century murder. Since the victim is a paying guest, the least Quill and Meg could do is investigate . . .

BURIED BY BREAKFAST

CLAUDIA BISHOP

BERKLEY PRIME CRIME, NEW YORK

THE BERKLEY PUBLISHING GROUP
Published by the Penguin Group
Penguin Group (USA) Inc.
375 Hudson Street, New York, New York 10014, USA
Penguin Group (Canada), 10 Alcorn Avenue, Toronto, Ontario M4V 3B2, Canada
(a division of Pearson Penguin Canada Inc.)
Penguin Books Ltd., 80 Strand, London WC2R 0RL, England
Penguin Group Ireland, 25 St. Stephen's Green, Dublin 2, Ireland (a division of Penguin Books Ltd.)
Penguin Group (Australia), 250 Camberwell Road, Camberwell, Victoria 3124, Australia
(a division of Pearson Australia Group Pty. Ltd.)
Penguin Books India Pvt. Ltd., 11 Community Centre, Panchsheel Park, New Delhi—110 017, India
Penguin Group (NZ), Cnr. Airborne and Rosedale Roads, Albany, Auckland 1310, New Zealand
(a division of Pearson New Zealand Ltd.)
Penguin Books (South Africa) (Pty.) Ltd., 24 Sturdee Avenue, Rosebank, Johannesburg 2196, South
Africa

Penguin Books Ltd., Registered Offices: 80 Strand, London WC2R 0RL, England

This is a work of fiction. Names, characters, places, and incidents either are the product of the author's imagination or are used fictitiously, and any resemblance to actual persons, living or dead, business establishments, events, or locales is entirely coincidental.

BURIED BY BREAKFAST

A Berkley Prime Crime Book / published by arrangement with the author

PRINTING HISTORY
Berkley Prime Crime mass-market edition / December 2004

Copyright © 2004 by Mary Stanton.
Cover design by George Long.
Cover art by Mary Anne Lasher.

ISBN: 0-425-19945-2

Berkley Prime Crime Books are published by The Berkley Publishing Group,
a division of Penguin Group (USA) Inc.,
375 Hudson Street, New York, New York 10014.
The name BERKLEY PRIME CRIME and the BERKLEY PRIME CRIME design are trademarks
belonging to Penguin Group (USA) Inc.

PRINTED IN THE UNITED STATES OF AMERICA

10 9 8 7 6 5 4 3 2 1

For Kate and Rebecca,
who run the best Inn in New York

CAST OF CHARACTERS

THE INN AT HEMLOCK FALLS:

Sarah "Quill" Quilliam	manager and owner
Margaret "Meg" Quilliam	her sister, chef and owner
Doreen Muxworthy-Stoker	head housekeeper
Dina Muir	receptionist
John Raintree	part-time business manager
Kathleen Kiddermeister	head waitress
Mike Santini	groundskeeper
Corisande Quilliam	Quill and Meg's cousin
Donald Dunleavy	president, The People's Police
Mitchell Moody	Chief Justice of the Supreme Court of the State of New York
Bouncer Muldoon	Juror #1, a truck driver
Muriel May Johnson	Juror #2, a civil servant
Sparky Stillwater	Juror #3, a software engineer
Brett Coldwell	Juror #4, retired Air Force pilot
Tony D'Agnetti	Juror #5, a mechanic
Maryann McAllister	Juror #6
Pat Pembroke	court liason; a housewife
Morgan Mwgambe	Juror alternate
Rebecca Galloway	for the prosecution
Porker Stuyvesant	for the defense
Max	a dog

And assorted court reporters, bailiffs, waiters, waitresses, and housemaids

CITZENS OF HEMLOCK FALLS

Myles McHale	sheriff and investigator
Davey Kiddermeister	acting sheriff
Elmer Henry	the mayor
Adela Henry	his wife
Andy Bishop	an internist, Meg's fiancé
Marge Schmidt	a businesswoman
Betty Hall	Marge's partner
Dookie Shuttleworth	minister, Hemlock Falls church
Miriam Doncaster	the librarian
Howie Murchison	town attorney
Harland Peterson	president of the Agway
Esther West	owner, West's Best Dress Shoppe
Carol Ann Spinoza	tax assessor
Harvey Bozzel	an advertising executive
Corliss Hooker	president, Friends of the Dead
Melvin Purvis	FBI (and no relation)
Ferris Rodman	CEO, ROCOR Construction

and others . . .

PROLOGUE

Nothing had changed about the cemetery. Nothing. It had been a different time of year, then. The leaves had been out on the beech trees, and most of the gravestones had been covered with thick spring grass. But snow blanketed almost everything now. The place where she'd been laid to rest was mounded high with white.

There was some saying—half-remembered, the way so many things were now—about the good being interred with the bones of the dead. It was the evil that lived after them, wasn't it?

The evil.

CHAPTER 1

"I'm so sorry I'm late, Quill," Mrs. Pembroke said. "You wouldn't believe how hard it was to get the green paint off my face. But you didn't have much else on this morning, did you? It isn't as though the Inn is bursting with guests this time of year." She settled herself into a chair at the conference table in Sarah Quilliam's office and smiled in a perfunctory way. "I'm afraid there's some remnants over my right ear." She opened her purse, removed a hand mirror, gazed intently into it, and pushed her silver curls aside. "There. Can you see it?"

Quill leaned forward. "There's a bit," she admitted. She suppressed a sigh. When Mrs. Pembroke had requested yet another planning meeting, she'd been pretty firm about keeping it to twenty minutes. Since Mrs. Pembroke was already twenty minutes late for her appointment, and then spent another twenty in inconsequent chatter, it looked as though her day was going to fray into its usual chaotic bits. "There's a ladies' room right off the foyer if you'd like to tidy up a bit."

"You seem to be in quite a hurry, this morning," Mrs. Pembroke said virtuously. "And a visit to the ladies' would take more time." She licked her forefinger and dabbed at the green spot, smearing it further along one wrinkled cheekbone. She looked into the mirror and turned her face from side to side. "I think that's it."

Quill refrained from reaching for a tissue to scrub the green goo away; Mrs. Pembroke had been coming to the Inn off and on for years, but she was the sort of elderly lady who found physical contact an intrusion. Instead she asked with a smile, "How *did* the Friends of the Dead protest go yesterday?"

Mrs. Pembroke pursed her mouth and said, "Pah! We're down to two members. Nobody has the guts to protest anymore. Corliss Hooker and I walked up and down the street in front of the cemetery for hours. And do you know what? Not one reporter showed up. Not one policeman issued a citation. Not one citizen of Hemlock Falls stopped to sign our petition. And we both went to all the trouble of painting our faces green and dressing up in those very drafty black robes. And I had made certain to e-mail the press releases *and* follow up with phone calls to CBS and CNN. 'I'm sorry,' I said to Corliss, 'but I am afraid I'm withdrawing my support.' I took off my robe and handed it over to him right where I stood. And do you know what he said to me?"

Mrs. Pembroke's white ruffled blouse swelled with in-dignation.

Quill shook her head and looked sympathetic.

"He said I was obviously not a true Friend of the Dead. I most certainly *am,* I told him, with my own dear daughter dead these many years, but I am not indiscrim-inant. I mean, am I a friend of the corpse of Adolf Hitler? I am not. Would I befriend the remains of Attila the Hun? I would not."

Since the list of the dead whom Mrs. Pembroke wouldn't befriend was certainly lengthy (if not exhaus-tive), Quill interrupted gently. "Not only that, Mrs. Pem-broke, but the F.O.D.'s protest, while noble in intent, is just not going to change Ferris Rodman's relocation plans. The courts ruled that he could move the Civil War cemetery to make room for a golf course, and it looks like that's just what's going to happen. I think you were right to turn in your robe and resign your membership."

"Who gives a damn, anyway?" Mrs. Pembroke said. "If it weren't for Elaine's dear memory, I never would have gotten mixed up with Corliss Hooker in the first place. You can't possibly know what it's like, to lose a child." Quill took some tissues from her desk and placed them in Mrs. Pembroke's hands. Mrs. Pembroke's daughter had died years and years ago, but the loss, it seemed, was still fresh.

She dabbed carefully at the corner of each eye, smear-ing her blue eye shadow into the green makeup. Quill couldn't stand the color combination—or the unexpect-edly fierce cast it gave to Mrs. Pembroke's rose-leaf features. "Excuse me," she murmured and leaned forward to gently dab at the makeup with a tissue.

"Thank you, my dear," Mrs. Pembroke said crossly. She sighed deeply. "Of course, you'll get some sense of a true mother's feelings when your cousin arrives tomorrow, won't you?"

Mrs. Pembroke had been delighted to hear that Meg and Quill had family coming to stay, "Because," she had said, "there's nothing quite like one's own blood."

"One's own family, at any rate," Quill had said cheerfully. Now she said, "Yes, Meg and I are delighted. Corisande wants to learn to cook, you know. Meg's spent all last week setting up lesson plans."

"I just hope she's not drug-ridden, like so many of these young people."

"I'm sure she isn't," Quill said, in mild protest.

"And she's not married?"

"She's quite young."

"Then she's sex-mad. They're all sex-mad these days, too. Hm! Well!" Mrs. Pembroke rummaged in her capacious purse, withdrew her PDA, and tapped at the tiny keyboard with expert, if gnarled, fingers. Despite her often-expressed contempt for modern music, modern politics, and the twenty-first century in general, she'd taken to computer technology like a goat to tin cans. "My time's valuable, Quill, and you're certainly wasting it with these sidebar chats of ours. The Tompkins County Court system is paying me fifteen dollars an hour to get things done, not to sit here gossiping with you."

Ten years of innkeeping experience had left Quill unfazed by a wide—and occasionally disconcerting—range of human behavior. So she merely said, "Of course. What can we do for you today?"

Despite her fluffy white hair, china blue eyes, and decorous navy blue suits, Mrs. Pembroke was one tough cookie. She leveled a laser-like gaze at Quill, and said firmly, "My room."

"Your room?"

"I feel that I should be here for the duration of the trial. The arrangements are bound to go wrong. You and your sister Meg have not undergone a sequestration before. And I may have mentioned how particular my son-in-law is."

She certainly had. Quill suppressed a second sigh. When she thought about it, she spent a lot of time suppressing sighs in Mrs. Pembroke's company. Retired for seven years as a court reporter in the Tompkins County Court system, she had strong-armed her way into a part-time job as a Facilitator. (Unfamiliar at first with the duties of a court-appointed Facilitator, Quill had asked Howie Murchison, the Town Justice for the village of Hemlock Falls. Howie had laughed and said, "Old Mrs. Pembroke? Doesn't have quite enough retirement money. Let's just say a grateful county has pensioned her off. And that she's Judge Moody's former mother-in-law.")

Mrs. Pembroke coughed delicately, her usual preface to an impossible request. "I was, of course, highly instrumental in advising the court to sequester the jury

5

here. And let's face it, Quill, the Inn's busy enough in the spring and summer months, but in winter, everyone avoids this place like the plague."

"We're always a little slow in March," Quill admitted. "But I hardly think—"

"It's not too much to say that I have made this month very, very profitable for you."

Quill bit her lip. The state employee who handled the per diem for sequestered juries clearly thought Silas Marner should have left little Effie in the snowbank. The state-supported presence of six jurors, three lawyers, a bailiff, and the notorious State Supreme Court Justice Mitchell "Time for Justice" Moody would barely pay the salaries of the staff required to serve them. On the other hand, Mrs. Pembroke had managed to stretch her consulting job into a full month of meetings and phone calls and conferences, so maybe the State had to make up the resulting budget deficit somewhere. Like insisting on BudgetInn prices for the Inn's lavish suites.

"So we're agreed? You will comp my room." This wasn't a question.

Quill made a last, admittedly feeble, stab to at least keep the Inn out of the red. "Then the State hasn't agreed to pay your per diem, Mrs. Pembroke?"

Mrs. Pembroke made a rude comment about the political party currently in office, then said briskly, "So that's settled. I will take the Provençal suite. Now, you have all the memoranda filed regarding the rules and regulations about the staff's rules of conduct?"

Quill tugged her ear a little nervously. "Umm, yes, of course."

"May I see the file?"

"It's in my apartment," Quill improvised freely. "I keep it up there in case I wake up during the night and need to review it."

"Very proper," Mrs. Pembroke said. "Now, if I might have a little tea before I drive home, we can conclude today's meeting." She checked her tiny silver watch and tapped into her PDA: "Meeting with Inn Management, 8:00 A.M. to 10:00 A.M." Quill glanced at the carriage clock on her desk; Mrs. Pembroke must be counting on either a half dozen cups of tea or sipping very, very slowly. It was only nine o'clock. It was also time for Kathleen to help ease Mrs. Pembroke out of the office so that Quill could begin her day.

There was a tap at Quill's office door. Quill called, "Come in," and Kathleen Kiddermeister, their head waitress, opened the door and stuck her head inside.

"Quill? You told me you wanted to be interrupted at nine. It's nine. I'm interrupting you."

"Yes!" Quill said a little too loudly. "The staff meeting. Thank you, Kath."

"There's a staff meeting?" Kathleen said. "Gosh, Quill, not another one. It's not about the jury business, is it? We've had this jury business up the wazoo."

"Would you take Mrs. Pembroke to the dining room, please? And ask the kitchen for a high tea?"

"But it's only nine o'clock in the—"

"And Meg has the information on the staff meeting. She should be in the kitchen."

"Where else would Meg be? Sure. Follow me, Mrs. Pembroke."

Quill got up, guided her difficult visitor straight to Kathleen, closed the door behind them, and sank back in her office chair. Her sister Meg would tell Kathleen, of course, there wasn't any staff meeting, remind their waitress that this was supposed to be Quill's day off, and curse a blue streak at having to prepare a high tea at nine o'clock in the morning.

But, hooray, hooray—Quill now had the rest of the day to herself. She could begin on that series of sketches she'd promised the gallery in New York.

Four hours, one tuna fish sandwich, and four cups of coffee later, Quill still didn't have any idea of what she wanted to draw. She had the whole afternoon to herself and she wanted to spend it sketching; she needed to spend it sketching and if she didn't come up with something soon, she was going to have to call her agent Claire in New York and tell her that was it—she, Quill, was never going to paint again, and the heck with her career as an artist.

Of course, if she didn't spend it sketching, she could also spend it taking a nap and sketch tomorrow.

She sat in an easy chair in the far corner of the Tavern Lounge. Max the dog was asleep on the floor next to her. Her empty sketchbook was in her lap, her charcoal pencil was in her hand, and her feet were propped on the ceramic pot that held a hibernating poinsettia left over from the holidays. The Inn was quiet, and she had time to work.

If she could think of something to work on.

"I'm drawing a blank," she said.

Max failed to express his opinion of this wordplay. And there wasn't anyone else around to groan. Quill tugged at her hair, scrubbed her face with both hands, and sighed. What about Mrs. Pembroke's face? Quill thought about it for a long moment. No. Too—something. Too self-absorbed. A true sketch of Mrs. Pembroke would be unkind.

Maybe looking for a human subject was a bad idea. Nature might have more to offer.

Quill regarded the poinsettia's naked stems. Nate the bartender claimed it was hibernating. It was Quill's own opinion that the plant was dead. Normally she liked the ironic in her work, but this was a bit much. She looked down at Max, who, as the world's ugliest (but smartest) dog, was equally uninspiring as a subject.

She yawned, stretched, and wriggled her toes. The Tavern Lounge was peaceful. Pine logs snapped cheerfully in the fireplace. Nate hummed "Take This Job and Shove It" happily through his nose while he polished wineglasses at the long mahogany bar. Nobody sat at the twenty or so round tables scattered across the oak floor; the Lounge didn't open until four o'clock in the winter, when the skiers and snowmobilers drifted in from the cold.

Max grunted, rolled, and began to snore.

Quill sat back in mounting irritation. Okay. Back to

work. If she could come up with some quirk of an image, some oddity of thought, she could start to draw.

Forget people, poinsettias, and pooches as inspiration. What about the view?

She looked through the French doors to the flagstone terrace outside. The Tavern Lounge had a full view of the falls. Sleet had turned the piles of snow on the stone to slush, and left melted indentations in the snow cover all the way down to Hemlock Gorge. The waterfall spilled over the lip of the ravine like an icy silver scarf. Quill had painted the waterfall once and bored herself silly in the process. She needed a weightier subject. Less sentimental. Something with gravitas.

Quill adjusted her charcoal pencil to the flat side. Then she adjusted it back to the pointed side.

She hadn't yet explored the fantastic in her work. Think Swinburne and his glamorous monsters. Or maybe Aubrey Beardsley and that weird way he combined precision of line with the baroque. She pushed out her lower lip. What about graphic novels? There was some wonderful work being done these days in comics. She could do a superhero dressed in one of those finicky Edwardian tea gowns, maybe. Terrific. This would stretch her artistic vision. And about time, too.

Pleased, Quill finally started to draw.

"That's bizarre. Don't tell me *you've* joined those idiots."

That tin-whistle, prim little voice could only belong to one person. Quill looked up at Carol Ann Spinoza, Hemlock's Falls' nastiest (and only) tax assessor. Quill should have been warned of her approach by the scent of soap—one of the creepiest things about Carol Ann was her fanatic cleanliness—but she'd been too absorbed in her drawing. "Which idiots?" she said.

"The Friends of the Dead." Carol Ann's clear blue eyes were guileless. Sometimes Quill thought the most dangerous thing about Carol Ann was that she had the face of a high school prom queen. "That drawing you're making looks like a fat skeleton."

"That's an oxymoron," Quill said.

Carol Ann's peaches-and-cream complexion flushed bright red.

"An oxymoron is two words with opposite meanings," Quill said hastily, "I wasn't calling *you* a moron."

"Right," Carol Ann said flatly. "Anyway. It's just like you, Quill, to join something like the Friends of the Dead."

"I haven't joined the Friends of the Dead."

"Who are you people, anyway, trying to prevent the Civil War cemetery from being moved? You're all a bunch of crackpots, if you'll excuse the expression."

"I won't excuse the expression, and I *haven't* joined F.O.D. I'm not drawing a skeleton. It's a superhero in Edwardian dress." Quill frowned at the drawing. To her annoyance, it did look like a fat skeleton. She added a large feathered hat to her superhero and erased some of the ribbing on the cape.

"It's not just me that thinks the Friends of the Dead are a bunch of crackpots," Carol Ann said. "Everybody else does, too. When the town gets bigger it's better for everybody, and who cares if a bunch of hundred-and-fifty-year-old corpses get dug up and stuck somewhere else so we can add a nice new hotel there?"

"Hotel?" Quill said, startled. "What hotel? I thought the resort people wanted to use the land to build a golf course."

"Oops!" Carol Ann covered her whiter-than-white teeth with her clean pink hand. "Forget what I said about the hotel."

Quill looked at her skeptically.

"Really. Forget I said that. I promised not to say a word. And here's silly me, blabbing all over the place. I keep telling myself, 'Carol Ann, you've got to stop being so impulsive.'"

Right. Carol Ann was as impulsive as a stalking ninja. Quill counted backward from ten. Silently. While she counted she thought: What hotel? How big a hotel? Someone is building a new hotel in Hemlock Falls? Will there be enough visitors for two hotels? She'd have to get down to the village as soon as she got rid of Carol Ann and talk to their business manager, John Raintree. John would be the first one to know if a hotel were going to be built not a quarter mile from the Inn and bankrupt them all in two weeks.

Carol Ann waved her hands in front of Quill's face and said, "Hel-lo. Earth to Quill," which irritated Quill so much she almost stuck her charcoal pencil up Carol Ann's nose. "So," she said shortly, "What's up, Carol Ann?"

"You crazy people from F.O.D., for one thing," she responded huffily. "All that marching is very disruptive."

Quill, who had refused to be drawn into any discussion about the propriety of relocating the cemetery with any of Hemlock Falls' citizens ever since F.O.D had started their protests a month ago, wasn't about to start with Carol Ann. She said, somewhat repetitiously, "Is there a specific reason why you're here?"

Carol Ann ignored the question and peered over Quill's shoulder at the sketch pad. "I could never figure out why you're supposed to be so famous. My six-year-old child Ashley could do better than that stuff."

Quill shifted away from Carol Ann's penetrating eye and kept on sketching. She added a coiled snake around the feet of her superhero. Then she drew a little bomb next to the snake and lettered in "tick-tick-tick."

"Although, now that I think of it, I can see why you joined F.O.D. You and your sister might not want a hotel there. Too much competition, perhaps?" Carol Ann tossed her head so that her blond ponytail bounced. She smiled sweetly. Quill smiled sweetly back.

"The ROCOR resort people want the land for a golf course. The hotel's going up next to the beach on Hemlock River ten miles from here. And I'm *not* a member of the Friends of the Dead."

"Right," Carol Ann said. Then, with spurious kindliness, "Forget I said a *thing* about the hotel."

"And it wouldn't matter if ROCOR *did* put a hotel there," Quill added recklessly. "People who come to the

Inn at Hemlock Falls come here because they don't want to go to hotels. And what is it that brings you here anyway?"

Carol Ann's voice, always high-pitched and precise, went sticky-sweet. "As a matter of fact, I do have a small request."

Quill nudged Max awake with her toe. Carol Ann hated dogs, especially large, multicolored former strays that spent a lot of their spare time in Dumpsters. She sent Max a mental message: Jump! Paw! Slobber! Max gave Quill an aggrieved stare, rolled on his back, and went back to sleep.

Carol Ann rustled crisply into the armchair next to Quill. She didn't actually starch her clothes—nobody starched their clothes these days except maybe indicted chief financial officers so they wouldn't look wilted on the six o'clock news—but her chinos never wrinkled even when she moved, which irritated Quill almost as much as Carol Ann herself.

"You'll want to get in on the ground floor of this," Carol Ann said flatly. "It's going to be good for the whole town. And you want things that are good for the town. Even that new hotel. Right? You're just like me, Quill. We both want to help Hemlock Falls. And I've got a great way to do it."

Quill would sooner shave herself bald than ask how Carol Ann was going to help Hemlock Falls; nobody in his right mind offered a tax assessor that kind of opening. And she didn't want to ask Carol Ann how she could help her personally, either; Quill didn't care what happened to

Carol Ann, unless she had a terminal disease, in which case Quill would be more relieved than sympathetic. There was, now that she thought of it, absolutely no conversation of any kind that she wanted to have with this woman: not about her health, not about the village, and certainly not about her job.

Except for this ridiculous rumor about a new hotel. The resort people were trying to move the cemetery to make way for a golf course, and they weren't going to move the hotel. Carol Ann was just trying to drive her crazy. She gritted her teeth and injected a modicum of warmth into her voice. "Did you stop by for anything in particular?"

Carol Ann wriggled smugly. "You would call yourself a public-spirited person, wouldn't you, Quill?"

Quill hated these kinds of questions. "I suppose so."

Carol Ann smirked and blinked slowly, like a snake on a warm rock. "Then that's settled," she said.

"What's settled?"

"That you'll let me use the Conference Center for these very important meetings I'm holding next week."

"Important meetings?" Quill asked. "Well, I'd love to, but we're all . . ." She stopped herself just in time. If she said the Conference Center was all booked up with paying conference-goers, (as opposed to Carol Ann's conference-goers, who were obviously looking for a free ride) Carol Ann would file that away as a factor in assessing the taxable value of the Inn. Property taxes in New York state were already the highest in the known universe, as Quill and her sister Meg knew to their sorrow. "What kind of important meet-ings?"

"I'm starting a community police patrol."

Quill opened her mouth. Then she closed it.

"I contacted this very important guy in Syracuse and he's coming in to help us get started. I told him all about the Friends of the Dead and all the flak over moving that stupid cemetery and how vandalism was taking down the property values of this town and he's agreed to help."

"We're really understaffed this time of year," Quill said. "You know the Inn is a seasonal business and we tend to, umm, downsize in the winter. We wouldn't have anyone on staff to help serve coffee or clean up afterward . . ." She stopped right there. One of the most horrible parts of Carol Ann's horrible personality was that she exulted in cringing, whining, importunate taxpayers. Brave responsible taxpayers made her vengeful. Quill didn't consider herself especially brave, but she abhorred whining, and cringing made her back muscles cramp. Plus, she was lying when said they were short-staffed and Quill didn't lie unless it was absolutely unavoidable, and it almost never was. Social fibbing, on the other hand, was perfectly permissible. "As much as I'd like to, I don't think we can help you with this," she said firmly.

"You don't want to keep the citizens of Hemlock Falls safe from vandals, then." Carol Ann delivered this state-ment with triumph. Quill had a brief vision of Carol Ann plumped in a booth at the Croh Bar in the village, telling everyone who'd listen that Sarah Quilliam supported Berserkers and Visigoths.

"I'm not totally comfortable with the idea of a vigilante police force," Quill said, with less than scrupulous honesty. Actually, she thought they were a terrible idea. So did Myles McHale, her longtime and much-beloved companion. And Myles, retired from the NYPD and a consultant on terrorism for an international security firm, was certainly qualified to hold an opinion on vigilante police forces. "But it's not that. I don't know if we'd be allowed to have outside meetings here in the next few weeks anyway." This, as Quill knew very well, was an out-and-out fib, rather than the socially acceptable kind. She'd square it with her conscience later, because it was a fib that would get Carol Ann out of her hair and if she had to talk to the tax assessor one more minute she'd smack her right in her shiny white teeth. "You know that the State has asked us to house the sequestered jury for the *ROCOR v. Meecham* trial. The Chief Justice wants the jury to be able to walk to the site downriver, and we're the closest hotel there is to the site. The voir dire is today and tomorrow, and the jurors and the judge will be checking in by Wednesday at the latest. We can't have any other guests at the Inn while the jury's here. The state," Quill added a little lamely, "said so."

"Of course I considered that, *dear*," Carol Ann interrupted with vicious emphasis. "But as a town official, I'm not exactly an outsider, am I, *dear*? And if the town thinks what I decide about taxes is good enough for them, *dear*, so should you."

Carol Ann was never subtle. She was stupid, but she was direct.

17

"Carol Ann," Quill said patiently. "Voir dire is the term the courts use for jury selection. I didn't call you dear, and I certainly didn't mean to condescend."

"So you say." She stood up with a crisp crackling of her meticulously ironed shirt, lips thinned, hair wafting the scent of shampoo and Irish Spring. "You let the Chamber of Commerce use the Conference Center for free, and it's just sheer prejudice if you object to my meetings. And we all know what to do about sheer prejudice, don't we?"

Tax it? Quill sighed. She tugged at her hair. She weighed the annoyance of letting Carol Ann use the conference room for free against her urgent desire to discover more about the rumor about the new hotel at the Civil War cemetery. "Sit down, Carol Ann. Let's discuss this a little. Would you like some coffee? Or tea? On the house, of course, since we'll be discussing town business."

"I missed lunch," Carol Ann said, settling carefully back down at the table. "So I'll have the special. The one with the fresh crab. As long as that Finn in your kitchen knows enough about crab to rinse them three times in running water."

Quill firmly suppressed the image of Bjarne rinsing Carol Ann three times with a fire hose and motioned to Nate the bartender to come and take the order.

Carole Ann had let the facts about the proposed hotel fall in infuriatingly slow drips until well after she'd eaten the most expensive dessert on the menu. (Crème Puffs Saint-Honore.) ROCOR had decided it'd be good to give the vacationers coming to the new resort an option for gourmet weekends. It's just a small, exclusive hotel, she'd said. They were going ahead with the big, cheaper hotel downriver. The new place would have a European chef. It would cater to a small, upscale trade.

Quill winced. Except for the fact that her chef—her sister, Meg—was as American as *Monday Night Football*, it was a perfect description of the Inn at Hemlock Falls.

The thing was not to panic. Especially in front of her sister, the staff, and anybody else connected with the Inn.

Quill banged through the swinging doors to the kitchen an hour later and cried, " 'Beware the Ides of March!' "

"It's the twentieth." Her sister Meg stood frowning at the long birch prep table, a file folder in her hands. "Not the fifteenth. And who cares, anyway?" A low fire crackled in the cobblestone fireplace, and the scent of the dried herbs Meg strung from the kitchen rafters wafted through the air. Several of the sous chefs and one dishwasher worked peacefully at the stoves and sinks. Quill looked at the familiar, comfortable scene with a pang. How long would it take before it would all disappear into the rapacious maw of the bank?

" 'There's a voice in the crowd shriller than all the rest,' " Quill continued, improvising freely. "And it cries, 'Beware! Beware the Ides of March!' " She sat on a stool at the prep table and regarded Meg with affection. "Although I haven't been spending the last hour with the soothsayer in *Julius Caesar*."

"You haven't been spending it with Mrs. Pembroke? She ate about a gallon of whipped cream with her scones and took off somewhere. Her gastro-enterologist, I shouldn't wonder."

"Much worse than poor Mrs. Pembroke, who only drives me batty. I spent it with Carol Ann Spinoza, who is going to drive me to homicide. If I'd only recalled the soothsayer's warnings while I was looking for inspiration, I would have been out with Max for a walk when she slithered on in."

"Phooey." Meg tossed the manila folder into the trash basket.

"If you mean phooey on Carol Ann, I couldn't agree more. If you mean phooey on me, all I can say is, little do you know what battles with the barbarian hordes— that is, Carol Ann—I fight on behalf of our team, while you remain here in the kitchen, serenely cooking." She eyed Meg doubtfully. Her sister's short dark hair was standing straight up and the frown on her face had deepened to a scowl. "Well, you aren't cooking and you don't look all that serene, come to think of it." She peered around the edge of the prep table. Meg's kitchen footwear alternated between a pair of clogs in the summer and running shoes in the winter. Both shoes required socks and the color of her socks was invariably an indicator of Meg's mood. These were an irritable yellow-green. "Is Andy okay?"

Andy Bishop, Meg's long-time fiancé, was the best-looking internist in Hemlock Falls.

Meg's frown lifted. "He's fine. I'm fine."

"It's us that ain't fine." Doreen Muxworthy-Stoker, the Inn's elderly housekeeper, stumped out of the small office off the kitchen that she shared with Meg, and slapped the clipboard containing the linen count on the prep table. "She thinks we're boring."

Quill digested this in silence.

Doreen dropped onto the stool next to Quill and glowered at both sisters from under her scant gray eyebrows. "Meg's been complaining for the best part of the day about the boring weather, the boring town, her boring boyfriend, and boring old you."

"Hey!" Quill protested.

"Just cool it, Doreen," Meg said. "You're blowing this all out of proportion."

"And she's been boring the bejesus outa me. Says the only guests to cook for are that there boring jury comin' in tomorrow. And that crazy Judge Moody."

"The menu for the jury is *prix fixe*." Meg pointed a disdainful finger at the manila folder in the trashcan. "Two entrees, two vegetables, and the state won't spring for anything but cookies for dessert. You call that interesting? I call that boring as hell."

Quill nodded in sympathy. "It's March. The weather's boring. It's off season. The Inn is thin of company, as Jane Austen would say. But we should be happy we have the business, Meg, even if it *is* boring. The jurors won't be a lot of challenge for the best chef on the Eastern

21

Seaboard, I admit. So I can see why you might be bored. And we've been corpse-free for a considerable period of time, too. So there's no opportunity to exercise our underappreciated skills in detection. No wonder you're a little bored."

This reference to their shared, not very successful forays into solving several murders that had occurred at the Inn in the past, brought a faint smile to Meg's face and a snort of derision from Doreen.

"But," Quill continued, "we'll be meeting our long-lost cousin Corisande tomorrow and you'll be able show her the great secrets of your kitchen, Meg. You won't be bored then."

Doreen's second snort smacked of skepticism. "She's talked herself into a regular snit, this one. And as for that cousin of yours, Corisande—What kind of name is Corisande?" Doreen interrupted herself. Her wild gray hair haloed her head like the coxcomb on a rooster. "Corisande," she said again, in case they had forgotten.

"Aunt Eleanor was fond of the Elizabethan poets, Doreen," Meg said. "Corisande's just lucky her name isn't Philomena. And I may have mentioned this before, Quill, but I'm not all that thrilled about teaching some teenager kitchen basics." She tugged ferociously at her hair.

"She's not a teenager," Quill said. "She's nearly twenty-three. I thought you were as thrilled as I am to have her here. Besides, Meg, how many members of our family have visited us here at the Inn in the past?"

"None!" Meg shouted. "We're too *boring*!"

"Far as I knew until now, you two didn't have any family," Doreen said with acertain disapprobation. "I always thought you were orphans." Doreen's three marriages—or perhaps it was four, Quill wasn't entirely certain—had resulted in a bewildering number of children, grandchildren, and in-laws who occupied her time in a very satisfying way. Doreen didn't hold with orphans. So she'd always treated Meg and Quill as close— if somewhat embarrassing—additions to her own family.

"We do have family, Doreen. We have Aunt Eleanor," Quill said. "We've always had Aunt Eleanor. Who has never visited here because she lives in Italy with a lover twenty years younger than she is, and more power to her, I say."

"Now, living in Italy," Meg said. "That's not boring. I mean, this kid's coming all the way across two continents from a place where she can have five-star food from a vendor on any street in Rome to Hemlock Falls?!"

"Aunt Eleanor wants Corisande to learn from the best chef around," Quill said. "And that's you, Meg. And I think I'm insulted that you think we'll bore Corisande."

"I don't even remember Aunt Eleanor," Meg said glumly. "And all of a sudden we're supposed to take this long-lost cousin in. We're nuts."

"That's because you were only eight when Eleanor took that job with the *Times* bureau overseas," Quill said. "I remember her very well." And she did remember her tall, elegant aunt. Quill had her hazel eyes and abundant red hair. "She and Mother were very close, Meggie."

"And I don't remember Corisande, either."

23

"She was only two. And you should remember her. She bit you at least twice and threw your Astronaut Barbie down the toilet."

"So how the hell is she going to behave in my kitchen?" Meg tugged her short dark hair into cranky spikes. "I mean, a kid who would toss a Barbie into the toilet at two is going to need a lot more excitement as an adult than this place can give her."

"Family," Doreen said to no one in particular. "Can't abide with 'em and can't abide without 'em. But it's only right to take the poor soul in. Past time, if you ask me."

"She's not a poor soul," Quill said, feeling guilty for absolutely no reason at all. "These past three weeks is the first time we've heard from Aunt Eleanor for years, Doreen. It's not as though we've been neglecting her on purpose."

"She'll think I'm an idiot," Meg said, dragging the conversation back to the first order of importance—Corisande's imminent arrival in her kitchen. "She'll think my reputation's inflated. If she's even aware that I have a reputation at all."

"That's just stupid," Quill said crossly. "You're a master chef. Our menus are loaded with your original recipes. If that doesn't impress her, cook in your toque. That's sure to impress her, if you don't fall into the soup because you can't see anything with the hat over your eyes."

"Cook what?" Meg demanded. "What the heck am I going to show her, Quill? We don't have any real guests booked until the season starts up in late April."

"The jurors are real guests."

Meg kicked the wastebasket containing the balled-up remains of the State of New York's menu suggestions. "Phut! I just got this RFR thing from the State of New York for those jurors and my hands are tied there, too. Two entrees. Two! Plus there's a cash limit. I'm supposed to cook fabulous food on a limit of twenty bucks a head per day? And Mitchell Moody's going to expect something more than tuna-fish casserole. That's what the buggers are going to get on twenty dollars a day."

"They'll only be here for a week or two. Then we can open the Inn back up to the real guests." Quill, her patience eroding fast, aware that she was driven by the need to get down to the village and see John about the rumors over the hotel in the cemetery, put her hands on top of her head and pushed down hard. It didn't help. Her head had started to pound and it wasn't going to stop.

"Oh, sure," Meg said bitterly, "and who travels to Upstate New York in March? Deer hunters, that's who. Catch them ordering something really interesting to eat."

"That Mitchell Moody!" Doreen, who had apparently been brooding about the notorious State Supreme Court Justice, smacked her fist on the prep table. "That bozo won't take a step without TV cameras stuck in his puss."

This, Quill thought, was very true. Mitchell Moody's flamboyant style made good copy. He wore a waistcoat and an ornate pocket watch. As he was about to deliver a judgment from the bench, he'd draw the pocket watch from beneath his robes and say, "It's time for justice," which drove the reporters silly with delight and everyone else to exasperation.

Doreen grumbled on. "Why don't you fancy-feed all them reporters that'll be crawling all over the place. They're all on expense accounts, anyways."

"The Meecham trial's over real estate," Meg said, "And if that isn't boring, I don't know what is. So forget the reporters. And it's not just the food," Meg grumbled, getting back to her original point. "There's nothing *in* Hemlock Falls."

"That's just not true," Quill said.

"Oh! So we can hang out at Nickerson's hardware store on Saturday? Drink Rolling Rock beer at the Croh Bar?"

"You *like* drinking Rolling Rock beer at the Croh Bar."

"And what about the Friends of the Dead?" Doreen demanded. "There's pretty exciting times around here, missy, I can tell you right now."

Meg rolled her eyes. "Right. As if a bunch of lunatics with their faces painted green aren't boring."

Quill was startled. "I don't think they're boring, Meg. Two bricks shy of a full load, maybe. But not boring."

"Well, most of them have quit the protest ever since the temperature dropped below freezing," Meg said sulkily. "So I won't have the opportunity to show her good old American peaceful protest in action. Corisande can walk the streets of Hemlock Falls totally stimulus-free. Boring, boring, *boring*!"

"You're a downright snob, missy," Doreen said loudly.

"There's more than enough excitement around here for Miss I-Want-to-be-a-Famous-Chef-Too. I'll take her to my Bingo night, how's that? And Stoke can give her a tour of the *Gazette*."

"Corisande has no interest in a small-town newspaper," Meg said loftily. "You think she gives a hoot about the Ladies' Auxiliary meetings? Or the high school basketball scores?"

Doreen bridled at this description of the contents of her husband's weekly publication, although it was absolutely true. "How do you know what she gives a hoot about?"

"Because it's BOR—"

"Stop," Quill said, for whom the penny had belatedly dropped. "You don't think *we're* boring. You think *you're* boring. Meg, you are not a boring person. Anyone who smashes six eight-inch sauté pans a month out of sheer . . . umm . . . exuberance isn't boring. Anyone who has earned three, then two, then three stars back from *L'Aperitif* isn't boring."

Meg looked around for something other than an eight-inch sauté pan to throw at her; Quill was familiar with the signs.

"Look. Maybe John will agree to taking a bath on the twenty dollar per diem for the jurors," Quill improvised. "You know, we could go into the red a little bit this month. Use the slack time for experimenting with new recipes. Put the expenses down to R&D."

"You think so?" Meg said doubtfully. "You mean, I could show Corisande some really interesting stuff and

27

not have to worry about overhead costs and all that garbage? Because all that cost analysis crap is so bor—"

"Stop," Quill said. "I'll talk to John. If it's a question between letting you loose with the menu or paying for all the stuff you throw when you're mad, I'll bet he'll go for the menu. So," Quill said briskly, "is everything okay, then? I'll take a walk down to the village and talk to John right now."

Meg looked at her suspiciously. "You were supposed to be painting today. You spent the last six months complaining you never have time to paint because the Inn is so much work and now that you do have some genuine free time you're going to walk downtown to see John? Call him on the phone!"

"I need the exercise," Quill said evasively.

"You took Max for a two-mile hike down the Gorge at seven o'clock this morning. If you get any more exercise you're going to fall over dead. Go paint!"

Quill, who had a strong suspicion that she'd have far too much time to paint if Carol Ann's sly gossip about the new hotel were something more than spite, gave her sister an affectionate pat. "I just need to clear my head a little. And while I'm clearing my head, I'll just run over the March budget with John. It'll help if you can give me a rough estimate of what you'll be doing. All right? Good. I'll be back in an hour or so."

Meg, whose eyes held that distant look that meant she was conjuring up amazing things to do with out-of-season fish, gave her an abstracted nod. Doreen, whose concern for both Meg and Quill's welfare was more rooted in the here and now, said darkly, "Not in this weather, you won't. And not with them green-faced goons walking the streets."

"The weather's fine," Quill said. "It's just above freezing. And the Friends of the Dead are just that, Doreen. They could give a hoot about the living and they aren't even picketing in this weather. Mrs. Pembroke told me they quit. Besides, I'll take Max with me."

"That durn dog!" Doreen's beady black eyes sharpened with malice. "Hey! I got a suggestion on how to keep Miss Fancy Pants Corisande from being bored. She can follow that mutt around and keep him out of the Dumpsters."

"Now, don't *you* start, Doreen," Meg flared. "All I need is you on Corisande's case and that'll be just *it*."

"Doreen, maybe you should check on the rooms for the jurors one more time," Quill said diplomatically. "Just to be sure. And Meg, sit down, make up a possible menu, and then run some numbers for me. Right now, I'll go talk to John about the budget."

"How can you talk about the budget when I don't know what I'm going to need?"

"I'll just get a ballpark figure on how much we can afford to lose. Okay, Meg? Okay, Doreen?"

Doreen stomped off, clearly in a mood to harass the maids into recleaning perfectly clean rooms out of sheer bossiness. Meg pulled a large, untidily stuffed file from beneath the prep table, dumped out a fistful of scribbled sheets of paper, and started to sort through them. Quill took her winter parka from the peg at the back of the kitchen, and called for Max, who bumped through the swinging doors from the dining room with his usual unapologetic air.

"You're supposed to stay out of the dining room," she reminded him.

Max flattened his ears and pawed imperatively at her skirt. Quill wondered, not for the first time, what accidental mix of breeds had given him his spectacularly ugly coat: it was ochre, muddy, gray and an offensive off-white. At least he didn't shed. She'd decided, after an evening spent paging through various books devoted to real dogs, that he was a mix of standard poodle and collie, with perhaps a touch of giant schnauzer about the ears and muzzle.

"And how come you didn't bite Carol Ann Spinoza when I wanted you to?"

Max barked in an offhand way.

"I don't believe that for a minute. She's awful, but she wouldn't bite you back. You're not antiseptic enough. C'mon. Let's go for a walk."

Quill let herself out of the kitchen door. A fine skein of sleet stung her cheeks, but the air was fresh and cool. Twilight was already settling in. The light changed from season to season in Upstate New York in a way that never failed to delight her. March in Upstate New York looked back to the cold hard sun of mid-winter and forward to April's grudging spring. Its aspect changed from week to week. Tonight, the sky over the Falls was awash with lavender as daylight waned and evening crept in.

The Inn perched on the lip of Hemlock Gorge. Quill walked to the edge to watch the waterfall. To the west were twenty acres of pine, birch, maple, and cherry. To the east, the Hemlock River wound its way through the Gorge, then past the halfway-completed construction site of the new resort. In the failing light, Quill could barely see the gate to the old cemetery. As far as she could tell, no protesters paraded outside its low gates.

Directly south of the Inn, the grounds gently sloped down toward the village itself. She whistled to Max and set off.

Quill took the graveled path through Peterson Park. The park held the quiet particular to winter. Chilly water dripped off the pines. No birds sang. Small animals rustled in the twiggy brush. They went past the statue of General C. C. Hemlock. Max saluted the General with a lifted leg, a brisk scrabbling of his paws in the slushy snow, and a brief wag of his scruffy tail. Quill threw a few slushy snowballs for Max to chase, and found herself out of the park and in the village before she was quite ready to leave.

It was close to four o'clock, and already lights shone in the village houses and offices. Quill turned onto Main Street, splashing her boots in the snowy puddles. She loved the village. When she and Meg had first driven down Main Street, she'd lost her heart to the cobblestone buildings, the wrought-iron lampposts, and the sound of the Falls nearby. And there was always some fresh perception, some trick of light or shadow, to keep her interest.

Claudia Bishop

John Raintree's accounting offices sat in the middle of Main, next to Marge Schmidt's Insurance and Realty Company. Quill passed Esther West's Best Dress Shoppe. The window was filled with plastic daffodils in addition to the usual polished cotton shirtwaists, and a hand-lettered sign noted hopefully: SPRING'S ABOUT TO SPRING. She paused, then decided against stopping at Esther's to say hello. Esther didn't much like Max. As a matter of fact, nobody in town much liked Max, primarily because of his affection for their Dumpsters.

She stepped around the display of snow shovels and snow blowers in front of Nickerson's hardware store, then waved to Marge Schmidt, who sat at her desk behind her large plate glass window. Marge's stout figure was almost obscured behind painted gold letters that proclaimed SCHMIDT'S PROPERTY AND CASUALTY, Inc. (FINEST INSURER IN HEMLOCK FALLS. ALSO REALTY SALES.)

John's sign RAINTREE ASSOCIATES, GENERAL ACCOUNTANCY, was less obvious, but then, John had no need to advertise his presence in Hemlock Falls. Except for the Inn, his clients were corporations headquartered in Rochester or Syracuse. Several years before, he'd given up his small equity in the Inn and his full-time job as business manager to take on larger clients. Quill missed his daily presence, but she'd learned enough about general accounting practices to handle the monthly accounts payable and receivables on her own, and a full-time business manager just wasn't necessary for a twenty-seven-room Inn with a heavily seasonal business. But a business consultant was an absolute necessity. She'd refused to take on the responsibility for the yearly budget or financial forecasting. In the years before John had taken the Inn's finances in hand, her business decisions had proved almost fatal more than once. (On good days, John characterized them as charitable; Quill herself was humbly aware they bordered on the profligate.)

The offices of Raintree & Associates were dark. Max pawed at the glossy blue door, then looked at her, his ears tuliped forward.

"It's Monday, Max. I totally forgot. He's in Syracuse Mondays."

"Why aren't I surprised you don't know what day of the week it is?" Marge stamped out into the street and pulled the door to her offices firmly closed behind her. "Ha-ha," she added. Marge was short, round, and popularly supposed to be the richest citizen in Hemlock Falls. Quill suspected that Marge was the richest person in the whole of Upstate New York, not just Hemlock Falls, but Marge kept the true facts to herself. She shrugged herself into her down coat and sent a disgusted glance skyward. "Weather's been lousy all day." She narrowed her eyes at Quill. "What're you up to?"

"A walk, mainly," Quill said. "I need to talk to John, but it'll keep."

Suddenly amiable, Marge poked Quill in the side. "Let's go down to the bar. Buy you a beer."

"Sure." Quill regarded her dubiously. Marge generally cultivated all the amiability of a Sherman tank. "Are we celebrating something?"

"Like what?" Marge shot back. Her genial smile disappeared. "Like that yahoo Justice Moody hauling that circus of a trial to town? You really goin' to keep those buggers up at the Inn?"

Quill fell into step beside her. If anyone in Hemlock Falls knew anything about the purported hotel, it would be Marge, so her time at the Croh Bar wouldn't be wasted. "It is going to be a bit of a circus, I suppose. Justice Moody doesn't exactly hide his light under a bushel."

"It's not him I'm worried about. It's the other buggers. We cross here," she added unnecessarily.

Quill followed her across the street to the Croh Bar, a favorite of Marge's, primarily because she owned it, and said, "I wouldn't call them buggers, exactly, Marge. Do you mean the attorneys?"

"You got them coming, too?"·

"Six jurors, the judge, the court reporter, the bailiff, and both sets of lawyers. It's not usual for us to be at capacity in March. Doreen thinks it means we're going to have a really good summer."

Marge shoved her way into the close, warm darkness of the bar and didn't answer. Quill let Max precede her, then joined Marge in the booth closest to the door.

"You're getting cocoa," Marge said. She pulled her knit cap off and unzipped her coat. Her cheeks were bright red, which made Quill wonder a little. It wasn't that cold outside. "So am I. Betty's fiddled some with this new recipe." Betty Hall, Marge's junior partner in both the Croh Bar and the EAT, AMERICA! Diner, had Meg's respect as a cook, and Quill's, as well. "As for you," Marge said to the hopeful Max, "sit down and shut up and maybe you'll get a soup bone."

Max sat.

"Now, see here, Quill." Marge drummed her fingers on the tabletop. "I've been meaning to get on up to the Inn to have a little chat with you. So it's a good thing you dropped on by."

"Actually, I had something I wanted to discuss with you, too."

"Yeah?" Marge eyed her narrowly. "You first."

Quill took a deep breath. She was never sure where she stood with Marge. If you fell into a gloppy pond, Marge would laugh herself pink before she offered to pull you out, but pull you out she would; if you owed her money and couldn't repay it, she'd stop short of taking the shirt off your back—but not by much; she never, ever lied about business deals, but she didn't talk about them, either, which made inquiry difficult.

"Is there any reason why Meg and I wouldn't have heard about a new hotel going up in the Civil War cemetery?"

A deep line appeared between Marge's ginger eyebrows. "I can think of a few reasons why you *would* hear about somethin' like that. But no reason why you shouldn't."

"Carol Ann came up to see me today. And she thought

the ROCOR people were planning on using the cemetery as the site of a new hotel."

Marge made a noise like "umpha," which Quill took to be a sign of commiseration. She blinked once, then pursed her lips and gazed at the ceiling. This, Quill knew, presaged a serious exchange of information. It had taken Quill far too long to figure out how to get information of substance from the long-time residents of Hemlock Falls, but she once she got it, she had never returned to her old impetuous ways. So now, rather than giving in to the desire to shriek, "Why the heck didn't anybody *tell* me!" she simply waited.

"Yeah? So no golf course, huh?" Marge's tone was casually disinterested, which meant A: she hadn't known about any hotel and B: she was eaten up with curiosity.

"Guess not." Quill rubbed her neck with an air of unconcern. It was time to pretend neither one of them was interested in the subject at hand. "Do you think we're in for more snow?"

"*I'm* about ready for spring," Marge admitted.

"Me, too. You knew that Meg and I have a cousin coming to stay?"

"Might have heard something about it," Marge agreed cautiously, which meant she knew to the second when Corisande's train was due to arrive. "Ought to be fun for you two."

"We think so." Quill smiled with genuine warmth.

"Okay. Well, I'll check into that other matter for ya. See what's going on."

"Thank you. As you might imagine, Meg and I are pretty concerned. That is, I am. I haven't said anything to Meg and I hope that Carol Ann doesn't either . . ."

Marge held up a cautionary hand. "Got ya. Might take a bit of time, but I'll let you know."

And this, Quill knew, was as far as she was going to get today. She hoped that John had more information, but if Marge herself was baffled, it wasn't likely.

"Reason it's gonna take a little time is I'm gonna be going out of town for a few days." Marge, now clearly out of her business mode, relaxed into a ferocious scowl and into her usual confrontational style.

"Oh?"

"And there's somebody I want you to keep a bit of an eye on while I'm gone."

"There is? I mean, you do? I'd be happy . . . why me?"

"You and that sister of yours aren't too bad as detectives." This last was delivered with a grudging truculence that meant Marge was impressed indeed.

"Well," Quill said in a pleased way. "Thank you. So you want us to, um, tail somebody?"

Marge laughed rudely. "Like he wouldn't notice a tall skinny redhead followin' him around? Or a brunette the size of a dwarf and her with a mouth on her?"

Betty put two mugs of cocoa in front of them, which gave Quill a moment to count backward from ten. "So it's a 'he,' is it?"

"It's not a 'he,' it's a low-down sneaky rotten son of a gun who went and got himself a place on that jury."

Claudia Bishop

"You want us to spy on a juror?!" Quill set the cocoa down with a thump. "Marge, I don't think we can do that."

"Name's Bouncer Muldoon." Marge took a huge gulp of cocoa and gave Quill a glare that would have stopped the German tanks advancing on Stalingrad.

"He's my ex-husband."

CHAPTER 2

❧

"Marge Schmidt's ex-husband's name is Bouncer Muldoon and he's a juror on the Meecham trial?" Meg goggled at Quill over the scrambled eggs. "Wow." She bit into a piece of cinnamon focaccia. It was just after seven in the morning. The dining room at the Inn was empty, except for two snowmobilers who'd been at the Inn for a week. Quill was grateful for the lull. She hadn't slept well. She was grouchy. Despite a call to John, she hadn't been able to find anyone who could confirm Carol Ann's gossip about the new hotel.

"And she wants us to what?"

"Just keep an eye on him." Quill sipped at her coffee, which was hot, freshly ground, made at the table, and smelled delicious. One of the best parts of her life, which she liked a great deal, was that her sister was a gourmet chef. A better cook, she thought fiercely, than any imported chef from any European country anywhere.

"Just keep an eye on him?" Meg looked doubtful. "How can we do that? They'll be out all day at the trial until the closing arguments and then they'll be shut up in the Conference Room until they come to some decision about the Meecham case and they sure as heck won't let us in there. And besides, what has the poor schmuck ever done that we should spy on him?"

"That's what I told Marge. Politely, of course."

"And what did she say to that?"

"How could we call ourselves detectives when we couldn't even do a little information gathering?"

"And what did you say to—"

"I said," Quill interrupted a little impatiently, "that we don't call ourselves detectives as such because we aren't and that I was sorry we couldn't help her."

"We *could* keep an eye on him," Meg said. "I mean, Bouncer Muldoon. What kind of a name is that? And I never even knew Marge had an ex-husband."

"He's a wrestler," Quill said, "from what I gather."

"And aren't you at all curious about him?"

"Of course I am. But the poor man deserves the same kind of personal privacy everybody else does."

"Did Marge say why they got divorced? Or when they got divorced? Or even where . . . "

"Meg. All I know is that Marge doesn't want to run into him, which is why she's going away for a couple of days, and no, I don't have any idea where she's going. And she most especially doesn't want anyone to know that she has an ex-husband named Bouncer Muldoon who's a juror on the Meecham trial. So I told her I would forget it and not say a word to anyone but you and she said 'fine' and I said 'fine' and that's it. And we should respect her desire for privacy for two reasons. One, because she asked us to and two, because if we do tell anyone and she finds out she'll . . . " Quill waved her hands, trying to think of a legitimate second reason. "Call in our mortgage or cancel our life insurance or something."

"So," Dina Muir said as she bounced up to their table, "Did you guys hear about Marge's Schmidt's ex-husband?"

Quill sat back in her chair and sighed. Dina had been their receptionist for a long time, and normally, Quill rather liked her irrepressible nature. But she wasn't in the mood for it this morning. "Who told you?"

"It's all over town, I guess. Davey heard about it over coffee at the Croh Bar."

Quill eyed her receptionist with annoyed affection. "Marge doesn't want it all over town. Which means it's only kind to drop it." She looked at her watch and her brows rose. "You're in awfully early. It's not just to tell us about poor Bouncer Muldoon."

Dina, who'd been the Inn's receptionist for as long as she had been a graduate student at nearby Cornell University, didn't have to be at her station in the foyer until ten o'clock in the winter months, a requirement, she'd pointed out more than once, that should apply to all the other months as well.

"Davey and I were out kind of late last night. So I didn't go back to the dorm. I figured you'd want me here when the press started showing up anyway." She sat down next to Meg. "Besides, I'm so starving I woke up early. All I had to eat yesterday was popcorn at the movies." She pushed her large, horn-rimmed glasses up her nose with one finger, and peered at the breadbasket. "Cinnamon focaccia? Is there any butter?"

Quill handed over the butter dish. "The press is showing up already? Have you heard anything about the trial?"

"The last juror is being picked this morning. There's just six, you know."

"I know," Quill said.

"I mean, a jury's supposed to be twelve people, isn't it? And it'd be a lot better for the Inn if we had twelve because we'd make *some* money on this, Quill."

"It's a civil suit," Quill said. "Mrs. Pembroke said there's only . . . Dina, please just get to the point."

"Right. The bailiff left a message here late yesterday. The whole six will be here by lunchtime." Dina swallowed a large mouthful of bread. "And the only thing I know about the trial is what you know. It's *ROCOR v. Meecham* and they're squabbling over the ownership of that piece of land Meecham owns that's smack in the middle of the resort development. It's like the billionth lawsuit that construction company's brought. It's the suing-est company I've ever seen, not that I've seen all that many, and—"

"And it's *really* boring," Meg said flatly.

"You are so right!" Dina said sunnily. "Except that the jurors will be here and that should be kind of fun. So what's this about Ms. Schmidt? An ex-husband? Who knew?!"

"Everyone, apparently," Quill said. "But it's nobody's business but Marge's. So we should just forget about it, okay?"

Dina blinked her big brown eyes at Meg, who shrugged. "Don't ask me why she's grouchy. Maybe she had a telephone fight with Myles."

"Oh," Dina said. "Telephone fights are such a bummer. You can't really make up over the phone. Making up is more personal than that. Now, it's funny how you can *fight* over the phone. No problem there. But making up's gotta be, like, face-to-face. What did you and Myles fight about, Quill?"

"We didn't have a fight," Quill said stiffly, because they had. Or rather, she'd gotten mad at Myles, who never got mad, just silent.

"She misses him," Meg said. "He's been overseas for two months and he won't be back until June. And she can't make up with him until he calls back because she's not supposed to know where he is."

"I *don't* know where he is," Quill said.

"So if he's really steamed you just have to wait around until he decides he's not steamed anymore?" Dina shook her head sympathetically. "Double bummer, Quill. And it's not like you can get another boyfriend just like that, either. I mean, it's harder at your age."

Quill, who was thirty-six, said, "Oh?"

"I mean, it's hard enough for me, and there's all these cute guys my age at Cornell. There's just not all that many single guys over forty rolling down the streets of Hemlock Falls, that's all I meant."

"I don't want anyone other than Myles and I have really, really had it with this discussion."

"You're a lot prettier than I am," Dina said with disastrous honesty, "so maybe, like, the age thing doesn't matter all that much, but hey, who knows?" She shook her head sorrowfully. "The world is just strange."

"You are extremely pretty. And as of now, we're officially changing the subject." Quill poured the last of the orange justice into a clean glass and set it in front of Dina with an authoritative thump.

Dina nodded vigorously, which made her glossy brown hair switch back and forth over her eyes. "I'm cool with that. So, like, why isn't she called Mrs. Muldoon?"

"You mean Marge?" Meg said. "Why she calls herself Schmidt? Good question. Did she tell *you* why, Quill?"

Dina's eyebrows went up. "You mean you talked to Ms. Schmidt about this guy?"

Quill had not only talked with Marge, but with Myles McHale about Bouncer Muldoon. Which is why they'd had the fight over the telephone, or rather why Quill had gotten mad and Myles hadn't. Myles was a highly paid private investigator (and, when he was in Hemlock Falls, head of the sheriff's department) who did all he could to discourage Meg and Quill in the detective business. He had pointed out the inadvisability—from both a legal and a moral viewpoint—of poking their noses into the life of an (presumably) innocent citizen. He'd even, in his mildly sardonic way, hinted at nosiness. Quill, embarrassed, had gotten defensive.

"What Marge said to me was that she'd be truly happy if no one ever mentioned Bouncer Muldoon to her again. We all like Marge—"

Meg coughed.

"Well, we all respect Marge all the time and like her some of the time, when she isn't laying down the law to some poor debt-ridden soul . . ."

"Which is us, part of the time," Meg said.

"So we will all leave Marge's marital history alone. That is an official order from me, Dina, who, may I remind you, is your boss. Unless you've decided to seek other employment?"

Dina grinned, swallowed the last of the focaccia, and pushed away from the table. "I'll just go make sure we've got the Conference Room set up in case the judge wants to inspect it."

"Terrific," Quill said. "But it's Justice Moody, Dina. And you should address him as 'your Honor' when he checks in. Mrs. Pembroke gave me another memo from the State about not talking to the press. Please remember that."

"Yep. I'll be back in a flash. I want to check that the tape recorder's working. The one I hid under his chair." Dina, by now, had moved out of missile range. "The tape of the jury deliberations I'll sell to CBS has got to be perfect!" With a wave, she disappeared through the foyer.

"I don't know why we agreed to having these jurors," Meg grumbled.

"I don't know why we put up with Dina," Quill said. "She was just joking about the tape to sell to CBS, right?"

"We put up with Dina because if she didn't act like a giddy idiot at work she'd go bananas from writing her thesis and who wants to spend time visiting her in the rubber room at the hospital?" Meg said. "I swear, Quill, I'm buying you a T-shirt that reads: WARNING! I DIGRESS. Listen to me, please. About these jurors. I mean, sure, we can always use the business this time of year, but this might turn into a very big pain in the neck."

"It shouldn't," Quill said. "I talked to one of the corporate guys at the Marriott, and they said as long as the housekeeping staff stays mum about anything the jurors do until the trial is over, there's never any real problem with these things. And Doreen has briefed her staff more than once about it. She threatened them," Quill added absently, "with the mop."

"What does Myles think?"

"Why should I care what Myles thinks?" Quill said crossly.

"Oh no. So I was right. You *did* have a fight with Myles."

"The subject of this conversation is now something completely different," Quill announced. "I'm really sorry, but I'm not going to be able to go with you to the train station to pick up Corisande."

Meg straightened in alarm. "You want me to go by myself!?"

"Why can't you go by yourself?"

"It's rude, that's why. It's inhospitable. She's going to feel rejected before she even gets here."

"I don't see how I can go, Meg. If the jury's checking in at noon, one of us has to be here, and since I'm the manager, it has to be me. Not only that, there's a Chamber of Commerce meeting this afternoon." Where, she thought, she could find out more about the hotel. She hoped.

"You hate Chamber of Commerce meetings. You do anything you can to avoid Chamber of Commerce meetings."

"I'm secretary," Quill pointed out.

"Let Miriam Doncaster take the notes. She's a librarian."

"What does being a librarian have to do with taking notes?"

"As far as you're concerned, a lot. Max could take better notes than you do."

Quill, who'd regretted losing her temper with Myles, had gotten up that morning resolved to remain charming, gracious, and even-tempered with everybody else. She took a deep breath. "I need to be at this Chamber of Commerce meeting."

"Why?" Meg's face was pink.

Quill hadn't taken the time to look at Meg's socks, but she was willing to bet they were an anxious orange. And she didn't want to bring up the hotel until she had more facts. "Because Carol Ann Spinoza's going to be there. She's trying to start a community policing program."

"Community police?!" Meg closed her eyes. "Oh, my goodness."

"Exactly. Vigilantes in Hemlock Falls." Quill tugged at her hair. Now that she'd brought it up, there *was* more than one urgent reason to make the Chamber's meeting that afternoon. "Can't you just see all those guys in pickup trucks zipping around town with their shotguns loaded? And with everyone so upset about the Friends of the Dead protesting at the cemetery—the mind boggles." She waved both hands in the air. "Mayhem will ensue."

"Yikes. Did you mention this to Myles?"

"Yes. He's a little concerned. It depends on how it's run, he said. He was going to give Davy a call."

Meg didn't say anything in response to this. Davy Kiddermeister—the youngest brother of the Inn's best waitress—was the town's earnest, if not very confident, deputy sheriff. He'd grown up a lot since he and Dina had started dating, but he didn't command the respect among Hemlock Falls' rowdier element that Myles himself did. And Myles was an ocean and several continents away.

"Okay," Meg said grudgingly, "I'll pick Corisande up all by myself. But Quill, what am I going to do with her?"

"Show her to her room, for starters. Show her around town. You'll be supervising dinner for the jurors this evening so she can get a head start in the kitchen." Quill threw up her hands. "Ask her about Aunt Eleanor. I don't know, Meg. It can't be that hard."

"I have no conversation skills," Meg said glumly. "None. You know I can't chat, Quill."

"Let *her* chat, then. And I should be able to join you for dinner. Can Andy come, too?"

"He's at a pediatric conference today in Buffalo."

"Maybe Dina would join us, then," Quill said tactfully. "She's about the same age as Corisande. And there's nobody fuller of chat than Dina, who," she added, glancing at the entrance to the dining room, "seems to be headed this way for more chat right now."

"Quill? Sorry to interrupt." Dina suddenly looked very much like the serious grad student she actually was. "There's someone here for you. I put him in your office and called the kitchen for coffee."

Quill got to her feet immediately. A polite, courteous, efficient Dina meant some sort of trouble, usually minor, but as Dina herself often pointed out, you never could tell.

"Hey, Dina," Meg said. "Do *you* want to come with me to the train station to pick up Corisande?"

"Sure," Dina said. "If the Feds haven't locked us all up by then. That's who's waiting in your office, Quill. A man from the FBI."

"You're from the FBI?" Quill sat down behind her desk and looked in dismay at the agent.

"Special Agent Melvin Purvis, ma'am."

Quill blinked.

"No relation," Special Agent Purvis said, with the air of a man who had been asked about it one too many times. He folded the wallet containing his badge and tucked it away in his suit coat. He was probably in his mid-thirties, Quill thought, with a pale, not-unattractive pudginess and dark hair. He had very beautiful, long-lashed hazel eyes. "I won't trouble you for long. But the Bureau needs to make sure that the site for the sequestration is secure. And we need a list of your employees and anyone else who's going to be at the Inn while the chief justice is here."

Quill moved the cloisonné bowl on her desk from one side to the other. "My goodness," she said. "The guys from the Marriott didn't say anything about the FBI." She concentrated on suppressing her excitement. A real FBI agent. Who even looked a little bit like David Duchovny, if she squinted.

He gave her a sweet, somewhat absentminded smile. "It's just routine, ma'am."

"You're not going to be staying here, too, are you?" Quill said.

He looked hurt. "No, ma'am. I just need those lists in case we need to do background checks. I'll be out of your hair in no time."

"I don't mean that quite like it sounded. It's just . . . FBI? I thought the Meecham case was just about real estate."

Purvis frowned slightly, and said, reprovingly, "Twenty million dollars represents quite a bit of real estate, ma'am. But you're right. We wouldn't normally assign an agent to jury sequestration, but there have been several credible threats against Justice Moody's life."

"But I thought . . . " Quill bit her lip.

"That Moody was pulling his usual Barnum & Bailey? That his demand to have the jury sequestered was part of the circus that surrounds this guy? That he pulled it so he could get a few weeks here at the Inn on the state? So did we, at first. But I did say 'credible'."

"Credible," Quill repeated. She didn't know much about the FBI, but she was vaguely aware that the Bureau could only be called in on federal crime. Which meant kidnapping or organized crimes or domestic terrorists.

She put her head down on her desk. There was a definite downside to meeting a real FBI agent under the current circumstances.

"Are you all right, ma'am?"

Quill sighed. "I was just thinking how innocent I was yesterday afternoon."

Purvis's beautiful hazel eyes sharpened. As a matter of fact, they didn't look beautiful so much as lethal. "And you're not innocent anymore? Ma'am?"

"I didn't mean that the way it sounded, either," Quill said hastily. "I meant that things seemed so quiet yesterday. And now they don't."

His gaze traveled around her office. The couch was upholstered in a comfortable bronze and terra-cotta. The carpeting was warm cream. Her cherry desk and small cherry conference table were gently curved in the Queen Anne style. The tin ceiling dated from the nineteenth century—as did much of the rest of the Inn—and lent the whole room a gently nostalgic air. "It's a nice place," he said, "but crimes happen everywhere, Miss Quilliam. Even here."

Quill hunted in her desk for the Inn's employee list, gave Special Agent Purvis the names and addresses of the snowmobilers who were the Inn's only current guests, then waited (hopefully) to be interrogated.

"Thank you," he said. "I'll be off, now."

"That's it?"

"That's it."

Quill, conscious of disappointment, tugged at her hair. "You know," she began modestly, "my sister and I aren't totally unacquainted with crime, Agent Purvis."

One eyebrow went up.

Quill laughed hollowly, "I don't mean that we're crooks, of course. I mean that we've had some—very moderate—success in your line."

"My line?"

"Criminal investigations." Quill sat back in her chair and crossed her legs in a casual way.

"You're referring to the murders of Boomer Dougherty, and others."

"Yes." Quill, taken aback. Of course the FBI would know about the cases she and Meg had been involved with in the past. "So, ummm, if there's anything at all we can do to help, Agent Purvis . . . "

He leaned forward. "I've got a message from Captain McHale."

"Myles? My Myles?"

"Yes. It's this," He patted his suit coat pockets,

pulled out his notebook, paged through its contents and read. " 'No.' "

"You know Myles? What am I talking about?" she asked herself bitterly. "Practically everyone in law enforcement seems to know Myles."

"He thought you'd feel like that. So the second half of the message is: 'Relax.' " He tucked the notebook away. "Really, Miss Quilliam. My presence here is just routine." He got to his feet. "It's highly unlikely you'll see me again. We don't anticipate any real trouble. This is precautionary."

"You couldn't stay for coffee?" Quill asked a little wistfully. "I was hoping we could sort of swap stories about cases?"

"He didn't stay for coffee?" Dina said a few moments later, as she carried the tray into Quill's office.

"Nope. He's gone."

Dina set the coffee tray down on Quill's cherry table. "Was he really from the FBI?"

"He was really from the FBI."

"Are we, like, in any kind of trouble? I mean more than the usual?"

"We're not in any trouble," Quill said. "Are we?"

Dina bit her lower lip. "It depends on what you mean by trouble. The reporters are gathering outside and they want to come in to get warm, but you said not to let them come inside, so I didn't. And the Friends of the Dead heard about the reporters so they're gathering outside, too, maybe because they hope they'll get on the six o'clock news, and"—Dina drew a deep breath—"Mayor Henry said he's decided to bump the Chamber of Commerce meeting up to eight o'clock."

"Eight o'clock in the morning? That's right now!"

Dina looked at her watch. "Yes, it is."

"Did Elmer say *why?*—Never mind," Quill interrupted herself. "I know why. It's those darn reporters. Elmer's a politician and politicians are always running for something and if they're running for something they're dying to be on television."

"Yep," Dina said brightly. "Anyhow, they're all gathering in the Conference Room and I said you were being interrogated by the FBI and might be a little late. So they'll understand if you are."

"Thank you," Quill said. "Thank you very much."

"You sound a little, like, sarcastic."

"Just because you told Mayor Henry I was being interrogated by the FBI," Quill said. "There isn't any other reason, really."

"*More* sarcasm," Dina said in a resigned way. "I think I'll take this coffee out to the reporters."

"It'll just keep them hanging around, Dina. I'll take it into the Conference Room."

"There won't be enough for everybody."

"So maybe it'll help shorten the meeting. Come and get me when the justice shows up."

The Conference Center was a short hallway away from the reception area, which itself was just outside Quill's office. She propped the tray on one hip, waited to

see Dina out of the office and safely ensconced behind
the big mahogany sign-in desk, then stopped for a criti-
cal look at herself in the mirror outside the ladies' bathroom. In the spring, summer, and autumn months, when
the Inn was filled with guests, she made it a point not to
leave her own suite of rooms unless she was suitably
dressed. (Most days, elegance was too much to hope for.
She settled for suitable.) The quiet winter months were
different. She'd anticipated another slow March day this
morning, which meant she'd pulled on jeans worn to pale
blue, a cream colored fisherman's sweater, and loafers
without socks. Her hair was piled in a careless knot on
top of her head. She looked like last week's laundry and
she didn't have a second to change.

She nudged the door to the Conference Center open
with one hip and carried the coffee tray into the room.

The Conference Center was a long, large room with
wood wainscoting and pine floors. This part of the
Inn dated from the late eighteenth century, and the ceilings were low. Quill had painted the walls above the
wainscoting white and protected the floor with a cream
Berber runner to bolster the sense of spaciousness. An
eighteen-foot-long table occupied most of the space. At
the moment, the room looked emptier than she'd expected; Mayor Elmer Henry sat at his usual spot at the
head of the table, but there were only four other Chamber members there: Howie Murchison, the town's attorney; Harland Peterson, a local farmer and president of
the Agway; Miriam Doncaster, the town librarian, who
looked half awake and grouchy to boot; and Carol Ann

Spinoza. Sitting next to Carol Ann was a tall thin man Quill had never seen before. Her first impression was beige; he had lank beige hair, a beige face, and small, beige-colored eyes.

"So the FBI let you go, Quill?" Carol Ann said sweetly. "There's some food between your teeth, by the way."

" 'Lo, Quill," Elmer said.

"Hi, guys." Quill set the coffee tray on the credenza, and resisted the impulse to scrub her teeth with her fore-finger. She'd just looked at herself in the mirror, and surely she would have noticed if she had food stuck in her teeth.

Carol Ann leaned back in her chair. "I hope that cof-fee's hot. And I thought there was going to be rolls."

Quill smiled and restacked the coffee cups, mostly to stop herself from pulling Carol Ann's hair out by its bleached-blond roots. "Help yourselves to coffee." She took a seat next to Harland Peterson, who smelled pleas-antly of cows. "Are we expecting the others, Elmer? I can call for more coffee if we are."

"Goodness knows we should be," Elmer said fussily. "Adela called everybody. But this FBI stuff musta scared people off, Quill. What did you want to go getting mixed up with the FBI for?"

Quill didn't point out that it was the hour, rather than the FBI, that was responsible for the poor turnout, be-cause nobody had known about the FBI until fifteen min-utes ago. "I'm not mixed up with the FBI, Elmer. It was just one very nice agent who was making some routine inquiries regarding the Meecham case. Those newspaper stories about the death threats against Justice Moody appear to have some substance after all."

"I guess I heard about that," Elmer said disingenuously. "You got a fair number of reporters out front, Quill. Kinda a surprise, comin' here like I did in my capacity as mayor of this town."

Harland, a big man in his sixties with a weathered face, went "Uh-*hunh*" with such meaningful skepticism that Elmer blushed.

"Perhaps we might adjourn the meeting until more people can come," Miriam Doncaster yawned. "I know all of us are busy this morning."

"*I* have important business," Carol Ann said. "And I don't want to adjourn this meeting just because you want to go back to bed, Miriam."

The beige man sitting next to her nodded.

"Don't have a quorum," Harland pointed out. "No use in passin' on important business if we don't have a quorum."

"We don't need a quorum, thank you very much," Carol Ann said.

"This is business that could be very important to this town," Elmer said with a self-important air. "We'll need to make announcements to the press and everything. So I say we go right on ahead and listen to Carol Ann."

"So you can get out there before them reporters leave?" Harland suggested with heavy sarcasm. "Bull hockey, Elmer. We got to have enough people to vote on whatever it is you want to vote on. And we don't.

There's twenty-four members so we need at least eighteen present and accounted for."

"We don't need this quorum or whatever you call it," Carol Ann said. "I asked you, Mayor, and you said we could take a vote on this right now."

"So whatever this idea is, you and the mayor got your heads together about it?" Harland popped a piece of gum in his mouth and chewed thoughtfully, all the while gazing at Carol Ann's visitor. "Can't say as that hits me too good."

Carol Ann's eyes narrowed in a cobralike stare. "I don't see that that matters much to me, Mr. Peterson. Mr. Murchison, do we have to have a quorum to vote on my bill?"

"Your bill?" Harland said. He slapped his knee. "That's a hoot."

Quill, wondering at Harland's temerity in facing down the awful Carol Ann, suddenly recalled that his farm had been reassessed several months ago. Carol Ann could hold no terrors for him for another two years, at least, unless he decided to add another hundred heifers to his dairy herd.

"What d'ya think, Howie?" Elmer asked the attorney anxiously. "Can we vote on this-here idea of Carol Ann's and mine or not?"

"You didn't have a thing to do with this, Mayor," Carol Ann said briskly. "And if anyone is going to be talking to reporters about this bill it'll be me. So, Mr. Murchison?"

"This isn't a legislative forum," Howie Murchinson

said. "So 'bill' wouldn't be an appropriate term. However, most of our chamber members seem to think that Robert's Rules of Order has to do with take-out Chinese, so sure, go ahead." Quill noticed that Howie never really looked at Carol Ann, in the way that most people do when they can't stand the person they're addressing. Quill herself couldn't stand to look away from her. You had to watch sneaky people every minute.

"I thought so. I don't know why you people had to waste all this time." Carol Ann sat up a little straighter and folded her hands on the table. "Now. I have with me some alarming statistics about the rise of crime in Hemlock Falls—"

"Just hang on a minute." Harland lumbered to his feet and headed for the coffee. "Let's bide a bit and see if we got any latecomers showing up."

"You're looking for Marge Schmidt," Carol Ann said in her flat, brook-no-argument way. "Well, she isn't even in town, Mr. Peterson. I know that for a fact. And besides, people are starting to say that the only reason you're sucking up to her these days is because of all the money she's got. I'd be flat-out embarrassed to hang around Marge Schmidt the way that you do. Besides, what I have to say is a lot more important than your supposed romance with Marge Schmidt."

This—as it was clearly meant to do—silenced Harland completely and he carried his coffee cup back to the conference table without another word. There was a light tinge of red on his cheekbones, although it was hard to tell since, like most farmers, he had skin like tanned leather. Quill, who happened to know that Marge liked Harland as much as he liked her, and that money had nothing to do with it, wished she'd given in to her earlier impulse to pull Carol Ann's neat little ponytail right off her scalp.

The only good thing about Carol Ann's deliberate malice was that it woke Miriam Doncaster out of her usual morning fog. Miriam, like many of Quill's older woman friends, had just gone off hormone replacement therapy and had been in a damn-the-consequences mood for a couple of weeks. "Who *is* this person with you, Carol Ann? If this is an official Chamber meeting, and if we're going to discuss official Chamber business, you can just tell him to step outside." She frowned. "Now."

"Mr. Dunleavy has important information to add to my bill."

"Then he can wait until we invite him to do so. Good morning to you, Mr. Dunleavy."

"Miriam has a point," Howie said. "If you would excuse us, sir."

Mr. Dunleavy stuck a toothpick in his mouth, got to his feet, hitched his trousers up, and shambled out the door.

"Where do you *find* these people, Carol Ann?" Miriam asked crossly.

"I met Mr. Dunleavy online."

Miriam's eyes, which were wide, blue, and by far her best feature, widened even further. "No one was sorrier than I was to hear about your divorce. But if you will persist in Internet dating, you ought to at least run a background check on these guys before you invite them into town." She tilted her head toward the ceiling, as if recalling Mr. Dunleavy's unprepossessing features. "And here's a tip. They *never* post real pictures of themselves."

The only part of Carol Ann that moved in response to this was her right thumb, which struck the mahogany tabletop with short, ominous taps. "Mr. Dunleavy is president of The People's Police."

"The People's Police?" Howie said. "What people?"

"Any people," Carol Ann said crossly. "He's here to help to help us organize a citizens' patrol."

"You mean like the Guardian Angels, or whatever they're called?" Miriam said. "Vigilantes?"

"You got it," the mayor interpolated happily. "So the citizens of Hemlock Falls can be vigilant in the pursuit of peace in our time. Hang on a second, that's pretty good. Peace in our time. I got to write that down, in case I forget it."

"Neville Chamberlain was there before you," Miriam said. "And what are you thinking, Carol Ann? A citizens' patrol? Here? I've never heard of anything more ridiculous in my life."

"You won't feel that way once you hear my complete report on the alarming rise of crime in Hemlock Falls." Carol Ann waved a manila folder in the air.

Harland Peterson snorted. "What crime? Kids sliding down Main Street on their butts? The only crime we got is that that lazy son of a gun Eddie Morris can't get his ass off a bar stool and onto the snowplow often enough. So I have to agree with you about volunteer police, Miriam. I got enough work on my hands without running around town half the night looking to bust some sorry-ass kids, and sure as heck if there's a volunteer police force, I'll have put in some hours and I ain't got the time."

This, the longest speech anyone had ever heard from the taciturn Harland in any Chamber meeting Quill had attended, was followed by an impressed silence.

Howie Murchison shook his head. "There are a lot of liability issues as well, Carol Ann. I wouldn't recommend the town take this on at this point."

"I have with me," Carol Ann said, "some alarming statistics about the rise of crime in Hemlock Falls."

Miriam muttered, "Shut up, shut up, shut *up*" in an increasingly violent tone. Quill half rose to her feet—it looked as though the rise in crime in Hemlock Falls was going to begin with Miriam smacking Carol Ann with her purse. She was debating diversionary tactics, when the door to the conference room opened and provided one for her. Everyone turned toward it with a sense of relief.

Dina stuck her head inside, drew back at the sight of six faces staring at her, and hissed loudly. "Quill?"

"I'll be right with you, Dina." Quill stood all the way up. "I'll cast my vote right now, and you can record it *in absentia*. Or that I wasn't here, but I voted. Whatever. Anyway, I can't see the need for a volunteer police force in Hemlock Falls, either. That's how I'm voting. So, if you'll excuse me, it looks as though we have guests arriving."

"The rest of those reporters here?" Elmer said eagerly. "And the judge? Hmm. Well, I'll tell you what, Carol Ann. I think mebbe we ought to wait a bit to discuss this until we got the rest of the members here."

"But you said we didn't need a quorum!"

"Yeah, but I didn't think this idea would go over like a lead balloon, either," Elmer said frankly. "And besides, as mayor of this town, I should be here to officially welcome Chief Justice Moody. We can't have a man like that come to Hemlock Falls without an official welcome. Oh, Quill?" By this time, Elmer was halfway across the room, and narrowing in on Quill like a SCUD missile. "Maybe you could see that the judge and I have a chance for a little cup of coffee together. He's not goin' to have all that much to do while the jury's off on its confab."

"Elmer, I don't think—"

"Mr. Mayor!" Carol Ann was furious. "You stop right there!" She grabbed Elmer by the sleeve of his Husky Man's All-Polyester washable sports coat. "I did *not* rearrange my schedule this morning to be put off like this."

"We'll meet at the regular time this afternoon, Carol Ann. You can talk about it then."

"There isn't *time* to meet at the regular time," she wailed. "Those reporters are going to get a statement from that judge and then they'll be gone!"

While Elmer (futilely) tried to disengage the sleeve of his sports coat from Carol Ann's clutches, Quill took her chance and followed Dina out the door.

"What was that all about?" Dina said, peering over Quill's shoulder into the Conference Room.

"The usual sort of argument. But you arrived just in time, like the cavalry. I'll have to get you a horse." Quill looked at her watch. "It's only nine o'clock. It's too early for the jury to be checking in, isn't it? They can't be here already."

Dina shook her head.

"Thank goodness! I am really really, glad you got me out of that meeting, Dina, but the only thing that's supposed to happen today is that the jury's checking in. Please don't tell me that the plumbing's backed up or that the kitchen staff is going on strike."

"Nothing like that," Dina said reassuringly. "It's a guy from the Friends of the Dead. He's here about a body."

"Aha."

"Aha?"

"It's another detective job, isn't it?" Quill said, pleased. "That's amazing. Two jobs in less than twenty-four hours. Even if we had to turn down the first one."

CHAPTER 3

Corliss Hooker had a round, prosperous face and wore a navy-blue polyester blazer with flat black buttons. He didn't look like the kind of man who painted his face green and spent most of his days slogging up and down in front of the gates of the Hemlock Falls Civil War Cemetery carrying a sign that read LEAVE 'EM LAY. He didn't look like the kind of man in need of detective services, either, but Quill cherished a hope anyway. He looked like the kind of man who sold Hondas.

Quill, in full detective mode, assumed at once that he wasn't married. A wife would have known to replace the flat black buttons with brass. A clean white handkerchief spilled over his breast pocket. The tops of his tan chinos were stuffed into a pair of green rubber boots. (So he was a sensible unmarried protester.) The boots left snowy puddles on the waxed foyer floor. (A sloppy, sensible, unmarried protestor.) He carried a red anorak over one arm. (Who must be from Upstate New York, since anyone from downstate would have carried a fur-lined parka.)

He extended his hand when Quill came into the foyer, and she shook it, giving him an appropriately keen and incisive glance. She'd read, recently, that all the best cops could memorize a face with one careless yet penetrating glance.

"This is Ms. Quilliam, Mr. Hooker," Dina said as she settled herself behind the big reception desk. "But if this is about a body, I can give the sheriff's office a call as quick as anything."

The thick front door opened a crack and a guy with a ring in his nose and long black hair stuck his head inside.

"Out," Dina said.

"But it's friggin' *cold* out there!"

"Camera guy from WPEG, Quill," Dina said. "These reporters are *merciless*. Out!"

"When's the bar gonna open again?"

"Not until four. Out!"

The camera guy grinned appealingly and slammed the door shut.

"So," Quill said to Mr. Hooker. "You said something about a body?" The brief interruption had given her time to think, and she wasn't at all sure than this sounded like the kind of detective job at which she excelled. "Perhaps we *should* call Deputy Kiddermeister." She wasn't at all sure that she wanted to look at a body. As a matter of fact, she was very sure. "If this is about a body, I don't know that I can help you, Mr. Hooker."

"It isn't a recent body," he assured her. His voice was high-pitched, and curiously flat. He smiled timidly. The smile changed his face. Instead of looking like a prosperous Honda dealer he look both anxious and defensive.

"You didn't tell me *that,* Mr. Hooker," Dina said with a faint note of reproof. "You said it was extremely important that you talk to my boss about a body and what with the way things go around here, naturally I thought it was a fresh one."

Corliss Hooker stared at Dina in considerable consternation.

"Dina just meant . . . well, the explanation would bore you," Quill said.

"No, it wouldn't," Corliss Hooker said simply. "My organization is very interested in bodies."

"Oh." Quill didn't allow any of her dismay to show in her face. Years of dealing with the broad spectrum of human behavior had forced her to control her usual impulsive sympathy, but she still felt a little helpless when confronted with the farther reaches of people's nuttiness. "Then, if it's about a contribution to the Friends of the Dead, I'm afraid I'll have to say no, Mr. Hooker," she said firmly. "We have a great deal of sympathy for your cause, of course. But we can't—"

"We don't need funds," he said, with the same degree of simplicity he'd shown before. He turned away from Dina and looked at Quill. "I need to speak to the judge."

"You mean Justice Moody?" Quill didn't run her hands through her hair, but she wanted to. The endless stream of memoranda Mrs. Pembroke had written about security and employee leaks and the general nature of a successful sequestration had been stern on the issue of Justice Moody's personal privacy, which was the main reason that the reporters were languishing outside the Inn's front door rather than inside in the warmth and cheer of the private dining rooms. "I'm afraid I can't help you there, either."

"Well, either they will or you will." He jerked his thumb over his shoulder to indicate, presumably, the swarms of reporters outside. He looked, suddenly, unpleasantly cunning.

Quill temporized. "I'm not sure I know what you mean."

"There's something about one of the bodies in that cemetery that the judge's gotta know about. F.O.D's spent a lot of time checking out each and every one of the graves and the bodies of those poor soldiers in them and we've come up with some pretty important stuff."

"Then it'd be much better to talk to the sheriff's office," Quill said. "I'm afraid I don't see how Justice Moody could help you."

"He could get us one of those injunctions to stop the desecrations of those sacred grounds."

"The case has already been heard, Mr. Hooker," Quill said patiently. "And Justice Moody couldn't give you an injunction even if he wanted to. It's not his jurisdiction." Quill was a little vague on this point, so she added,

"I think that's the right term. Anyway, the court has already approved the relocation and I am so sorry things didn't go your way. But I'm truly doubtful that anything can be done here. Perhaps if you called your own legal counsel?"

"It's past all that," he said darkly. "If you don't let us in to see the judge, we'll just bring our folks right on up here to the Inn. Everyone's getting too used to seeing us at the cemetery. And this seems to be the only place where stuff's going on. We got," he added, "a couple of tubas."

"Tubas?"

"Since we don't seem to be getting folks' attention like we used to we got to be doing something a little bigger, if you get my drift."

"Tubas," Quill said intelligently. "I didn't know you played."

"Well, that's the point, innit? We don't. But they make one hell of a honk."

"Oh, shit," Dina said.

Quill sent her a reproving glance.

"I didn't mean 'oh, shit' about the tubas. I meant 'oh, sh—I mean—shoot,' here comes Carol Ann."

Carol Ann minced into the lobby, trailed by the mayor, Harland Peterson, and the anonymous Mr. Dunleavy. The mayor's winter coat was lined with two-inches of acrylic fur and he looked like a hot, swaddled baby. "We're adjourned, Quill. Adela's gonna call all the Chamber members and we'll hold the meeting at the reg'lar time." He stopped short at the sight of Corliss Hooker. "Oh," he said unenthusiastically, "it's you, Hooker. What're you hanging around here for?"

"None of your beeswax," Hooker said with dignity.

"That's *just* what I was talking about, Donald," Carol Ann said vindictively to Mr. Dunleavy. She threw a contemptuous glance at Quill. "This Hooker person is just the *kind* of person we don't want hanging around Hemlock Falls. If we had a People's Police Patrol, you can just bet this jerk wouldn't be standing here dripping mud all over me."

Donald Dunleavy transferred the toothpick in his mouth from the left side to the right with a flick of his tongue, but otherwise made no comment. "This Inn is supposed to be so exclusive," Carol Ann continued. "Ha!"

The front door cracked open, but before the cameraman from WPEG could stick his head through again, Dina yelled, *"Out!"* then, somewhat sheepishly to the rest of them, "Reporters."

Carol Ann zipped open her purse, took out a hand mirror, a comb, a small bottle of Aqua Net hairspray, and began to redo her perfect ponytail. The mayor squared his shoulders. Harland Peterson, still without saying a word, spun on his heel and disappeared through the archway, apparently intending to leave by way of the Tavern Bar. Corliss Hooker smiled at the disappearing journalist, and gave Quill a look so pregnant with meaning that her temper slipped and she snapped, "Blackmail is illegal in all fifty states. And tubas would be the last straw," to the confusion of everyone except Corliss Hooker. She followed this up by stepping to the oak door, throwing it open, and stepping aside. "I think you should all go out there and announce a press conference at the Croh Bar in fifteen minutes." To Corliss Hooker, the last to leave, she added. "The justice and the jurors won't be here until tomorrow. Whatever you do, Mr. Hooker, don't tell the reporters that. It's highly confidential information."

She slammed the door shut and leaned against it.

"The *ROCOR v. Meecham* trial people won't be here until tomorrow?" Dina said. "Shouldn't you tell the kitchen? And Doreen?"

"It was a ploy, Dina."

"Oh."

Quill turned and peered through the bubbled glass of the sidelight. "A successful ploy, I might add. Corliss Hooker is tugging on the cameraman's sleeve. Now the cameraman is tugging on the WPEG anchor's sleeve. Now the WPEG people are strolling casually away. And everyone else is noticing. And they're all going after them! Ha!"

"Ha?"

"Ha," Quill said with enormous satisfaction. "My first success of the day. Yippee. I can go get Corisande with Meg. Now listen to me, Dina. If anybody wants me, I've gone to Beloit."

The phone rang. Dina looked at it dubiously, then at Quill.

"Unless it's Myles. If he calls, I'm here."

Dina picked the phone up and said, "This is the Inn at Hemlock Falls. May I help you?"

"No, no, no," Quill said, "I've changed my mind. If it's Myles, tell him—"

"Hang on a sec." Dina held the receiver out.

"Is it Myles?" Quill hissed.

Dina made a face Quill couldn't interpret, but whoever it was, it probably wasn't Myles. Dina liked Myles. As a matter of fact, practically everybody liked Myles, except the people he'd put in jail. So the phone call probably had to do with Inn business. On the other hand, Dina wouldn't say "hang on a sec" to someone she didn't know well, unless she held them in mild contempt, which meant it was probably Carol Ann Spinoza on her cell phone in front of a raft of reporters trying to grab free space for her stupid volunteer police force. Quill took the receiver and said crossly, "What?!"

"It's me," Doreen said. "That cuckoo Judge Moody's bangin' away at the kitchen door. Should I let him in?"

CHAPTER 4

"We'll be out of your hair in a week or two," Mitchell Moody said. "And lovely hair it is, too." He reached forward, hand extended, and Quill resisted the urge to smack him over the head with her clipboard. She'd been resisting the urge to smack somebody over the head with the clipboard for the past forty-five minutes, and Mitchell Moody's playful pass was the last straw. It didn't help that—except for his eyes—he was one of the most physically attractive men she'd met since she'd fallen in love with Myles McHale eight years ago.

Mrs. Pembroke sat on the couch and blinked at them both like a little silver owl. Quill moved from her cherry conference table, where she'd been sitting with the State Supreme Court Justice, to the safety of the chair behind her desk. "I appreciate your help with registration—both of you—but it really isn't necessary."

"Oh, but it is," Mrs. Pembroke said. She had her PDA open on her knee, ready to key in another hour's worth of consultation.

Moody noticed Quill's glance at the PDA and grinned maliciously. His eyes were very dark, as close to a true black as human eyes can get. It was a theatrical, almost unnatural color that exaggerated his expressions and reminded Quill of the remorseless shark in *JAWS*. When he frowned (a frequent occurrence) Quill had to make a deliberate effort to squash her impulse to cower.

"We can't have either the prosecutor or the defense sitting with the jurors at meals, or next to each other in the Tavern Bar," Mrs. Pembroke said officiously. "Mitchell wouldn't like it."

"I'm well aware of potential problems in that area," Quill said politely. "As I may have mentioned before, we've been careful to read all memos about the sequestration procedure. You can be sure that we'll follow the protocol as well as is humanly possible. The memos cover every possible contingency—"

"Except being refused entrance into the Inn by that remarkable woman with the mop. And there's no reason to lose your temper, Miss Quilliam." Justice Moody's smile widened.

"I just can*not* understand that Doreen," Mrs. Pembroke fussed. "She knows me. I explained the process to that woman over and over and over again. I marked those meetings in my time sheet. You can look it up, Mitchell."

"I'll be sure to, Louise."

Quill smiled graciously. She knew it was gracious because she'd fled to the bathroom and practiced it for five minutes in front of the mirror while Dina was registering the jurors after Quill had disarmed Doreen and let the jurors into the kitchen. "Doreen expected you to come in the front door. As a matter of fact, I expected you to come in the front door. But you *were* admitted, your Honor, and if you'd like me to, I will willingly apologize again for the whack Doreen gave your bailiff, but he really shouldn't have tried to strong-arm his way inside. Doreen," she added ruminatively, "doesn't respond to bullying. Nor, should I add, do I."

"Your cheeks are pretty pink for somebody who isn't in a temper."

"I'm not at all annoyed," she said, even more politely. "But my sister and I have been running this Inn for some time, your Honor, and I'm perfectly capable of remembering who's who."

"So we'll go over it again," Mrs. Pembroke said happily. "I want to be absolutely sure that you know the prosecutor from defense counsel from Juror Number Three."

Moody merely smiled. Quill pinched her knee. Hard. State Supreme Court Justice "Time For Justice" Moody was tall, slumped shouldered, and built like a long-distance runner. He had an attractive beak of a nose and the predatory, focused, intelligent look of an eagle and when he smiled he was dangerous. Quill reminded herself that eagles were almost as stupid as owls—and owls were

75

at the absolute bottom of the ornithological intelligence scale, and that was pretty stupid indeed. She reminded herself that she did *not* like Chief Justice Mitchell Moody. And she would give Myles a call as soon as she finished with this bozo, to tell him she loved him. If she could get a call through to him, wherever he was.

"Miss Quilliam? The *dramatis personae*? If you please." Mrs. Pembroke waved her silver pencil.

Quill decided she didn't like Mrs. Pembroke, either, even if she was an elderly lady who deserved respect on account of her age if nothing else. She stopped pinching her knee, which, she could tell, was going to have a nice purple bruise in a few hours. "Certainly. Rebecca Galloway is the prosecutor. She's the thin blonde with the mole. Porker Stuyvesant is attorney for the defense and he's a big blond Dutchman who seems to have combined the Atkins and low-fat diets in the hope that two diets are better than one. Now the jurors . . ." Quill, perplexed, scanned her notes. "We seem to be missing Juror Number Five." Absently, she picked up her pencil and began to sketch little caricatures next to the names on her list. "Let's see. I have Mrs. Muriel May Johnson, she's an African-American and she works for the civil service, and the rather, ummm, portly twenty-something, Sparky Stillwater, who's a software engineer. And then Mrs. McAllister . . ." Quill stopped a moment to think about Mrs. McAllister. Mrs. McAllister had been shrilly outraged at being locked out of the Inn. She was in her early forties and used, she'd assured Quill in no uncertain terms, to better treatment. "Anyway.

Mrs. McAllister is the one with the expensive hair. And there's Mr. Mwgambe," Quill smiled, "who told me that jury duty is his first real contribution to this country. He was made a citizen just last year, you know. And Louis D'Angetti, the car mechanic. But what happened to Mr. Muldoon?"

"You know Mr. Muldoon?" Mitchell Moody asked sharply.

Mrs. Pembroke was oddly still.

"I know *of* Mr. Muldoon," Quill said, feeling as if she were on the witness stand. "I believe he used to live here, in Hemlock Falls. Let's see, that's four. And the retired Air Force guy, Brett Coldwell." She added a colonel's epaulettes to Brett Coldwell's sports coat, then tugged at her hair. "That makes six. But I don't recall meeting Bouncer Muldoon. He's supposed to be Juror Number Five. It's on one of the endless, I mean one of those very clear memos." She flushed, embarrassed. "Good grief. I have a very good memory for faces, you know. How could I have missed him? And I wanted especially to meet Mr. Muldoon."

"Oh?" Mitchell Moody's voice was so cold that Quill looked up, startled.

"Because he used to be married to a good friend of mine," Quill said. "I was just . . . I mean, I've never met him, but I was going to give him Mar . . . I mean welcome him back to Hemlock Falls. I am," she added with a touch of asperity, "a professional innkeeper, you know. It's my business to make people feel welcome."

Mitchell Moody shoved himself away from the

conference table and sat on the edge of her desk. He took the clipboard from her hands and looked at her list. He scowled at the caricatures. "Oh my god," he said, "you're *that* Quilliam."

Quill didn't say "which Quilliam" because it would have been disingenuous. "Yes, I am."

"What the hell are you doing running an inn?"

Quill had heard this question often over the years. "I like it," she said.

"I recall reading that you'd left New York and retired to the country." He tossed the clipboard onto the desk. "Well, whatever suits you, I suppose."

"It suits me quite well," she said. "But it doesn't suit me at all to have missed Bouncer. Was he removed from the jury for some reason?"

Moody didn't answer for a moment. "No," he said. "Mr. Muldoon didn't show in court this morning. I had the locals look him up. He lives in an apartment at the south end of Ithaca. He wasn't there. As a matter of fact, he seems to have skipped on us."

"Oh." Quill thought this through. "Does that happen often?"

Moody ran his hand over his chin. "Once in a while. I issued a bench warrant for his arrest. We'll find him sooner or later. It's interesting, though. I announced the jury's venue from the bench, and I could swear the man turned pale."

"You mean when you told the jury that they'd be sequestered here?"

"That's right."

"They hadn't known before? I mean, everybody in town—" Quill bit her lip.

"I, of course, said nothing," Mrs. Pembroke said sharply. "This is not a good sign, Quill. Not at all."

"They hadn't known before, no." Moody's black eyes turned darker still. "You wouldn't know of any reason why he'd want to avoid this beautiful little village, would you?"

A five-foot three-inch one-hundred-and-forty-pound reason, Quill thought. Oh dear. Poor Marge. Poor Bouncer. Both of them galloping off in all directions.

Perhaps they still loved each other.

Quill brooded for a long moment on the possibilities. What if the divorce had been a terrible mistake? What if they both had been lonely for each other all these years? And who would break the news to Harland Peterson?

"Miss Quilliam? Am I boring you?"

"She does that," Mrs. Pembroke complained. "Just goes off once in a while. I think it may be drugs."

Quill made an effort, and focused. "You're going to arrest poor Mr. Muldoon for not showing up for jury duty?"

"Damn straight. We have an alternate, of course. Mr. Mwgambe."

"Who should be listed as Juror Number Five," Mrs. Pembroke said. "*I* got it right, of course."

Moody tapped his finger impatiently. "But if you know anything about Muldoon's whereabouts, you'd better cough it up now."

Quill decided the only sensible response to this was to say nothing at all.

"Not one word more?" Moody grinned unpleasantly. Still firmly ensconced on her desk, he pulled his pocket watch from his waistcoat and clicked open the gold case. "Well, well . . . just about time for lunch." His eyes ran over her face. "You'll join me for lunch? Court resumes in the morning, but I have the afternoon free."

"I don't," Quill said pleasantly. "I'm due to pick up a cousin of ours at the train station in a few minutes, so if you'll both excuse me . . ." There was a tap at the door, and Dina opened it and said, "Quill?"

"Do you have a bell under your desk? That was a fortuitous entrance, wasn't it?" Moody clicked the watch shut, then shrugged and slid off the desk. "Time to go, Louise. You can rack up another couple of hours on your time sheet while we have lunch." He helped Mrs. Pembroke off the couch and stood there, his gaze sardonic.

Quill stood up and edged her way past them both. "Has Meg left yet to get Corisande, Dina? Would you let her know I can come with her after all?"

"That's what I came to tell you." Dina stepped out of the way to allow Moody and Mrs. Pembroke to pass. "Corisande called and said that she missed the train from New York and she's not going to be able to get here until tomorrow. So Meg's crashing around the kitchen in a—" Dina eyed Moody a little dubiously "—anyway, Meg's disappointed that she's not coming because she, Meg that is, is making this really cool appetizer for tonight and she wanted to show Corisande how it's done which is *not*"—Dina took a deep breath— "why

I came to see you. The mayor wants you in the Conference Room for an emergency Chamber of Commerce meeting."

Moody looked at Quill over the top of Dina's sleek brown head. "Another time then."

"I'm pretty busy, as you can see," Quill said. "All the time, actually. But thank you anyway."

Dina craned her neck and followed Moody and his former mother-in-law until they disappeared through the archway to the dining room. She turned to Quill. "I mean like, wow."

"What do you mean, 'wow?' "

"I've seen him on the news, of course. Everybody has. But like, wow. He's gorgeous."

"He's an arrogant jerk," Quill said with determination. "He's driving me crazy. And I hope Mrs. Pembroke's right—that the jurors will only be here for two weeks at most."

Dina looked doubtful.

"I know. The O.J. trial lasted for a year. But this is a civil matter, Dina. And what's in dispute is the interpretation of a deed. So the jury looks at it, listens to the arguments from both sides, and then decides. There's just not that much documentation to review."

"Okay."

"That's what Mrs. Pembroke said, at any rate," Quill ended a little lamely.

"Hmm. Well. So, if Myles calls you'll take the call, right? This guy isn't, like, capturing your interest?"

"Absolutely not," Quill said, and went to find out

why Corisande missed the train and to forget all about the arrogant justice.

Meg didn't know why Corisande had missed the train.

"I don't know why Corisande missed the train." Meg, clearly in a temper, flung spinach into a clear broth bubbling on the Aga, watched it for a long second, then dumped it down the sink. She refilled the pan from a bowl of broth sitting on the birch counter, and slapped it back onto the stove to heat again. "Just want it to wilt. The spinach, I mean. Even a couple of seconds is too long," she explained. "And our connection wasn't very good because she was on a cell phone, Corisande, I mean."

"But how did she sound?"

"Sound?" Meg rubbed her forehead. "Sort of glum," she admitted. "And Quill, she sounds *young.* I started to worry about her being stuck in New York—that train station there's not the best place to be stuck, you know, but then we lost the connection."

"Did you get the number of her cell phone?"

Meg looked a little stricken. "Shoot. No, I didn't."

"If she calls in again, get it. And maybe we should drive down and bring her back ourselves. It's only a few hours."

"She's due in at eleven tonight. Unless she misses that train, too, she said. For sure she'll be here in the morning. She said."

"Oh, dear," Quill said, "Well, whenever she gets in, I'll go with you. I'm off to a Chamber meeting at the moment. Let me know if you hear from her."

"Quill?"

Halfway out the kitchen door, Quill turned back.

"What about Bouncer Muldoon? You know . . ." Meg glanced from side to side and whispered, "You know. Our tailing job."

"He never showed up."

"He never showed up?!"

"Nope. Mitchell Moody put out a bench warrant for his arrest, too."

"No kidding." Meg's brows rose. "Think he was scared of running into Marge?"

"You know what I think?" Quill patted the swinging door with a thoughtful hand. "I think that both of them are scared to see each other. And that can mean only one thing, can't it?"

"I think it can mean a whole pile of different things."

"Love lasts, doesn't it? I'm just wondering if, after all these years, they still . . ."

"Love each other? Phut! Didn't she refer to him as that low-down, dim-witted son of a sea cook?"

"Or words to that effect," Quill admitted.

"It sounds more like she didn't want to be arrested for hitting him up the side of the head with a two by four. Some love lasts, Quill. But not all of it. Whatever, if he's skipped, it means she didn't have to leave town after all."

Quill nodded. "There might be a tactful way to let Marge know he's chickened out. I'll ask Dina to let the information drop when she's down at the Croh Bar with Davey." She checked her watch and sighed. "Right now,

I have to keep Carol Ann from arming half the citizens of Hemlock Falls."

The Conference Room was almost full. She'd expected Carol Ann, of course, who was accompanied by the inarticulate Mr. Dunleavy. Carol Ann was looking snakier than usual, which meant she had something awful up the sleeves of her starched white shirt. Quill greeted Dookie Shuttleworth, the elderly minister of the Hemlock Falls Church of the Word of God, and smiled at Esther West. Esther sat next to Harvey Bozzel, Hemlock Falls' best (and only) advertising executive. Harvey had a sheaf of papers in front of him, and a large, battery-operated tape recorder. Even Axminster Stoker, editor and publisher of the *Hemlock Gazette* was there. Almost all of the usual crowd. But, seated in between Howie Murchison and Nadine Nickerson (Hemlock Falls House of Beauty), was someone Quill hadn't expected: Ferris Rodman, CEO of ROCOR, Inc. And chief plaintiff in the *ROCOR v. Meecham* trial.

Quill had met Ferris Rodman, of course. Everyone in Hemlock Falls had at one time or another. The resort on the Hemlock River had been under construction for donkey's years. It started and stopped, clogged by a series of delays due to weather, litigation, and whatever else stopped huge construction projects from going forward. The project was far enough away from Hemlock Falls so that the noise and dust didn't bother the village, but close enough so that everyone expected to benefit

from the influx of tourists drawn by the riverside de-
lights promised in the glossy four-color brochures. And
except for his bulldozers and backhoes, Ferris Rodman
was a pretty quiet presence in the village. Even when the
Friends of the Dead began their futile demonstration
against the removal of the Civil War cemetery, Rodman
stayed well away from the furor.

He didn't look like the largest commercial contractor
in Upstate New York (which he was). Quill was pretty
sure he had his hair cut at Nadine's beauty salon; it was
a Ward Cleaverish buzz cut. This, with his wire-rimmed
glasses, short-sleeved white shirts, and plastic pocket
protector made him look like a very nice accountant, or
a mild-mannered electrical engineer. The only clue to
his profession was his tan: his face was as weathered as
any farmer's, and his hands were calloused. He had very
small, very sharp gray eyes. He nodded at Quill and his
ears turned red.

"Late again, Quill," Elmer Henry said in a sadly un-
surprised way. "We tabled reading the minutes, seeing
as how this is a special session. Quill? You hear me?"

Quill, who'd been staring at Ferris Rodman (which,
now that she thought of it, was probably why his ears
were red) jumped a little. "Oh, certainly, Mayor. The
minutes. Ummm. You don't need them. Right." She sat
down next to Miriam Doncaster, who promptly shoved
a steno pad into her hands. "But I'll take minutes of the
special session, shall I?" she said brightly.

"That's what the secretary does," Miriam said dryly.
Elmer whacked the mayoral gavel on the polished

surface of the mahogany table, to the inevitable distress of Esther West. "Welcome everybody. And a big Hemlock Falls welcome to Mr. Ferris Rodman, who's here because this is going to affect him, too. So, to get right down to it. Carol Ann's made a motion to consider the formation of a volunteer police force. You got that, Quill?"

Quill wrote: ASK FERRIS RODMAN ABOUT THAT DAMN HOTEL! Then: CONFLICT OF INTEREST? (JURORS!!!!) THROW HIM OUT?

"Quill's got it," Miriam said in her astringent voice. "What I hope we don't get is a lot of bogus 'crime in Hemlock Falls statistics' from Miss Carol Ann, here."

Carol Ann bridled at the word bogus.

"Vandalism is a bit of a problem for us," Ferris ventured mildly. "We have some mischief at the site, you know. Nothing major, but we'd like to see it stopped."

"You could hire a security firm," Miriam said tartly.

"Those green buggers," Elmer said. "I knew we were going to have trouble with the Friends of the Dead the minute they rolled into this town. I swear we ought to lock them up and throw away the key."

"They have a right to free speech," Howie Murchison reminded them all. "And I haven't found them to be too disruptive."

"I can tell you one thing," Nadine Nickerson said spitefully. "They're scaring the you-know-what out of my kids. I think we ought to run them out of town."

The rumble of assent that greeted this took Quill aback.

The mayor cleared his throat. "We got to get to this business at hand, now. Carol Ann's not going to bother us with the crime statistics, Miriam. We pretty much know what they are, and pretty bad, too."

Quill, who had assumed that the extent of the crime wave was a little graffiti and some overturned trash cans, raised her hand in protest.

"Not now, Quill," the mayor said. "We'll have time for discussion later. Anyway, Carol Ann and Harvey got up a real nice presentation for our guest speaker. Harvey, as you know, is the president and CEO of Bozzel Advertising, the best ad agency in Hemlock Falls. Seems like after our meeting this morning, Carol Ann figured she needed a little help to get us all the facts about having peace on the streets in our time. So, thank you Harvey. And Carol Ann Spinoza is, as you know . . ." Here Elmer faltered. Even Elmer, politician that he was, couldn't find anything praiseworthy about Carol Ann. "So we want to thank her, too. Carol Ann, you want to introduce your man from Syracuse?"

Miriam snorted derisively into her coffee and muttered something about online dating.

Carol Ann rose to her feet and said sweetly, "Everybody? I'd like to introduce Mr. Donald Dunleavy. Get up, Donald." •

Donald Dunleavy rose from his chair, rolled his toothpick from one side of his mouth to other and said, "Uh."

"One second, Donald," Carol Ann said. "Harvey? Hit it."

Harvey smoothed his scrupulously styled blond hair back with one hand, and punched the button on his tape recorder with the other. An erratic piano version of the "The Bowery Grenadiers" blasted the Chamber members into momentary immobility. Harvey twiddled with the volume button and the music sank to an irritating whisper.

"So," Donald Dunleavy said, squinting at some three by five cards in the palm of his hand. "We all know how the streets of cities up and down America run with the blood of crime."

"The what?" asked Dookie Shuttleworth, who was getting a little deaf.

"Crime, rev'rund," the mayor said. "Go on, now, Donald."

"Yeah. Right. And we all know about the heavy burdens carried by our fine boys in blue."

The music on the tape changed tempo and tune. "The Volga Boatmen," Quill thought, but the pianist was playing while grunting in a burdened boatmanlike way, so she couldn't be sure.

"That is, our p'lice," Dunleavy persevered. "The ones with the burdens. Now, you all know about the taxes we burdened taxpayers bear, right?" He looked up sharply, cutting off the murmur of assent from the Chamber members with the ferocity of his glare. "So, you got a choice. You pay for protection, or you do it your own self."

The pianist on the tape moved into a more or less stirring rendition of "The Battle Hymn of the Republic." Harvey began to hum and waved encouragement to the Chamber members to join him. "The Battle Hymn of the Republic" is a hard hymn to resist. Elmer, humming too, began to beat time with the gavel. Harland Peterson shrugged, and joined in, then Nadine and most of the others. Quill's notes of the proceedings became increasingly erratic, mostly because the buzzing of "The Battle Hymn of the Republic" through ten or fifteen noses drowned out the rest of Donald Dunleavy's speech. She caught "service to others", "the right to keep and bear arms", and "pound the little bastards flat" (although she wasn't sure about the last one). Dunleavy's timing was good. He sat down just as the Chamber hit "his truth is marching on!" or would have, if they'd been singing instead of humming.

"Little loud on the back-up there," Harvey said with a considering air. "But I think we got the gist of it." He sprang to his feet. "Ladies. Gentlemen. Mayor. I would like to make a motion that the Hemlock Falls Chamber of Commerce sponsor the first-ever volunteer police force in Hemlock Falls!" He punched the tape recorder and "Men of Harlech" boomed into the room. "All those in favor . . ."

"You're kidding," Meg said.

"Nope. Fifteen for. Three against."

Meg set her glass of wine on the oak chest that Quill used as a coffee table. "I know *you* didn't vote for it. Who else didn't? Don't tell me. Howie and Miriam. What about Dookie?"

"I think he thought he was voting on the music."

"Jeez." Meg sat back with a sigh. "Now what?"

"Elmer was elected Volunteer Police Chief. Adela's going to be president of the Ladies' Police Auxiliary. The Nickersons offered to sell handcuffs at cost to the volunteers; Esther's going to design the uniforms. You know. The usual."

"Did you tell Myles?"

Quill glanced at the clock on the wall. "I haven't heard from him. Yet."

She leaned back and closed her eyes. Meg bounced her wineglass gently on her knee.

It was late, after twelve o'clock, and they were sitting in Quill's small living room. Max was prone in a corner, snoring peacefully. Quill wished she were prone in a corner, sleeping peacefully, too.

Ferris Rodman had scooted out of the Chamber meeting so quickly after it was adjourned that Quill was convinced he was planning a small, elegant, gourmet hotel instead of the golf course. He absolutely did not want to talk to her and refused to catch her eye. She'd promised herself to visit him at the construction site as soon as she could get an hour away from the Inn.

She'd spent the rest of the day after the Chamber meeting handling the usual complaints from staff and guests, paying bills for the month, talking with John about Meg's plans to inflict the results of her research and development on the hapless jurors, and avoiding Mitchell Moody's invitations to pre-dinner cocktails, dinner, after-dinner cocktails, and a nightcap.

She was exhausted. And then Meg had bounced in for a talk about Corisande.

Although both of them had suites at the Inn, Meg rarely used hers, preferring to stay evenings with Andy in his small house near his clinic. But Andy was away for a three-day conference on childhood autism, and Meg was spending the night in her own quarters, across the hall from Quill.

Quill opened her eyes and stared at the ceiling. "So Corisande wasn't on the eleven o'clock train."

"She called, though," Meg said anxiously. "And I couldn't hear exactly, over all the music, but she did say she'd met up with some friends she'd known in Europe. And she will be here tomorrow, Quill, I know it." She bit her lip. "Do you think we should e-mail Aunt Eleanor?"

"I tried earlier. Her server seems to be down. It's just as well. We'd tell her what? Corisande's off whooping it up instead of staying with her staid and . . ."

"Boring," Meg supplied gloomily.

"Cousins?" Quill got up and moved restlessly around the room. "I think we should remember that Corisande's almost twenty-three years old and we can't do a thing about it." She took a sip of her wine, "Do you remember Uncle Erhard?"

"Why should I remember Uncle Erhard? We've never met Uncle Erhard."

"Mother didn't like him."

"Well," Meg said stoutly, "He must have been a miserable S.O.B. to divorce Aunt Eleanor."

"It was more than that. He had visitation rights to see

Corisande, of course. And from what I can gather, he did his best to set Corisande against Aunt Eleanor. Eleanor wasn't all that forthcoming in her e-mails to me, but she implied she was worried about Corisande's lifestyle."

"And the reason you didn't mention this to me before was . . . ?" Meg said.

Quill sighed and put her feet up on the chest. "It wasn't really anything you could pin down. I just got this . . . feeling."

They both fell silent.

Quill looked wistfully at her toes. When she and Meg had first remodeled the Inn, she'd kept the colors and furnishings of her own apartments neutral and undemanding. The Berber carpet was a pale ecru. The walls were a soothing cream. A leather couch in saddle brown faced the French doors that led to her small balcony. Her living room was sparsely furnished; there was an Eames chair in the north corner, with a good lamp for reading craning over it, and a tall bookshelf, painted with the same cream as the walls. She'd placed two pieces of art on the walls: a black-and-white photograph and a small charcoal sketch of herself and Meg. The very neutrality of the rooms allowed her imagination free rein. It was here that the ideas came for her most complex paintings. It was here that she came to rest. Right now, she wanted some peace.

"Well, I think Corisande's visit is going to be wonderful." There wasn't a lot of conviction in Meg's voice.

"Yes," Quill said. "Well, Meggie. It's time I turned in."

She slept hard, and there were no calls from Myles.

She woke at seven to find Doreen standing over her, a look of grim satisfaction on her face.

"I *told* ya there was going to be trouble."

Quill pulled the pillow over her head.

Doreen removed it.

"What?"

"It's that bozo Corliss Hooker."

Quill yawned and blinked fuzzily up at her. "Mr. Hooker? The Friend of the Dead?"

"Yep. And that's what he is now. Dead as a doornail."

CHAPTER 5

"So what's this murder got to do with us, anyways?" Doreen slapped an omelet down in front of Quill, a second in front of herself, and sat down at the staff table in the corner of the dining room.

"Not out here, Doreen. Not with everybody listening," Quill hissed. "And it doesn't have a thing to do with us. Why do you keep saying that? I don't know why you're in this early anyway. You're not supposed to be here until nine. Just eat your breakfast. Okay?" She lifted the omelet's puffy golden lid and looked inside. Chopped lox, sour cream, mustard and chives. Muriel May Johnson, sitting with Jurors Two, (Sparky Stillwater), Three (Brett Coldwell), and Five (Morgan Mwgambe), cried, "Honey! It's the best thing you're ever going to eat. And did you try those potatoes?"

"It's my sister's potato soufflé," Quill said, raising her voice a little. "It's wonderful, isn't it?"

"That it is," Mr. Mwgambe agreed.

"I'm so glad you're enjoying it." There was a general murmur of assent.

Doreen put her fork down and cast a disapproving eye over the dining room. "Why are they all sitting like that?"

"Like what? Oh, you mean the lawyers in one corner, the judge and the bailiff in the other, and the jurors in the middle? They aren't supposed to fraternize."

"Makes a load of work for the waitstaff," Doreen grumbled. "You smush 'em all together and you can save some walking, that's for sure."

"Well, we can't smush them all together. Anyway, everybody gets the same thing, so there's less traffic to the table and back."

"That Mrs. Pembroke says she can't eat eggs," Doreen said indignantly.

Quill looked over at Mrs. Pembroke, who was eating by herself. Her PDA lay open on the table. For some reason, she looked very cross. She stabbed her spoon into a bowl as if she were killing cockroaches. Maybe Justice Moody had told her he wouldn't accept any more time sheets.

"Meg had to make oatmeal, special. So don't you tell me about traffic."

Quill looked at her housekeeper with affectionate concern. Doreen hid a loving, loyal disposition behind a grumpy demeanor, but there was something edgier than usual about her this morning. "Are you okay? Is there anything wrong?"

"You said not to talk about it."

"About"—Quill leaned forward and lowered her voice—"Mr. Hooker? I'm so sorry. I didn't realize that you knew him, Doreen."

"Didn't know him from a hole in the ground, did I? Stoke found him, is all."

"Your husband found the body? Oh, dear. Oh, my. Here. Let's take our plates into the kitchen."

"What?" Meg demanded as they came through the swinging doors. "You can't bring your food back. It's not allowed."

"I'm not bringing my food back." Quill put her plate on the prep table. "I'm bringing my food in here to eat it so we can talk. Did you know Stoke discovered Corliss Hooker's body?"

Meg grabbed Quill's fork and sliced off a piece of her omelet. "Yes."

"Stop that. That's my breakfast." Quill sat down and began to eat. She stopped and put her fork down. "So why didn't you tell me?"

"I was going to tell you," Doreen said, in the tones she normally reserved for the most irritating of her teenaged grandchildren. "I woke you up to tell you. But what happened when I woke you up? Leave me alone, you said. I gotta get a shower and we have to get Corisande this morning and I don't want to hear about it right this minute. Then I started to tell you again out there," she jerked her thumb toward the dining room, "and you told me to shush right up."

"I didn't think we should talk about it in front of the jurors," Quill said feebly.

"Why not?" Meg said. "Everybody's talking about it. You know Hemlock Falls. Word gets around like that." Meg snapped her fingers.

"But how could I guess that you'd found the body? I mean, you sat right out there, Doreen, and you said 'so what's this murder got to do with us, anyways?' It doesn't have a thing to do with us. Does it?"

"Had a note addressed to you right on the body, didn't it," Doreen said with immense satisfaction.

"A note to me?!" Quill sat back. "I don't believe it."

"Hang on a bit," Meg said. "We don't know that it was addressed to Quill." She patted her sister's arm reassuringly. "But it did have your name on it, that's true."

As delicious as the omelet was, Quill couldn't eat any more of it. She shoved the plate aside and sat down at the prep table. "Why don't you start at the beginning, Doreen."

Doreen folded her arms and nodded approvingly. "That's more like it. Okay. Here's what happened. Thing is, Stoke always takes a walk at night just before he turns in. Helps his legs. Gets aches in 'em, from standing around the news office all day. He went out 'bout his regular time, eleven or so. And see, he walks the dog from our place down to the cemetery and back.

Every night. Like clockwork. You know where I mean."

Quill did. Doreen and Stoke lived in a small bungalow on a side street about a quarter of a mile from the Civil War cemetery. The offices of the *Hemlock Falls Gazette* were located about five blocks in the other direction. Stoke was a familiar sight on the streets of the village, striding along in his khakis (shorts in the summer, trousers in the winter) from workplace to home and back again, the little Lhasa apso at his side.

"So he gets to the cemetery like usual, and all of a sudden, Cosette takes off like a bat out of hell. Jerked her leash right out of his hands." Doreen lowered her voice and said dramatically, "Run right into the cemetery, she did. Went straight to this grave. And Stoke? He finds this Corliss Hooker a-laying there, all dressed up in his black robes and his face painted green."

"Oh, my," Quill said.

"So Stoke kneels down and takes a look. Poor guy's head's all bashed in. Stoke gets on the cell, calls the amb'lance and the deputy and while he's waiting he takes a few pictures of the scene for the newspaper."

Quill bit her lip.

"It's news, missy. And Stoke runs a newspaper. So don't you get hoity-toity with me!"

"I didn't say anything."

"Looked like you might."

"Well, I didn't." Quill rolled her eyes at Meg.

Doreen sighed. "So, anyways. Davey gets there and the EMTs from the hospital and when they roll the body over, guess what they find."

"A note addressed to me?" Quill hazarded.

"A crumpled-up notebook with the pages tore out."

"I thought you said—"

"That comes later."

"How *much* later?" Quill asked, exasperated.

Doreen, who had a literal turn of mind said, "About one o'clock."

"And what time is it now? Not," Quill added hastily, "right this minute, but the time when Stoke and the police found the empty notebook."

"It's about midnight, because Stoke calls me on the cell and tells me he's going to the hospital to follow up on the story."

"And then?" Quill prompted.

"That's what I know from Stoke. He come back home around three and we both got up early. He's down at the paper writing the story right now. It'll be a special edition."

Quill poured herself a glass of orange juice from the pitcher on the prep table and drank it before she said carefully, "What. About. The note. Addressed. To me!"

Meg giggled, and then responded to her sister's glare with a meek, "Sorry. It isn't funny, is it? A death never is. Although Andy said it was very, very quick. Just one blow to the side of the head."

Quill swiveled and glared at her sister. "Do *you* know anything about this note?"

"Of course I do. Andrew found it in Mr. Hooker's jacket pocket. When Doreen came in this morning, I told her all about it."

"And I came in to tell *you* all about it," Doreen said in a very satisfied way. "So now you know."

"I don't know anything!" Quill said. "You haven't told me anything at all! I want to know about this note!"

The swinging door to the dining room whacked open and Mitchell Moody—followed by his large, balding bailiff—walked into the kitchen. "Everything all right in here? We heard a scream."

"Everything's fine, your Honor," Quill said a little stiffly. "How was your breakfast?"

Moody ignored this attempt at diversion. "I understand there was a homicide in the village last night?"

Meg, Quill, and Doreen all exchanged glances. Quill knew why. They were closing ranks against an outsider. "Apparently," Meg said. "It's the poor old guy who was the head of that group protesting the relocation of the cemetery."

Moody's black eyes glittered. "Oh? I ruled on that case a while ago. ROCOR versus"—he snapped his fingers—"some acronym. F.O.D., that was it."

"The man's name is—was—Corliss Hooker," Quill said.

"Yeah. I remember now. Bit of a loony tune."

Quill looked at her thumbs. This seemed like very unjudicial behavior to her, but Moody wasn't on the bench and he could reveal all the insensitive prejudices he wanted to. On the other hand, he was standing right in the middle of their kitchen. Which, according to New York State Health codes, was off limits to guests. "You'll have to excuse us, your Honor. We don't allow guests back here."

Moody raised his eyebrows. "I do seem to get under your delightfully smooth skin, Miss Quilliam. Your local bobby able to handle it?"

This Britishism annoyed Quill profoundly.

"Deputy Sheriff Kiddermeister is perfectly able to handle things, thank you."

"Just let me know if you want me to make a few calls." Moody jerked his head at his bailiff, and the two of them left the way they'd come in.

"'Delightfully smooth skin?!'" Meg said. "Jeez, Quill."

Doreen flexed one skinny arm. "He been giving you any trouble, Quill?"

"No mop," Quill said immediately. "And I can handle Mr. Chief Justice Moody. What I can't handle is not knowing a thing about this note!"

"Oh," Meg said. "Sure. Well, Andy couldn't actually touch it, of course. Davey swept it away to take to the forensics people in Ithaca, but Andy managed to read it and said something like. 'Quill. K-47.'"

"Mean anything to you?" Doreen asked hopefully.

"K-47?" Quill rubbed her nose. "'K' as in Keuchal, maybe? I think K-47 is the one of the horn concertos. Oh! Of course! The tuba!"

"What tuba?" Meg said. "Mozart didn't write for the tuba. The tuba wasn't even invented yet."

"So what's going on?" Doreen huffed.

"Mr. Hooker threatened to play tubas in front of the Inn since his protest at the cemetery wasn't getting any attention," Quill said. "I guess he was planning on playing one of the Horn Concerti. Hence, the note."

"Hence bull hockey," Doreen said. "That note's a clue, missy."

"What kind of clue?" Quill asked reasonably.

"We won't know until we find out who murdered him and why," Doreen said.

"If we find out who murdered him and why, we won't need the clue," Meg pointed out.

"And we aren't going to investigate this murder," Quill added. "We can't."

"I can," Doreen said.

"None of us can. We're all too busy."

"But that clue was addressed to you! I'm telling ya. We're up to our ears in this mess."

"It wasn't a clue, Doreen. It was part of poor Mr. Hooker's protest plans."

"Well, if you ain't interested in following this clue up, I am."

Quill clutched her head with both hands for a long moment. She peered up at Doreen. "Let's list the reasons why we should leave this up to the police."

Doreen pushed out her lower lip; it made her look like a sulking chicken. Quill patted her arm. "Honestly. We're up to our ears in work here."

"No mor'n usual."

And that, Quill thought, depends entirely on what

Ferris Rodman has to say when I finally catch up with him. We may have to go into the detective business full-time just to pay the bills.

"Well?" Doreen said. "You just gonna sit there, I got things to do."

"Yes. Of course. Sorry. For one thing, we have Corisande arriving today. How's she going to feel if her nice, reliable cousins are up to their ears in a murder investigation?"

This made an impact on Doreen, Quill could tell. Meg, on the other hand, brightened up. Murder wasn't boring at all.

"She's here to learn to cook, after all." Quill continued doggedly. "How would Aunt Eleanor feel if we drew her only daughter into this? Detective work can be dangerous, as both of you know."

"True," Meg said, reluctantly.

"Not only that—we're smack in the middle of hosting a sequestered jury. What if something we did wrecked the outcome of the trial?"

The skepticism on both Meg's and Doreen's faces made Quill hurry on to the next point. "Finally, if, and I say if, the note on Mr. Hooker's body was addressed to me, I'd prefer to stay as far away from this as possible. I mean, the last time I got mixed up as a suspect in a murder case, I actually spent time in jail."

"It'd give you more time to draw," Doreen offered. "Jail's pretty quiet. Nothing else to do."

"And that's another thing. In case you've forgotten, I

promised to send Upton Gallery a few new pieces by the end of the year. Now when am I going to find time to do that?" Quill did her best to look pitiful.

"I still think . . ." Doreen began.

Quill got to her feet and assumed the physical position advised by her latest course at the Cornell School of Hotel Management—Authority-Based Kinesics. She stood with both feet slightly apart, folded her arms, lowered her chin to her breast, and said "No," in her lowest voice. Professor Wjoucski had called this stance "the Trump."

"Gonna get a crick in your neck if you keep that up," Doreen said, unimpressed. "I'm going down to the Croh Bar for coffee. Let ya know what I find out later." She grabbed her parka from the coat rack, jammed her knit cap over her gray curls, and left the kitchen with a loud slam of the back door.

"She's just going to go right ahead and poke her nose into that murder," Quill said.

"I told you that kinesiology stuff wouldn't work with people," Meg said. "Dogs, maybe. You should try it on Max. I don't know why you waste your time on these stupid courses." She grabbed the remains of Quill's omelet and carried it back to the dishwasher. "And aren't you just a little curious about why Corliss Hooker died?"

"There's something I'm more curious about than that." Quill bit her lip. "What time is it?"

"About nine o'clock."

"Corisande's due at the train station at ten, right?"

"I hope so."

"Let's leave now. We'll be a little early, but some-times the train is, too. I've got something I want to tell you, and I'd rather not talk about it here."

"I'm ready anytime," Meg said. She raised her eye-brows. "Wait a sec. Talk to me about what? You haven't broken up with Myles again, have you?"

"No? Why? Did he call you? Why did he call you in-stead of me? Is there something wrong? Does he want to break up?"

Meg rolled her eyes, removed her apron, and grabbed the small backpack she used as a purse. "Isn't there a course at Cornell on dealing with insecurity?"

"Very funny."

"If there is, I think you should take it." She broke off abruptly, "How do I look?" Meg scrabbled through her backpack. "Should I put on a little lip gloss?"

"You want to take Insecurity 101 at Cornell with me? You look fine," Quill took a step back and looked at her sister. She'd been so caught up in Corliss Hooker's mur-der that she hadn't had time to look at Meg. "As a mat-ter of fact, you look pretty glamorous. Isn't that the outfit you used to wear for Lally Preston's TV show?"

Meg glanced down at herself. She was wearing a cherry chenille sweater, elegantly draped black trousers, and an expensive pair of black leather Italian boots. She tossed her head carelessly, "Oh, this?"

"Meg, you don't need to dress up for—"

"Need to what?"

"Nothing. Do you want me to drive?"

"I do not," Meg said emphatically. "Corisande should

spend her time here and not at Andy's hospital. I'll drive. But we'll take your car. It's newer."

The drive to the train station took them out of Hemlock Falls and almost to Ithaca. Quill was always mildly surprised to ride with Meg. Her sister was an excellent driver, exhibiting a controlled, athletic steadiness in direct opposition to her volatility in the kitchen. Quill, who cheerfully accepted her own incompetence behind the wheel, relaxed in the passenger seat for a few luxurious moments. When they turned onto Route 15 (which in turn led to the notorious Octopus intersection—a labyrinth Quill was perfectly happy to leave to Meg) she sat up, ready to tackle the most important of her worries—the possible threat to the Inn. "Okay, so here's the problem."

Meg listened in grave silence as Quill gave a pretty accurate account of her conversation with Carol Ann, and of her inability to find out anything else from John or Marge. The first thing she said was, "Which European chef?"

"Carol Ann didn't say. And the chef doesn't matter, Meg. We don't even know if it's *true*. After we pick up Corisande, I'm going to go straight over to ROCOR's site office and ask Ferris Rodman if there's any truth in it at all."

"What do you mean, the chef doesn't matter? Are you nuts?" Meg frowned, beat both hands on the steering wheel, then pulled to the side of the road and stopped.

"Why are you stopping?"

"Because I can't scream and drive at the same time. I

know that you're perfectly happy to scream and drive at the same time, but then, you're the one who's in the insurance risk pool." Meg killed the engine, rolled the window down, and shrieked.

Quill drummed her fingers on the dashboard. "Okay now?" she asked, after a long moment.

"No, it's not okay. But I don't have to scream anymore. Unless you tell me the chef is Claude de Courcy. If it's Claude de Courcy, I'm not only going to scream my head off, I'm going to shave my eyebrows and throw ashes in the air."

"I don't have a clue about the chef. If there even *is* a chef. Or even if there's a new hotel."

Meg reignited the engine and pulled back into the stream of traffic. "Have you heard anything from Marge?"

"Not a word. Nobody seems to know where she is. I hope by now someone's told her that Bouncer never showed up for the second day of the voir dire. My guess is she'll be back in town as soon as she knows the coast is clear."

"That was funny," Meg said.

"I don't think it's funny. I think it's sad. I told you, what if they . . ."

Meg waved one hand impatiently. "Not funny ha-ha. Funny peculiar. It's odd that Bouncer Muldoon disappeared."

"Mitchell Moody says that happens once in a while."

"It's odd that Corliss Hooker was killed."

"You think they're connected?" Quill shook her

head. "There's not the remotest possibility. How can there be?"

"And it's funny that Carol Ann's the only one that knows about this new hotel."

"Now *that's* odd," Quill agreed. "Marge said she could think of a couple of reasons why you and I would know about the new hotel before anyone else, but no reason why we wouldn't know. If it's true, why in the world does it have to be kept secret?"

"You're going to find out what you can, right? I mean, talk to Marge, poke around as much as you can."

"Right."

"And you'll let me know if we're going to be out on the street without a penny to our names."

"I will."

"And you'll especially let me know if that penultimate rat Claude de Courcy is the—"

"Stop," Quill said. "Not the car, Meg. If we don't get going we're going to be late. Just stop all that stuff about the European chef. We're going to pick up our long-lost cousin. We're going to welcome her with open arms. You are going to teach her all you know about being a great cook, and I am going to reveal the inner secrets of innkeeping to her. And we'll tackle the stuff about this new hotel when we have more information."

"Fine," Meg snapped.

"Fine to you, too."

They drove on in a charged silence.

Eventually, Meg relaxed. She expertly dodged an

ice-filled pothole and said, "Did you get any e-mails from Aunt Eleanor this morning?"

"Not since last week. The server's still down. But she hasn't gotten back from her tour of Turkey yet, anyway."

"I'd love that," Meg said a little wistfully. "Just being able to take off anytime you wanted. Go anywhere you wanted. Do anything you wanted."

Quill didn't answer that. Meg increased the Honda's speed to seventy. She divided her attention between the road and the rearview mirror.

"You're not nervous about this, are you, Meg? I think Corisande's visit is going to be fun."

"You would," Meg said obscurely. She hesitated a long moment, then said, tentatively, "Have you and Myles talked any more about having kids?"

"Some," Quill turned her head and looked out the window. She could almost feel Meg's gaze on the back of her head. "What about you and Andy?"

"When we do get married, we want two."

Quill imagined the word "when" as a bright blue balloon, floating over Meg's head and then turning into a question mark. "It isn't quite so definite for Myles and for me. He's older, for one thing. And I'm not sure how good a mother I'd be."

Meg reached over and clasped her hand briefly. "You'd be terrific. But I know what you mean, it's such a drastic change." She put both hands back on the wheel. "The thing is, Corisande's visit is sort of a trial run, if you see what I mean."

"A trial run? Meg, she's almost twenty-three years old."

"I know. But she's younger than both of us. And from what you've told me about Eleanor's e-mails, she sort of—you know—seems to look up to me."

"The Cornell co-op students look up to you."

Meg smiled reluctantly. "That's different. They have to, or they'll get fired." She shook her head. "Since Mom and Dad died, it's just been the two of us, as far as family goes. This is someone who looks a little like us—didn't you think so? From that picture she sent?"

Quill, who had downloaded the picture and studied the face of their cousin, had concluded that Corisande mostly resembled Aunt Eleanor's late—and highly unlamented—ex-husband Erhard, if anyone. "Maybe a little," she said cautiously.

"She probably has the same blood type as we do, and she has the same grandparents. It's a connection. A family connection. Our first!"

Quill nodded. "True. The turn for the train depot's about a mile ahead. You can slow down. We're early."

They were early, but the train from New York had been even earlier. When Quill and Meg walked into the terminal, Corisande rose from the bench where she'd been sitting among a litter of backpacks and gave them a tentative smile.

Corisande's picture hadn't prepared Quill for how large she was. She was tall, taller than Quill, who was close to five-eight. Corisande's face was gaunt, as if she'd lost weight recently, which made her look a lot older than twenty-three. Her hair was almost exactly the same color as Meg's. Her eyes, like Uncle Erhardt's, were a deep brown. After a brief moment of awkwardness between the three of them, Quill hugged her.

"Well," Quill said, surprised to find her eyes a little damp. "Just look at you, Corisande."

"Call me Cory. As soon as I landed at JFK I decided to call myself Cory. Since I'm in America now." Her voice was flatter than Quill had expected.

"Did you spend the night with your friends?" Meg asked. "Did you sleep well?"

Cory's eyes flickered. "Yes. Oh, yes. It was great to see them after all this time. Sorry I missed the train yesterday," she added in a perfunctory way. She tapped the palm of her hand lightly against her forehead. "My mother probably bitched about my being scatterbrained."

"Well," Quill said. "Well. Here we are. Is this all your luggage, Cory?"

She nodded. "I couldn't decide what to bring with me, so I brought it all. You want to get it to your car. Is your driver here?"

"We drove ourselves," Meg said. "Mike the groundskeeper drives the guest van when the guests need to be driven somewhere. But we drive ourselves."

"Oh. I thought you two were rich."

"No," Quill said lightly, "not rich. But we're very happy."

"So we have to lug this ourselves, huh? I'll take the duffle, then. Meg, you can handle those two there, can't you? And Quill, if you tuck the red canvas bag under your arm, you can get those other two." She looked a little bored. "Not too heavy for you, Quill?"

"Um, no," Quill said, staggering slightly. "We're over here. The silver Honda CRV."

"Uh-oh. A rice rocket, huh?"

"Excuse me?" Meg said.

"That's not what you call Japanese cars over here? Rice rockets?"

"Um," Quill said. "No. We don't call them that." She set the bags down, fumbled for her keys, and opened the back.

Corisande flung her duffle back into the cargo space. "I haven't been back to the States for years." She shivered. "I don't remember it being this cold."

"You didn't go to the University of California? Here—" Quill interrupted herself, as Corisande began to climb into the backseat. "You sit up front with Meg." She shepherded their cousin into the front passenger seat, then got into the backseat.

"U-Cal?" Cory gave a short, unpleasant laugh. "Well, that was my mother's plan. But no. I took off my freshman year. Well, it was supposed to be my freshman year."

Meg put the Honda into gear, and pulled out of the terminal parking lot. "Supposed to be?"

"Eleanor probably told you that I mostly lived with Papa while I was growing up."

"Yes," Quill said. "Meg and I didn't know a lot about the divorce, of course, but I remember our mother mentioning how unfair the custody agreement was." She put her hand on Cory's shoulder. "I'm sorry. I didn't mean to imply that your father was . . . I mean—"

" 'Eleanor?' " Meg interrupted. "You don't call your mother Mom?"

"Well, she wasn't around enough of the time for me to call her Mom, was she?" Cory said sullenly. "I mean, I saw her on school holidays when I was little and for a month in the summers. But it wasn't until after Papa died that I went to live with her on a regular basis, and by then, I was grown up and it seemed stupid."

Meg, who was driving much more slowly than usual, tilted her head thoughtfully. "You really grew up without a mother, then."

Cory gave a very European shrug.

"So you never got to U-Cal," Quill said sympathetically.

"Nope. Seemed a waste of time. I backpacked around Spain for a while, though. That was pretty cool."

"Oh!" Meg said enviously. "That must have been wonderful."

Cory shrugged again. "Met a lot of guys. Smoked a lot of dope. Yes, it was fun. But then Eleanor dragged me back to live with her and that was the end of that." She looked out of the window. "Is it always so shitty here? Looks like East Berlin after the wall came down."

"It's beautiful in the spring," Quill said. "You aren't seeing us at our best." Then, in defense of Hemlock Falls, she said, "March is lovely in its own way, I think. The colors can be wonderful."

Cory craned her neck over the front seat. "Eleanor

told me you're a famous artist. What do you find to paint out here? What kind of art do you do?"

"I work in acrylics, primarily," Quill said. "Although I've been thinking recently of . . . "

Corisande turned punched Meg lightly on the shoulder. "And you're supposed to be the chef! What do you cook, anyway? Do you have a specialty?"

"I started with classical French. Most of us do. And I'm really looking forward to getting started with you, Cory. I've planned out the next ten days so that you can get a nice head start, without feeling overwhelmed."

"Whatever." She slumped back into her seat, the brief bout of enthusiasm over. "Eleanor tells me I'm lucky to have such famous cousins!" She yawned widely. "But before we get started, I think I should tell you straight out—that's the American way, isn't it? Straight out that I'm not expected to scrub pots and pans and that kind of thing, right?"

"Scrub pots and pans?" Meg said.

"You know, like a skivvy. I'm supposed to be learning the top stuff, right?"

Meg cleared her throat. "Well, we all have to start with the basics, of course. But, no, you won't be washing dishes. As such."

"You have people to take care of that, correct?"

Meg kept her eyes on the road. Quill tugged at her hair.

"Correct," Meg said.

"Good. I'm glad we got that out of the way. I think Americans say something like, 'no offense,' correct?"

"Correct," Quill said. And conversation lagged until they turned up the main drive to the Inn.

"So you're finally here!" Dina sprang from behind the reception desk as the three of them walked through the front door of the Inn. "Hi! Welcome to Hemlock Falls!"

"Thanks," Cory said. She thumped her duffle bag onto the Oriental carpet that covered the foyer.

"This is Dina Muir, our receptionist," Quill said. "Dina, this is Corisande. Cory, I mean."

Cory nodded. "Do you think you could get the rest of my bags?"

"Sure," Dina said. "Is the Honda out front? Do you want me to park it, Quill?"

"Thank you, Dina." Quill was very aware of the extravagance of the warmth in her own voice. "Thank you very much. But I think that Cory can—"

"Oh, I don't mind schlepping bags. It's her first day." Impulsively, she gave Corisande a hug. "Look, you don't let them work you too hard, okay?"

"They'd better not," Corisande said.

"Later on, I'll take you around the village, and over to Cornell, if you want. Quill? Doreen checked her room ninety-six times or so, so everything should be all ready."

"I'd like to go to my room," Corisande said. "I'm pretty tired."

"You must be exhausted," Quill said in sudden sympathy. "And you flew into JFK what, just two days ago. You're probably half dead with jet lag."

"Speaking of dead"—Dina ducked down behind the mahogany reception desk to retrieve her purse, then reappeared, her face slightly flushed—"Davey wants to see you about poor Mr. Hooker. Did you know that there was this note to you under his body?"

"Umm, let's not talk about this right now, Dina."

Corisande's eyes flickered in that curious, sideways gesture that Quill had noticed before. "Body?"

"Yep. That's right. You've arrived in Hemlock Falls, murder capital of the world."

"Dina, I hardly think—" Quill protested weakly.

"You Americans all carry guns, I suppose," Corisande said with contempt.

"He wasn't shot. He was whacked over the head," Dina said. "And we're all very sorry about it, of course."

"Sure you are. I don't consider myself an American, you know. It's, like, worth your life to admit it around my friends. My French is good, so most of the time, I can fake it. Americans. Another day, another murder."

"I think," Quill said, in the tone of voice that usually silenced everyone within hearing distance, "that it's time for Cory to go to her room."

She led the way upstairs, Corisande dragging her duffle bag behind her, Meg straggling along behind. "We put you in 221," Quill said as they walked down the hallway. "We aren't using it for guests at the moment because we're going to replace the carpet and the drapes this year. That's one of the ongoing expenses of keeping up a hotel, of course. We can't afford to have the guest rooms showing wear." She opened the door and switched on the light.

Two twenty-one was a double, with one mullioned window looking out over the back gardens. Quill's disclaimer about the loveliness of the room had been automatic, since she hadn't wanted Corisande to feel intimidated by the luxuriousness of the small suite. The carpeting was a warm caramel, and the drapes, bedspread, and small settee were furnished in soft creams, bronzes, and blush. The effect was both elegant and warm. Someone, probably Doreen, had placed a bowl of hothouse roses on the mantel of the small brick fireplace. "Most of the central part of the Inn dates from the mid-nineteenth century," Quill said cheerfully. "That's why the ceilings are so low, of course. But I'm sure you're used to older buildings."

"There's a TV?" Corisande said.

"Yes, in the wardrobe."

"You get cable?" Corisande upended her duffle bag onto the bed. A tangle of makeup bags, T-shirts, jeans, sandals, and hiking shoes spilled over the spread. Her laptop looked very much the worse for wear.

"Not out here, no. The village is just out of range from the cable company in Ithaca . . ."

Meg, who had been silent until now, said, "There's a television in the Lounge that's on satellite. We put it in last year so the guests could follow football."

Corisande threw herself on the part of the bed not covered by the detritus from her bag. Meg sat down next to her. "You are exhausted, aren't you? Tell you what. You get a good nap," she drew in her breath, "and a shower, too, and then come on down to the kitchen. I'm always there. Then I can show you around."

"Right," Corisande said. She closed her eyes. Then after a long moment, she said, "Thanks."

Meg followed Quill out the door and shut it behind them both. "Well," she said.

"Correct," Quill said.

"She's bound to be a little shy. I mean, she doesn't know us at all."

"True."

"Well." Meg drew a deep breath. "This is going to be great."

Downstairs, they found Dina struggling with the last of the bags. Quill sent Meg off to the kitchen, and told Dina to wait for Mike to show up after snowplowing.

"I can get them upstairs," Dina protested.

"They're pretty heavy. And if Mike doesn't show, Corisande can get them up one at a time. She managed all the way from Milan."

"But I don't mind, Quill, honestly."

"I do."

"The jurors and all those other guys left for the courthouse this morning," Dina offered. "That gorgeous judge—"

"Justice," Quill said.

"Whatever, said they might be very late. So I told the kitchen."

"Thank you."

"And the mayor called. He wanted to know if he could use the Conference Room for the first meeting of the Hemlock Grenadiers this afternoon."

This got Quill's attention. "The what?"

"That's what they're calling the volunteer police force. I said yeah, it'd be okay for now."

"Okay."

Dina settled behind the reception desk and opened a textbook titled *The Life Cycle of the Copepod*. Quill broke off a wilted lily head from the flower arrangement in the Oriental vase to the right of the desk, and fiddled with the drooping ferns.

"Quill?"

"Yes, Dina."

"You want your other phone calls?"

Quill, whose universe had been knocked a little askew by the arrival of her graceless cousin, was relieved to have things back to normal. "Of course I want my phone calls. I always want my phone calls."

Dina handled over a pink sheaf of While You Were Outs and Quill paged through them quickly.

"Aha!" she said. "Marge is back."

"She was back last night," Dina said. "She was in the Croh Bar. She said she'd be there at lunch, which is in fifteen minutes, if you want to meet her. Are you going down to see her?"

"Well, I was planning on going out to the construction site but I think I want to see Marge first."

"If you are, will you stop and see Davey? He wants to ask you about your murder."

"It's not my murder. I didn't know Corliss Hooker any better than anyone else! Less, in fact."

"But you," Dina said, "were the only person he wrote to before he died."

"Phooey. It was a note to himself. I didn't have anything to do with it."

"Davey thinks . . . "

"Davey can just wait," Quill said callously, "I can take care of the interview with him over the phone. It's far more important that I see—"

The front door flew open. A very large, very bald, very fat man marched into the foyer and roared, "Hey! Anybody up here seen Marge Schmidt?"

CHAPTER 6

"Oh my gosh," Dina said. "It's Bouncer Muldoon. Oh my gosh! I've seen you on TV!"

"I don't give autographs no more," the huge man said, modestly. "Got a bad case of carpal tunnel. But I could come up with some kinda souvenir if you want, little lady." He stepped aside as Max pushed his way through the front door and said, "Excuse me, pal. Go right on ahead."

Max gave him a brief glance, wagged his tail in a "Later, I'm busy way," and trotted up the stairs to goodness knew where.

Quill immediately thought of her superhero sketch, left unfinished since her discussion with Carol Ann Spinoza. Bouncer Muldoon dominated the foyer like a sequoia in a bonsai garden. Quill was good at guessing heights; the former wrestler had to be well over six foot five. His neck started at his ears and sloped directly into his shoulders. He wore a tentlike leather jacket against the cold March day outside. It gaped open, revealing a t-shirt emblazoned with the legend FOLLOW THE BOUNCER'S BALLS! His tiny blue eyes, almost swallowed up by his huge, pink cheeks, swiveled in Quill's direction. "Margie here?"

"Marge Schmidt?" Quill said.

Dina, after that first, involuntary outburst, sat at her desk with her mouth slightly open.

"Schmidt. Right." Bouncer cracked his knuckles with a sound reminiscent of ball bearings flung in a hubcap. "She owns the place, right?"

"Owns? Oh! Yes, Mr. Muldoon, she did at one time. But she doesn't anymore. We bought it back from her a few years ago." Quill's manners, delayed by astonishment, suddenly kicked in. "I'm sorry. My name's Sarah Quilliam. My sister and I own the Inn now. Can I help you?" She walked toward him, her hand extended. Bouncer took it in his own, looked at it, and released it like a puppy dropping a ball.

"Well, if Marge don't own this place, what does she own?"

Quill, who had wondered about the origin of Bouncer's name this first time she heard it, wasn't wondering anymore. This man could bounce any normal-sized human being off any ceiling, if he chose to. But despite his fearsome size, he didn't look violent. For one thing, Max had liked him. For another, the look in his piggy blue eyes was befuddled, but kindly, and—for some reason this was the most reassuring to Quill—he didn't have any tattoos. Or none that she could see, at any rate. He also smelled pleasantly of Old Spice.

"Quill?"

"Yes, Dina."

"Would you like me to send any, umm . . . messages to the Croh Bar? To your lunch appointment?"

"Yes," she said. "Tell my lunch appointment I've been delayed and by . . . uh . . . whom. But be *sure* and get a phone number where I can reach my—"

"Lunch appointment. Got it. I'll call from your office, shall I? And Quill, I'll be *right back*."

"Lunch," Bouncer Muldoon said, with interest.

"Would you like some, Mr. Muldoon?"

"I want to find Margie. But I could eat, yeah."

"I could help you with finding Marge," Quill said mendaciously, "but there's some information you should probably have before you go out on the street again. Did you know, for example, that there's a bench warrant out for your arrest?"

Bouncer snorted. "That jackass Moody. Yeah, well, he ain't here, is he? He's in court."

"That's true." Quill bit her lip and regarded him for a long moment. "Look. Why don't you come with me to the dining room, and I'll see what the kitchen specials are today?"

"Chili'd be good. Wouldn't mind a burger."

"My sister's the cook. And her burgers are spectacular."

The dining room, as she'd known it would be, was empty. The jury was at the Tompkins County Courthouse for the trial, and the Inn, of course, had no other guests, since, as Mrs. Pembroke was fond of pointing out, inn-going travelers avoided Hemlock Falls in winter as if they had the plague.

Bouncer tested the strength of his dining room chair before he sat down by slamming it once or twice against the carpeting. He settled into it gingerly, looked around and said, "Nice place. You sure Margie don't own it anymore?"

"I'm sure. If you wait right there, I'll go place our order."

Quill slipped into the kitchen and closed the doors quietly behind her. Meg, poring over a sheaf of recipes, looked up eagerly as the doors opened. Her face fell when she realized it was Quill.

"She's still asleep?"

"Corisande? She hasn't been down yet? I'm afraid I didn't check," Quill said a little guiltily. "Look, I know the grills are off, but could you make some hamburgers?"

"Hamburgers? I don't have time to make hamburgers. I've got a whole lesson plan set up for Cory and it doesn't include hamburgers. If you want hamburgers why don't you go down to Marge's? Betty Hall makes the best—"

Quill help up her hand. "I know. But Bouncer Muldoon just showed up."

Meg's eyes widened. "You're kidding."

"I'm not kidding."

"And you want to *feed* him? Quill! The man's an escaped felon!"

"He didn't show up for jury duty, which is a misdemeanor with a fine attached. It's not a felony. I checked it with Howie. Just come and take a look at him."

Meg, with an expression so dubious Quill wished she had a camera, slipped off the stool and went to the swinging doors. She peered out, stood stock still for a moment, then turned around. "Okay," she said. "He's sort of cute, in a bull-in-the-china-shop sort of way. Hamburgers. Lots of hamburgers. But I think you're stark-staring crazy."

"Darn good burgers." Bouncer swallowed twice (one burger down) and picked up the second. "Pretty near as good as Betty Hall's." He chewed twice (second burger down) and paused to reflect before he picked up the third. "Maybe even better."

"I'll tell Meg."

"Who's she again?" He nodded to himself. "Your sister. Right."

Meg had quartered three large Idaho potatoes and fried them to crisp, puffy slices the size of a small banana. Bouncer picked one up, gazed at it in admiration and began to swallow them whole. He burped gently and said, "Thank you, ma'am," just like John Wayne in the movies.

Quill waited until he'd emptied three cups of coffee, then said, "About Marge."

"Yeah. That's who I came to see, all right."

"I don't mean to be intrusive, but you were married to her once, weren't you?"

"Oh, yeah."

"Did you come to see her about that?"

"About being married?" His brow wrinkled, which gave him the look of an elephant. "We were divorced," he said. "A while ago."

This was the tricky part, but Quill, with years of experience with the heights and depths of human fallibility, had to ask. "Are you? That is. Are there any money issues?"

"Money issues?" He pursed his lips. "On account of I asked about her owning this place? You think I'm after some bucks?"

"Sorry," Quill said gently. "But she's a friend of mine and if I put her in touch with you, I just need to . . . you know."

"Make sure I ain't got my hand out." He chuckled, suddenly, like a small volcano burping lava. "Hell, Miss Quilliam. I'm Bouncer Muldoon. Best wrassler on the Xtreme network before I retired. No, I don't need any cash." A sentimental smile washed over his mammoth features. "But I'm real glad you asked. Margie always had the gift, you know? A talent, like."

"You mean making money?"

"Well, that, too. I meant for making friends. Me? I was always too big, even as a kid. People were scared of me more often than not, which is one of the reasons I turned to wrassling. If you're gonna scare folks no matter what, you might as well make a pile of coin at it. But

Marge, she walks into a room, people warm right up to her."

"Um," Quill said.

Bouncer rose to his full height and pulled the second largest wad of cash Quill had ever seen from his jeans pocket. (The first largest came from the suit-coat pocket of the minister of the Church of the Rolling Moses.) "I thank you for the lunch, ma'am."

"Please," Quill said. She added, in the vernacular, "Your money's no good here."

Bouncer nodded soberly and tucked the wad back into his pocket. "Thank you again, ma'am. I surely owe you one. And I'm gonna need one more favor. What it is, I'd like to see Marge one more time. If you could just pass that on to her, I'd appreciate it."

Quill looked at him a little anxiously. He was the healthiest six-foot-six, three-hundred-pound wrestler she'd ever seen, but then, you never knew, did you? Some terminal diseases were silent and sneaky. It was just like an old movie: Bouncer was dying and he was lying low, dodging the police, until he could see Marge one more time. "Are you, um, running out of time?"

"Me? In a way. I'm off to Vegas with Corky. Just wanted to say good-bye before I left."

"You're feeling well?"

"Finer than a frog hair." He burped, and smiled peacefully. "Especially after this lunch."

Quill smiled at him. "We talked about that bench warrant out for your arrest over lunch. I can see why you want to avoid going into town and finding Marge for yourself. But we have a very good lawyer here in town who could clear that up for you and you wouldn't need to go through me to see Marge. You could just give her a call."

"It's like this. Last time I gave ol' Margie a call, she banged the receiver down so fast my ears rung for a week. Just tell her I want to say hi, that's all. And not to hang up when she knows it's me."

"I'll do that, and gladly," Quill said.

She saw him out the front door, and watched him climb into a large, long monster of a pickup truck. BOUNCER'S BALLS was emblazoned along the side in fiery orange-red letters.

Dina slipped out from behind the reception desk and stood behind her. "Holy crow, Quill. That's some truck. That's some *guy*."

"I know. But he's really . . ."

"What? Scary? Yes. Huge? Yes. Don't tell me he's sweet. I won't be able to stand it."

"No, he's not sweet. But he's not stupid and he's not after Marge's money and I'm positive he doesn't want to hurt her."

"So you were right? He's still in love with her? He wants to undo the divorce?"

"Maybe. I don't know. But he definitely still likes her a lot." She closed the door, then sat down on the cream leather couch in front of the foyer fireplace. "I don't know what he wants. Did you find Marge at the Croh Bar?"

"Yes."

"What did she say when you told her Bouncer was here?"

"She didn't say a word for a while. Then she said as soon as you got rid of the son of a b—"

"Never mind," Quill said hastily, "I get the picture."

"Anyway, she said you should come down to her office as soon as you can ditch him. She'll be there all afternoon."

"I'll go right now." Quill got up, took her purse from large drawer in the reception desk, and pulled out her keys.

"Quill? Will you stop and talk to Davey first? Please! The thing is . . . I think he might need your help."

"My help?"

"He's up a stump with this Corliss Hooker thing. And you and Meg have solved a couple of murder cases in the past. It's just—he doesn't want to call on the State Troopers—you remember that awful Lieutenant Harper. He's just a worm."

Quill made a face. In her opinion, Harper wasn't a mere worm; he was a full-blown sociopath. "So! Now Davey's interested in hiring us as detectives?"

"I didn't say that exactly," Dina said nervously.

"A third opportunity for a case," Quill said, in a pleased way. "Actually, I'm finding it kind of hard to stay away from this murder, Dina. I mean, I told Doreen and Meg that we shouldn't interfere, but if Davey really is asking for a hand, I'd be failing in my duty as a citizen if I didn't help, wouldn't I?"

"Right. Just . . ." Dina's face was pink.

129

"Just what?"

"Just don't let him know that you're helping him. Okay? And for goodness sake, don't let on that I asked you to help."

"Oh," Quill said, deflated. "I thought he asked for us."

"Not in so many words. And it isn't that you two aren't really, really super at detecting. You *are*," Dina said earnestly. "It's just hard for someone like Davey to admit it."

"Hmm," Quill said. "That's probably very true. Well, I'm off. And sure, I'll stop in to see him. Trust me, he won't even know I'm on the job."

Usually, Quill enjoyed walking to and from the village, even in weather like today's, which was just as sleety and gray as yesterday's. But she'd decided to drive. Who knew how much time Davey would want her to devote to the case? And she had to see Marge to give her a heads-up and to find out if there were any news about the new hotel. And no matter what information Marge had to give her, she wanted to talk to Ferris Rodman afterward, and that meant a drive south of the village. So she found the Honda where Dina had parked it near the toolshed, and drove the short distance to the Municipal building, where David Kiddermeister staffed the sheriff's office.

She parked in the lot and found herself looking for Myles' old green Jeep, which was ridiculous, because it was parked in the garage of his house and had been ever since he'd left for the Mideast two months ago. She got out of the car and went in the steel door marked SHERIFF'S OFFICE and found Davey at Myles' old desk, a little shorter, a lot younger, and much blonder than Myles himself.

Davy got to his feet as she came in the door. Dina had talked him into growing a mustache, which helped mitigate his extremely youthful appearance. He'd gotten over his habit of blushing whenever he talked to women, and he greeted Quill with polite gravity as she sat down in the single, shabby armchair that the village government allowed its law officers.

"Thanks for dropping by, Quill. Dina told me she'd get you here come hell or high water, but I would've come up to the Inn. I hope you didn't go out of your way. I just need to ask some questions about this note Mr. Hooker wrote to you."

"I have to see Marge a little later, so coming here first was no problem at all. And that note from Mr. Hooker wasn't for me. But we'll get to that in a minute." Quill took a glance at the pile of documents on the desk. "Can you fill me in on what's happened so far? Is all that paperwork on your desk related to Corliss Hooker's murder?"

Davy riffled the pile glumly. "Yep. We already have the autopsy report back. The coroner did it first thing this morning."

"Meg said Andy thought it was the blow to the head that killed him. Was that it?"

"Yeah. It was murder, and no mistake. Or at least,"

he added conscientiously, "it was manslaughter. We won't know for sure until we solve the case."

He looked at her a little hopefully.

Quill leaned back in the armchair and folded her hands over her stomach. Just like Nero Wolfe. "Any suspects yet?"

"Well, sh—I mean, shoot. As far as people that wanted him out of the way, you mean? You could just about suspect half the people in town."

Quill remembered the hostility at the Chamber meeting. "You're right about that. You know, I never paid too much attention to what the Friends of the Dead actually did. They just walked up and down in front of the cemetery didn't they? Holding those signs?"

"LEAVE 'EM LAY, yeah. At first. Then it got to be more than that."

"A lot more? Can you give me some examples?"

"I wouldn't say it was a *lot* more. He started coming in here bugging me a couple of times a week, usually with a copy of some old piece of paper he'd found in the library. A lot of it had to do with stuff about the soldiers. One of 'em was a deserter from the Confederate Army and shouldn't be there, another one some horse dealer from Poughkeepsie and shouldn't be there, that kind of stuff. Then he tried to stand outside the Croh Bar and get the people coming in to sign his petition. He pissed off Ferris Rodman something fierce, so we had to get an injunction from Howie Murchison to keep him away from people. That kind of thing. If you ask me, he just got awfully bored stomping up and down the sidewalk and just wanted a little change."

"I was never sure why the whole F.O.D movement started," she said. "Did it originate with any of the relatives of the, um . . . deceased?"

"Well, Adela Henry got her knickers in a twist about it right off. But Ferris Rodman went to each of the surviving families of the Civil War veterans that were buried there and had them sign off on moving the bodies, and the first person he talked to was Adela. Heck, there aren't more than twenty graves in the whole place, and about half of 'em are guys nobody's ever heard of. And most of the other half was related to the mayor's wife, and she shut up quick enough—sorry, Quill—she didn't have many complaints once Mr. Rodman gave her a check. The rest of the surviving relatives were Petersons, and *they* don't give a hoot. They thought it was crazy to get money for it. Although it didn't stop any of them from cashing the checks."

"What will ROCOR actually do with the bodies?"

"They're going right down the road to that acre on the north end of Peterson Park. There'll be a little ceremony. Mr. Rodman fixed it all up with the state and the historical societies."

"So whatever Mr. Hooker did, he wasn't going to prevent the relocation."

"No, ma'am. Not to say he didn't try like hell. He was in here every other week claiming he'd found some new research, like I told you, but it was all smoke. He couldn't even find a lawyer to take the case once the appeal was denied, and that's saying something."

Quill pulled at her lower lip. "He told me yesterday that he had important new information about one of the bodies there. He wanted me to introduce him to Justice Moody."

Davey shook his head. "Yeah. And last week he said he was writing the President. Week before that it had to do with"——He shuffled among the papers and pulled one out—"gravestones of significant historical interest." Seems like he thought they'd crumble into bits and lose the lettering when they were moved and there's some law against destroying historical artifacts. But Rodman had that covered, too. There was just no way Hooker could keep that from happening."

So Ferris Rodman and his resort consortium were a dead end as far a motive. And if Ferris Rodman had no motive to kill Mr. Hooker, perhaps his fellow F.O.D-ians did. "Do you have a list of the all the members of the Friends of the Dead?"

Davey snorted. "Basically, it was just Corliss Hooker, Quill. Oh, once in a while he'd get some university professor from Cornell to come down and walk around with a sign, but as soon as they heard the whole kit and caboodle was going to be preserved up the street, they went back where they came from. And that busybody Mrs. Pembroke—sorry, Quill—but you should have seen her fussing over security procedures for that darn trial. She even called the FBI."

Quill looked at him. "She did?"

Davey nodded his head. "As if I didn't have enough trouble handling this town. Yeah, she's got connections, so I had talk to some agent they sent down from Syracuse. Something about threats on Moody's life. Bogus."

"Mel—I mean the FBI agent told you it was bogus?"

"Said it was politics. Everything's politics."

Quill was miffed. She tugged at her lower lip until Davey said a little plaintively, "Quill?"

"Yes. Right. We were talking about Mr. Hooker." She drew a deep breath and narrowed her eyes like Lew Archer.

It was a maxim of detective fiction that the motive for murder was frequently found in the character of the victim. "Who *was* Corliss Hooker?"

Davey shrugged, and said, "Kind of peculiar," which made Quill think of Richard Corey. That fictional character always made her feel weepy. She pinched her knee to help her focus. "That's not kind, Davey."

"You're right." Davy shuffled through more papers. "Corliss Hooker. Aged 57. Retired early from a thirty-year job at Kodak. Divorced in 1991 from Beth Ann Livingston Hooker, now of Pasadena. One son—he's a career solider, assigned to Iraq right now. And that's it. Lived out near Covert. You know, it's about six miles from here, due west."

"Did he have any friends?" Quill asked. She was feeling quite sad.

"I got his neighbor to come and identify the body. Said Hooker spent a lot of time at the library and online—course, that's what those guys do. The researchers."

"Do you have some"—what had Myles called it?—"some theory of the crime?"

Davey's ear turned bright red. "Well, I'll tell you what some of them think around here. Some of them think there's kids running around loose whacking people just for the heck of it."

"What kids?"

Davy went *t-uh!* "Who knows? No kids I've ever seen or heard of. Anyway, some people in town are running around claiming there's some mysterious gang responsible for an 'alarming rise of crime in Hemlock Falls.'" He did a pretty good imitation of Carol Ann's sticky-sweet voice. "And then for God's sake, as if I didn't have enough to do in this job, some people went and took the law into their own hands, practically." He glanced at her sideways. "You heard about this volunteer police force."

Quill admitted she had. "But," she added, "they are legal, Davey. So it isn't fair to say that they've taken the law into their own hands. Besides," she added in a practical way, "you know what will happen."

Davey's voice rose and his whole face got red. "You mean I'll be out of a job."

"No, of course not! Everybody will get bored with it and go on to something else."

"Not soon enough for me," Davey said. "And I'll tell you something, Quill. If some people in this town keep on talking about a crime wave, we're going to go ahead and *get* a crime wave."

Quill made soothing noises. Then she said, "Just so

136

it's clear to me, you're pretty sure that some peo—"
Quill, exasperated, decided to go ahead and name
names, "—that is, Carol Ann Spinoza and Donald Dun-
leavey, have been running around town making false
claims about crime?"

"I don't know that the claims are false, as such,"
Davey admitted. (Myles had told her Davey's biggest asset was his honesty. Myles was turning out to be right. It
was always annoying when Myles turned out to be right.)

"Somebody *has* been messing around in the cemetery, digging around and pushing the headstones over,
and Ferris Rodman's got couple of vandalism problems
over at the site. But it's not all that unusual this time of
year. Everybody gets antsy waiting for spring."

Quill was struck with an idea. "Do you think that
poor Mr. Hooker ran into somebody at the cemetery and
tried to stop him or her or whomever and things got a
little out of hand?"

"Maybe."

Quill knew that cases like that could be almost impossible to solve. "I take it you canvassed the neighbors
about the night of the murder."

"Nobody saw a thing. Not even Stoke, and he's a
noticing old bird."

"And you're afraid that it was just somebody passing
through."

Davy nodded, his lips tight with exasperation.
"About this volunteer police force. You talked to the
sheriff yet? I mean, it's bad enough that I've got to
worry about you and . . . well. Hem. Never mind."

"I will talk to Myles," Quill promised. "Let's get back to the real police work, shall we?" She decided to ignore his pained expression, and she continued, "Hooker's murder occurred last night. And the Chamber voted on the volunteer police force yesterday afternoon." She smiled, suddenly. "As tempting as it is, I don't think we can pin this one on Carol Ann. Even she has her limits."

"Doubt it," he grunted. "I can tell you this. I'd sure like to know who's been trashing the construction site these last couple of weeks. Although if I had to bet, I'd say *that's* kids. I've staked out that site more than a couple of nights running and you'd think someone had tipped the little buggers off."

They both sat there, Quill thinking hard; Davey bending a paper clip into a fishhook.

"Wow," Quill said. "This is a tough one. And you have no leads at all."

"Just this one." He pulled a cellophane bag from the top of the pile. Inside it was a bloodstained piece of paper, torn from a notebook. "Do you have any idea why Mr. Hooker wrote a note to you?"

"Oh, dear. I'm sorry, Davey. I'm about to knock off your first and only clue."

Quill left the Honda in the municipal parking lot and walked down Maple to Main Street and from there to Marge's office. She wasn't any further along than Davy with the solution to Corliss Hooker's murder. Myles had told her the hardest crimes to solve were those committed by a random killer. She hated to think of someone like that passing through the village and killing Corliss Hooker on some sick whim. But it happened in other cities all the time which was one of the reasons she had left New York to come and live in Hemlock Falls.

"And it shows up here, anyway." She looked up and found herself in front of Marge's office. It looked much as usual, except for the bright red label plastered over the SCH in Schmidt. Puzzled, Quill bent forward to read it:

VIOLATION CITATION!!
VILLAGE OF HEMLOCK FALLS
HEMLOCK FALLS, NEW YORK

Failure to Pay Shall Cause A Summons to Be Issued to
Appear in County Court, Tompkins County, New York

ISSUED BY THE HEMLOCK GRENADIERS (HKVPD)

The door to Marge's office jerked open and Quill confronted Marge herself. For a moment, neither one of them said a word.

"I'll rip it off," Quill offered.

"Damn thing won't come off." Marge jerked a thumb at the label and Quill saw that she had, indeed, tried to pull it off her window. "Stuck on with Krazy Glue, is my guess. Come on in."

Quill followed her inside. Marge was looking tired. Faint purplish smears underscored her eyes, and her gingery hair was lank. "What's the citation for?"

"Letters on my sign are too big. Or so Miss Fancy Pants Spinoza says."

"Too big?"

"There's some damn regulation on the books about the size of signs." Marge sighed heavily and sank into her desk chair. "She pulled the whole town code out of the library, Miriam says. Right now, she's up to the A's. Laws regarding permissible advertising," she added in response to Quill's bewildered look.

"Holy crow." Quill realizing that this response was wholly inadequate, asked. "How much is the fine?"

Marge shrugged. "Who gives a rat's ass?"

"You aren't going to pay it?"

"Do I look like I'm going to pay it?"

"You look tired," Quill said frankly. "I came by to see if you've discovered anything more about the hotel— and for one other thing, that I'll get to in a minute. Marge, I've never seen you look so tired. Haven't you been getting any sleep?"

"Went down and checked into the Marriott on Route 15 for a while. It's a noisy place."

Quill, who knew better, said merely. "I'm sorry. Look. Would you like to go get some coffee?"

"I'm about coffeed out, thanks." Marge looked around her office. It was pleasantly furnished, with a ficus in the corner and dark maroon wall-to-wall carpeting, very unlike Marge's usual Salvation Army style. "There's some in the BUN over there, if you'd like a cup."

"Thanks. I'm fine. So . . ."

140

"Haven't heard a thing about the change in plans for the golf course," Marge said abruptly. "Old friend of mine in the county clerk's office would have let me know. Rodman's gotta file the blueprints with the zoning board, all that stuff. And there's nada."

Quill's shoulders sagged with relief. She hadn't realized how worried she'd been.

"But that's not to say it's not happening."

"Oh. But I thought . . ."

"You'd get a chance to talk to the zoning board? You will. Thing like this has gotta go public."

"I don't think we could . . ."

"Sure you could." Marge leaned back in her chair and put her feet on her desk. "You gotta be a bit of a hardnose in business, Quill. You get another place like yours within a couple miles, you're gonna be toast. If a request for a change in the zoning plans comes up before the board, you and your sister get yourselves a lawyer and come up with every objection you can find."

"Marge, I just don't think—"

"John'll tell you the same thing. You talked to him?"

"The day before yesterday. He's tied up in Syracuse for the rest of the week."

"Yeah." Marge rubbed her chin thoughtfully. "Guy with that kind of brain isn't going to stick around here too long, you know."

Quill smiled at her. "You did. I mean, you're not a guy, but John said you have one of the best business minds he's ever seen."

Claudia Bishop

Marge turned pink. "Hmm. Well. I'm different. Never really wanted to leave where I grew up."

"So, what would you recommend, Marge? Do Meg and I just sit and wait for Ferris Rodman to make a move to change the golf course to a small exclusive hotel? Do I talk to him about it?"

Marge's gaze sharpened. "Like I said. Your best bet is to complain like god-almighty."

"That's just not . . ." Quill trailed off. "The thing is, Marge, Ferris Rodman has just as much right to own a small hotel as we do."

"Principles'll kill you, every time," Marge said. "But you're gonna do what you're gonna do, I suppose. As for talking to Rodman himself? I don't know that I'd bring it up with him." There was a slight, a very slight emphasis on the pronoun.

"I'm not sure what you mean. Why shouldn't I talk to Ferris Rodman? And why wouldn't he tell me what he's planning?"

"Go ahead and talk to him if you want. I don't care. But he's not going to tell you a thing he doesn't want you to know, so why waste your time? As for the other— could be lots of reasons why he hasn't talked about it yet. Most probably, he doesn't have the zoning board sewed up."

"Sewed up? Marge!"

"What?"

Quill raised her hands in an "I give up" gesture. "I'm objecting to your view of the universe, I guess. Not everyone is for sale."

142

"Most everyone is," Marge said cynically. "And the ones that aren't, like that poor fella Hooker? They're the ones that screw everything up."

Quill took a deep breath, thought the better of it, and didn't say anything.

"Tell you what I would do, if I was him, I'd buy you out."

"We aren't for sale."

Marge ignored this. "Thing is, if he wanted to buy you out, all he has to do is make a big a noise about this new place, scare you to death, and take advantage of your panic."

"I do not panic," Quill said indignantly.

Marge ignored this, too. "Something's a little off," she mused. "I got a question for you. Why does Carol Ann know what she knows?"

"She wouldn't tell me," Quill admitted. "And I don't like to say this, but it did cross my mind that Carol Ann was just making this up for spite."

Marge used a word Quill never used in reference to other women, but had always wanted to as far as Carol Ann was concerned. "So of course she'd make it up if she could. But she was pretty specific, right? About the European chef and the size of the place and what the market is. Mean as she is, Carol Ann would be dangerous if she weren't so stupid. Get my drift?"

Quill got it. "She's not quite bright enough to make up a credible lie."

"Whatever. So the question is, where'd she get the rumor and why? Most likely Rodman or one of his people, right?" Marge nodded to herself. "Well, well, well. Guy like that, he's had an awful lot of lawsuits around the building of that resort. I've always wondered how come. Maybe it's time I put my oar in, find out a little more about him. I mean, heck. What do I know about him? He comes swanning in here with these plans for a big resort down by the river, everyone gets a piece of the pie, right? We all benefit. More people come into the area, property values go up, more businesses open up . . . once money starts circulating, everybody's better off."

Quill, thinking of the quiet of Peterson Park and the quality of the light as the sun rose over the woods next to the Inn, wasn't so sure.

Marge, her brow furrowed with thought, slapped her hand on her desk and said, "More I think about it, the more I know it just doesn't feel right."

"What doesn't feel right?"

"Never mind." She swiveled her gun-turret gaze on Quill, "Anyhow. I'll keep you in the loop."

"I'd appreciate it."

"And I wouldn't go asking him about it, either."

Quill raised her eyebrows in a noncommittal way.

"So, next item. Your Dina gave me a heads-up. Bouncer's back in town."

Quill couldn't tell if Marge's abrupt behavior was rooted in anxiety or a need to keep all of her interactions with people on a business level. "Yes. He came up to the Inn. He thought you still owned it and that he'd find you there."

"Birdbrain."

"I didn't think he was a birdbrain, Marge. I liked him."

"You did?"

"Yes. I thought he was gentle."

A very peculiar expression crossed Marge's face. Quill couldn't quite place it. Regret, maybe. Some anger, too. A lot of exasperation.

"The two of you just didn't agree? Marriage can be pretty tough." An image of her own ex-husband crossed her mind—and the thought of her marriage, now long dissolved.

"Us? Get along?" Marge pushed out her lower lip and in again. "Oh, we got on, all right. We knew each other in high school. Best quarterback that high school's ever seen, I'll tell you that for sure."

"I'll bet he was."

"Course he wasn't fast, Bouncer wasn't. But you get those kids from Covert seeing him running down to the ten yard line, they just as soon get out of the way as tackle him."

"I certainly would. He's *big,* Marge. At any rate, I liked him and he asked me to do a favor for him and I said I would. He's apparently moving out of New York and he'd like to say good-bye to you."

"So he can write me a letter."

"He meant in person. You know, I'm wondering if it wouldn't be a good idea if the two of you met over a meal at the Inn. If he calls, why don't you tell him you'll see him up there? It's not like we're as popular as the

Claudia Bishop

Croh Bar so . . ." Quill didn't finish the rest of the sentence, which was: you won't run in to anybody from the village if we time it right. "At any rate, I'd better be going. Thanks a lot for the advice. And as for Bouncer—"

"I'll think about it."

146

CHAPTER 7

Quill walked back to the Municipal building, sat in the
Honda and fumed. The more she thought about Marge's
casual acceptance of chicanery, payoffs, and backroom
dealings, the madder she got. If she weren't such a law-
abiding person, she'd start a crime wave in Hemlock
Falls all by herself. Nickerson's hardware store had a
games section, and in the games section was a whole
stack of Splatball. Splatball consisted of two water pistols and a supply of bright sloppy paint. You loaded the
pistols, aimed, fired, and splatted whomever you wanted.
She'd get Carol Ann first, then Ferris Rodman, and then
(unless he had a really good reason why he'd failed to
call her two days in a row) Myles McHale. While she
was at it, she'd splat the entire zoning board and anybody else who thought that big business was good for

Hemlock Falls. She fumed all the way back to the Inn and she was still fuming when she slammed the front door to the Inn and confronted a foyer full of six jurors, one bailiff, and Chief Justice Mitchell Moody.

This cooled her temper considerably. She'd gone into innkeeping with a few hard and fast rules. Number Three was Never Lose Your Temper in Front of The Guests (almost all of Quill's innkeeping rules were variants of Rule Number One: Don't Belt the Guests). Not only that, the sight of Mitchell Moody in full judicial rig—black robe and wire-rimmed glasses on his hawk-like nose—was very sobering.

Moody's demeanor was distant. "We're on our way out to the site, Miss Quilliam. Counsels for the defense and the prosecution have requested that the jury view the disputed property in the matter before this Court. Tompkins County has provided a bus for witnesses, plaintiff and defendant, but I want to travel separately."

"You mean you'd like to use the Inn van?"

"Yes."

"Mike's bringing it around." Dina peered around the bulk of Juror Number Two, Sparky Stillwater. He was, Quill recalled, a software engineer. She was starting to think her e-mails to Aunt Eleanor were getting lost in cyber space somewhere; maybe Sparky could help.

"So you'll have to drive," Dina said with an air of finality.

"I'm sorry, I didn't catch all of that. You'd like me to drive?"

"Mike's going into Syracuse to pick up those crabs

for Meg. I have a tutorial later today and Meg's in the kitchen, of course, so there isn't anyone else. I mean I checked *every*body."

"We need to get everyone to the resort site? All of the defendants will be there?"

"The lawyers, the plaintiffs, and defendants are traveling separately," Moody said impatiently.

Suddenly, Quill was very interested in spending the afternoon poking around bulldozers. Especially if Ferris Rodman were there. Which he would be, of course, because he was the principal defendant in *ROCOR v. Meecham.*

"I guess," Dina said. "the viewing or whatever isn't supposed to take too long and then everyone will be back here. Isn't that right, your Honor?" Dina sighed heavily, giving a fine imitation of an overworked employee. "So I told the kitchen never mind about what I said before, that'd dinner would be late. Now dinner's going to be early. Meg had a fit, of course, but I told her I was just . . . "

"Thank you, Dina," Quill said firmly. She turned to Moody. "I'd be happy to drive. If that's acceptable to you, your Honor."

"Just as long as you don't drive the Court into the ditch."

Quill didn't drive the van into the ditch, but after twenty minutes of enduring Mitchell Moody's driving instructions, she was ready to. The man was obsessive-compulsive. A control freak. She *had* seen the stop sign at the intersection leading to Route 15—she drove it every day, practically. She had the braking capacity of the van down to a science. And she was well aware of the speed limit on public roads in the state of New York; everybody knew the troopers let you go five miles over the limit without even blinking an eye.

By the time she parked the van on the graveled space cleared for parking equipment, she regretted not stopping at Nickerson's to buy Splatball. She didn't need the water pistol part, either; she'd just dump the paint on Moody's head.

Quill killed the engine, jerked up the parking brake and said, "We're here."

"Lordy," Muriel May Johnson fanned herself with one hand.

"You can say that again." Juror Number Three, whose short haircut and erect stance would have proclaimed his military background to the lost tribes of the Amazon, shook his head once, "Glad you're not in my motor pool, lady."

Coldwell, that was his name. Brett Coldwell. Quill smiled, but said only, "It's chilly out there. I hope everyone has a coat?"

Moody checked his watch impatiently. "The others should have been here by now."

"There they are." Quill pointed to a yellow school bus bumping down the access road to the site. Moody and his bailiff stepped out of the van and waved the school bus over. Behind the school bus was Ferris Rodman's black Escalade, which negotiated the gravel with insolent ease.

"So that's why Moody wanted to take the van," Quill muttered to herself, "I hate riding in school buses, too."

Brett Coldwell was sitting right behind her. He leaned over and said, "You're wrong there, Miss Quilliam. Haven't you noticed Frank, there? Guy shadows Moody like he was married to him."

"Frank? You mean the bailiff?"

"He's not a bailiff, he's a bodyguard. Moody doesn't take any chances. A school bus full of lawyers, plaintiffs, and defendants is a little too public for him."

Quill turned around and looked at Coldwell.

"You're skeptical." He smiled, suddenly. "I can tell by the raised eyebrow. You're better at skeptical than driving, if you don't mind my saying so."

Quill never minded criticism of her driving. "Do you really think someone's out to get the judge?" she asked him curiously.

Coldwell shrugged. "Who knows? Justice Moody's reputation for hogging the spotlight precedes him, certainly. On the other hand, a lot people don't like the guy. He's pretty arbitrary in the courtroom, that's for sure. What do you think?"

Quill gazed out through the windshield. Moody was gesturing toward the northeast end of the site, the sleeve of his black robe flapping in the wind. The two lawyers stood side by side, facing the justice, not looking at each other in the way that adversaries do. "I don't know, Mr. Coldwell. He asked one of our waitresses where all the reporters had gone this morning. She said he seemed quite disappointed to learn they'd packed up and left for more interesting stories. I guess they want more proof than just death threats. So, yes, I'd have to say that I don't think a bodyguard's necessary. Of course . . ." She broke off in midsentence. Perhaps Frank the bailiff was an FBI agent. The FBI was worried enough about the death threats. Melvin Purvis had said so. She squinted at Frank. He was a big stolid man, with a large belly. And quiet. Quill hadn't heard a word from him all the time he'd been at the Inn. Frank was awfully fat for an FBI agent.

"Miss Quilliam? Still with me?"

She turned her attention back to Brett Coldwell. "Sorry. Please call me Quill. His bodyguard's awfully chubby, don't you think? I mean, if I hired a bodyguard, I'd want one that could chase whoever was chasing me. I think he's just a bailiff."

"Well, you might be right. But there's a lot of people that want this guy dead."

Rodman parked his Escalade in front of the trailer that served as his offices and walked over to the group pacing through the sludgy snow. The jurors remaining in the van with Quill saw this as a signal that their presence was required, so they got out of the van one by one.

Quill waited until Moody had everyone assembled in a group at some distance from the van and the bus. She kept her eye on Rodman. He stood with his attorney, hands stuffed in the pockets of his jacket, shoulders hunched against the wind. She'd wait until the court session was over and catch him as he left.

The whole group wheeled around and headed up the access road. Quill zipped up her coat and stepped out into the slush. She hadn't visited the resort for some months, and she was surprised to see that not much had been accomplished since then. The foundation for the large hotel had been dug some time ago and the footers poured, but she couldn't tell how much more had been accomplished, since the pit was covered with huge swathes of blue tarp as protection against the snow and ice.

The bulldozers had taken more trees down, and tons of sand had been trucked in to line the narrow beach. Initial plans for the projects had included tennis courts, a large swimming pool, and cabanas along the beach that edged Hemlock River. There was very little to indicate any of these structures were going up any time soon.

She walked the short distance that took her to the water and inhaled its the clean cold scent. Large pieces of ice bobbed up and down the flowing water. She looked upriver to the Inn. A pale sun was out, and the light cupped the copper roof and dimmed the warmth of the cobblestones. She hadn't really looked at the Inn from this angle before. She could make a marvelous painting of this; the Inn high over the Gorge, and in the foreground, the stumps of trees, and the pits covered with plastic tarp, the raw chunks of earth left by bulldozers passing through.

Quill turned back to the site. The only sign of life was the group of lawyers and jurors pacing back and

Claudia Bishop

forth at the boundary of the hotel's foundation. She could do a series of paintings based on this site. Call it "A Note on the Twenty-first Century." She'd have to figure out how to represent the lawyers, which meant a foray into symbolism.

She stood still, ideas for the paintings whirling through her head. She patted her jacket; her sketchpad wasn't there. It must be in her purse, because she never traveled without it. She went back to the van, retrieved it and perched on the hood. Her charcoal pencil flew over the pages.

Outside the construction office, the Escalade roared to life, and Quill jerked herself back to the present. The group was breaking up. The jurors trudged toward the van in a tight cluster. Moody, the two lawyers, and the bailiff remained behind, heads bent forward in earnest conversation.

She broke into a jog as the Escalade drove by and held her hand up. The vehicle came to sudden halt, snow and gravel spraying from beneath its wheels. The driver's window rolled down and Ferris Rodman looked out at her.

"Good afternoon," Quill said cheerfully. She shoved her hands in her coat pockets with what she hoped was careless insouciance. Rodman didn't look like the evil goblin king of small hotels, but appearances could be deceiving.

He nodded. "Miss Quilliam. You're here with the jury, I take it."

"Yes. Just as a driver, though. Umm, I was hoping we

154

could get together fairly soon. I'd like to talk over a few things with you."

Rodman pushed the sleeve of his jacket back and looked at his watch. "I've got to get home right now. My youngest is in a hockey game this evening and I promised him I wouldn't miss it. And I'm in court the rest of the week."

"What about tomorrow night?" Quill suggested. "I'd ask you to the Inn for dinner, but of course, the jury's sequestered there, and Mrs. Pembroke would pitch a fit." She thought for a moment. "You live in Ithaca don't you? And of course, you'll be there for the trial. I could drive there and meet you at Estee for a drink. Or I could come out here, to the site."

"Not here!" he said sharply. He rubbed his face. "Sorry, I didn't mean to bark at you. I see enough of this place during the week. Estee is fine. Court wraps up at five. His Honor runs a tight ship." His mild voice held a hint of contempt. "I'll be there at five-thirty."

"Great." Quill rocked back on her heels.

"Anything in particular on your mind?"

"Well, yes, but it'll keep until tomorrow."

Rodman glanced over her shoulder. "Looks like your passengers are getting a little tired standing around in the cold. Better get a move on."

Quill turned around. Most of the jurors had already climbed into the van; Moody and the bailiff were in a close discussion some steps away. Everybody else had apparently boarded the yellow school bus, which was bumping back up the gravel road to the highway.

Rodman tapped his horn, perhaps to startle Moody, perhaps to aggravate him. Quill, thinking it over afterward, wasn't sure.

Then somebody fired a gun.

Quill didn't react at first; the countryside was filled with hunters, even in March. But Moody's bailiff pushed the justice flat on the ground, pulled a pistol out of his coat, and held it straight out in front of him as he revolved slowly backward. Just like the movies.

A second shot rang through the air.

"That's a rifle," Rodman grunted. Somebody screamed. Rodman reached back and shoved the rear passenger door open. "Get in and get down!"

Quill scrambled in the back and hunched down in the leather seat. In front of her, Rodman slumped down so that only his ROCOR cap was visible over the edge of the driver's window. Rodman put the car in gear, swung in a wide circle, and then headed straight for the van.

Quill, alarmed now, rolled over onto to her stomach so she could see over Rodman's shoulder.

Moody crawled rapidly toward the van, as if he were a soldier under fire; the door opened, and several hands helped him in. Frank, the bailiff—except that Brett Coldwell had been right and he was obviously a bodyguard—remained standing, his pistol at the ready. He backed himself to the van, fumbled for the driver's door handle and jumped in.

Rodman pulled up next to the van. Quill sat up, then hunched over again when Rodman snarled, *"Get down!"*

"I just wanted to know if anybody was hurt."

"You keep your head stuck up there like that, it might be you." Rodman spoke out the window to the others. "You all right in there?"

Moody's voice was edged with fury. "We're fine. Let's get out of here. I've already called the troopers, but I'm not hanging around to wait for them. Follow us, Rodman. We're going back to the Inn."

Quill heard Mrs. Johnson's slow, musical voice, "Your man driving, judge?"

"He is."

"Good. 'Cause I'd rather take my chances out there with the gunman than drive back with Ms. Quilliam at the wheel."

"The reporters are back," Quill drew aside the drapes at her office window to peer at the circular driveway. "And why is there a yellow police tape in front of our door? This wasn't the scene of the crime. If there was a crime." She let the drapes fall into place and sank into her chair.

Meg was curled in a corner of the couch. "As far as the reporters are concerned, why am I not surprised? Moody needs a circus like most people need breakfast. I'll bet he hired someone to shoot over his head. As for the yellow tape—who knows? It's probably there to keep the reporters out of our hair. Just be glad it's not German shepherds and barricades." Meg looked at her a little anxiously. "You're sure *you're* okay?"

"I'm fine." She was. Her pulse had returned to normal

Claudia Bishop

on the drive back to the Inn with Ferris Rodman. Neither one of them had talked much, except to speculate briefly on where the shooter had been located.

"Have some more sweet tea. It's good for shock." Meg refilled both their mugs, then curled back into a corner of the couch. She had changed into her working clothes after the brief foray into glamour when they'd gone to pick up Corisande. Her socks were a depressed gray. "Thank god nobody was hurt, at least."

"You're supposed to hear the whistle of the bullet passing," Quill said. "I didn't hear any whistle. I didn't hear any *thwack*, either."

"*Thwack?*"

"You know. When a bullet hits something, there's a whistle, then a *thwack*. Despite that, I think it was for real."

"Don't be silly. It's some bozo Moody hired to get those reporters back here and himself on the six o'clock news. And it worked."

Quill shook her head. "I don't think so."

"You know what I think? I think you aren't as calm as you think you are. Have some more tea."

"I hate sweet tea. The only reason you're forcing sweet tea down my throat is because you read too many English murder mysteries."

"You mean it's the sovereign remedy for shock." She glanced at the carriage clock on Quill's desk. "It's only eight-thirty, I know, but maybe you should go to bed."

Quill set the untasted tea down with a thump. "I'm perfectly fine, and I am not in shock. I am so far from

158

being in shock that I have a theory of the crime. And I'm so far from going to bed that I want to go out again. You want to come with me?"

"Are you crazy?"

"Far from it. Do you know what Ferris Rodman did just before the shots were fired?"

"Stood on his head and whistled 'Dixie'? Of course I don't know. I wasn't there."

Quill leaned forward. "He tapped on his horn."

"His car horn?" Meg sat up. "You mean, like a signal?"

"It wasn't like a signal. It was a signal."

"Wait a minute. I thought *you* thought that Mitchell Moody set this up so that the reporters would come back."

"What kind of idiot would set that up?"

Meg rolled her eyes.

"I'm serious. Marge is suspicious of him, too."

"Suspicious of whom? Mitchell Moody?"

"Ferris Rodman, Meg. Come on. Focus!"

Meg thought a bit. "You think Ferris Rodman is behind the death threats."

"It's obvious."

"Why would Ferris Rodman want to shoot the judge?"

Quill smiled in quiet triumph. "Why would Ferris Rodman want to kill Corliss Hooker?"

Meg beat her forehead gently with her fist. "I don't know! Why?"

"Well, that's why I want to go out again. Back to the site. And into that trailer ROCOR uses as an office. My educated guess is that there's significant evidence to be found there."

"Significant evidence of what? Based on what? Wild surmise? Why in the world do you think Ferris Rodman is behind all this?"

Quill held up one finger: "Hooker's body was at the Civil War cemetery, the very cemetery ROCOR is going to relocate." She held up a second: "Moody is presiding over a case between Meecham and—guess who?—ROCOR." She held up a third: "ROCOR is owned and operated by—*ta dah!*—you-know-who."

Meg held up her hand. "Stop. You do know, don't you, that there's a statistical correlation between sunspot activity and hemlines? Which is to say, Quill, that this is all coincidence."

Quill played her trump card. "Marge thinks there's something funny going on, and it has to do with Rodman. That's not a coincidence."

"It's not a fact, either." Meg scratched her nose. "But it's interesting."

"Let's face it, Meg. Without some cold hard evidence, we aren't going to be able to crack this case. And we just can't wait for evidence to fall into our laps. Why should it? I want to go back to the resort site right now and get into those offices."

"Twenty-four hours ago, you wanted to stay as far away from this case as possible. And now you're contemplating breaking and entering?"

"Twenty-four hours ago, I hadn't been caught between a bullet and the intended target. Twenty-four hours ago, the police hadn't called us in to consult about Hooker's murder."

"Consult? Oh. You mean your converasation with Davey. I wouldn't all that a request for a consultation," Meg said. "Is it?"

"Well, Dina told me that Davey needed our help, even though he'd rather walk naked into the Ladies' Auxiliary meeting than admit it. I think it's fair to say that we're unacknowledged consultants."

They grinned at each other.

"So," Quill began, "here's what I think we should do—"

Corisande flung the office door open and slouched in. Quill was startled into silence. Meg sat up with a smile.

"Hey," Corisande said, accusingly. "So here you are." She thumped down on the couch next to Meg. She hadn't taken Quill's advice about a shower, but she had exchanged her traveling clothes for tight black jeans, a cropped top that exposed a rather bulging stomach, and long dangling earrings.

Meg leaped to her feet and stood over her anxiously. "So you're up! Did you have a good rest? You must be starving! Have you eaten anything yet? I left word for you in the kitchen."

Corisande yawned. "No. I woke up and came straight down here. I suppose I could eat something, yeah." She twisted a lock of her hair and glanced at Quill. "What's going on? There's a TV truck in the drive and policemen all over the place."

"There was an incident outside the village today," Quill said. "It involved Justice Moody. And there's only one policeman here at the moment. He's interviewing Moody and the jurors in the conference room."

Corisande leaned back and swung her feet onto the couch. She'd changed her hiking boots for tennis shoes. The shoes were muddy. Quill winced. She'd recovered the couch last year with a beautiful—and expensive—chrysanthemum print.

"Let's get you fed," Meg said briskly. "You go on into the kitchen, Cory. I'll be with you in a minute."

Cory exited Quill's office with another careless bang of the door.

Meg started after her, then turned to Quill. "You don't mind, do you? If we don't break into the site offices tonight?"

"I can't believe you're chickening out on me."

"I'm not chickening out!" Meg said indignantly. "Sisters forever, right? And it's regrettable, but true, that I've long since abandoned any guilt pangs over breaking the laws regarding private property when we're on a case. But Cory hasn't even eaten, yet, Quill. I have to feed her. And the jury's going to want dinner after Davey's finished talking with them and I can get a head start on showing Cory some of those recipes I've been working on if she helps me in the kitchen tonight. Mike got back with the fresh crabs about four, and you know that won't keep. Besides, the state troopers are still out at the site, for all we know, searching for shotgun shells and crumpled packs of cigarettes so they can test the butts for DNA. We shouldn't go tonight anyway."

"I *have* to go tonight. Rodman's at his son's hockey game and I don't want to give him any opportunity to get back in there and destroy evidence."

"What evidence? We don't know that there's any evidence! We don't even know if he's involved!"

"We won't know until I look," Quill admitted. "But if I don't go tonight, I'll always wonder. And the troopers won't search for stuff in the dark."

"They'll be somebody on guard, though."

"I'll park downriver and walk up on the beach."

"What if you get caught?"

"I'll tell them I was out for a walk! I'll tell them I left my purse in the office this afternoon and I came back to get it and I didn't want to bother anybody! I'm getting pretty good at . . . at . . . covert operations, that's the term. And I won't get caught. Even if I do—how dangerous do I look?"

"You shouldn't go by yourself." Meg had her mulish look.

Quill considered her sister for a long moment. "You're right. I'm too tired to handle a break-in by myself anyway."

"You're sure?"

"I'm sure that you're right about doing it alone and I'm sure that I'm too tired to do it by myself. You go ahead."

"You haven't eaten yet, either. I've got a crab bouillabaisse going that you aren't going to believe."

"I'll be along in a bit. Right now, I'm going to check and see if Marge is at the Croh Bar." Impulsively, she got up and gave her sister a hug. "Have a lot of fun with Corisande. See you later."

She waited until she was certain Meg had crossed the foyer and gone into the kitchen. Then she let herself out of the office and darted upstairs to her rooms. She stripped off her wool skirt and sweater and pulled on a pair of dark jeans and a navy-blue sweatshirt Myles had left in her top bureau drawer. She swept her hair on top of her head, pulled a knitted cap out of her closet, and mulled over her jackets. The darkest was a navy pea coat, which wasn't much protection against the March cold, but if she added a thick scarf and gloves, she should be all right. She zipped up an old pair of boots and rummaged in her oak chest until she unearthed a laser flashlight, a set of screwdrivers, and a small camera with seven photos left on a 36-print roll of film.

She considered the least obvious way to leave the Inn. If she hadn't been dressed like a second-story man, she could walk out the front door, wave cheerily to the reporters shivering on the front lawn, and drive off with impunity. But she was dressed like a burglar. And since she didn't dress like a burglar except on those rare occasions that she burgled, she was sure to be conspicuous. What she needed was a covert exit.

Her rooms were right over the kitchen. She opened the French doors to her balcony. The balcony itself formed the roof of the external entry to the rear of the kitchen. She was five feet, seven inches tall and there was a huge pile of snow next to the kitchen door. If she climbed over the waist-high railing, and worked herself down to hang from the balcony base by her hands, she'd have a drop of perhaps five feet to the snow.

She did all of it with her eyes squeezed shut.

She landed hard in the snow bank. And despite her careful calculations, she'd forgotten that the snowbank was high because the garbage bins were there. So she landed hard and noisily.

The back door to the kitchen opened and Bjarne peered out. Bjarne had been a graduate student at the Cornell School of Hotel Management when he had come to work for Meg eight years ago. He had risen to the rank of Head Chef under Meg's astringent tutelage. He was a Finn and tended toward the phlegmatic.

Bjarne regarded her impassively. "Why are you sprawled in the garbage cans?"

"I was after Max," Quill said, grateful, for once, for the dog's recreational pastime.

"Why are you dressed like a burglar?"

"Because I didn't want to chase after Max in a skirt."

Bjarne nodded to himself and closed the door.

Quill pulled herself out of the snow and brushed herself off. She trotted around the end of the Inn to the tool shed, where her Honda was parked. She checked the glove compartment to make sure that her big flashlight was there and that the batteries were fresh. Then she drove down the village to the Croh Bar.

She was pretty certain Marge would be there. News of the shots over Moody's head—Quill still wasn't sure she wanted to think of it as an attempt at murder—would have brought the village out in force. And there was no better place to pick up information than the Croh Bar.

Quill parked in the only space available, next to the dumpsters at the rear of the building. There were large paw prints in the snow at the Dumpster's base, and a black garbage bag spilled its unsavory contents onto the ground. Quill sighed. She really did have to start keeping Max in at night.

Marge's Buick Century was parked near the dumpster, too, next to Harland Peterson's Ford Bronco. Quill walked around the building to the front door, and pushed her way inside.

The bar was jammed with villagers, as Quill had guessed it would be. She smiled at Howie Murchison, who was drinking white wine at the bar with Miriam Doncaster. She waved at Esther West, who was squashed six to a table with Betty Hall, Nadine Peterson, and three other Petersons whom Quill knew by sight, but whose first names she couldn't recall. She found Marge planted in her usual spot—the booth by the kitchen door. She sat across from Harland Peterson. At Quill's approach, Harland drained his beer, nodded a greeting at Quill, and disappeared into the crowd.

"How come you're all dressed up like a burglar?"

"Because," Quill whispered, "I'm about to burgle. I dropped by because I thought you'd come with me."

Marge took a long sip of beer and set the mug on the table. "Thought you only burgled with your sister."

"She's busy. And besides, I need you for this."

Marge pursed her lips. She gave Quill a steady, assessing stare. She nodded once. "All right." She got up. "Am I dressed okay?"

Marge wore chinos, cotton blouses, and a bowling jacket in summer. In winter she switched to chinos, wool sweaters and a lined bowling jacket. This year's sweater was green. Quill surveyed her and nodded in approval. "You're fine. But you'll need boots and gloves."

"Okay. I'll go put 'em on. Then I'll meet you out back."

Quill wound her way back through the crowd, fielding the questions thrown at her about the attempted shooting of Chief Justice Moody: no, he hadn't been hit; no, none of the jurors had been gunned down in cold blood; no, she hadn't gotten hysterical and flung herself into the path of the bullet to save Moody from certain death.

Out in the parking lot, Marge gave Quill a brief argument about who was going to drive and lost it, after Marge reminded her just who it was that carried her liability insurance. "Me, that's who," Marge said. "And I'm not having my claims rate go up any higher than it is already on account of you."

"Fine," Quill said.

"Not to mention you oughta be in the risk pool."

"Fine."

"So we'll take your car, but I'm driving it."

"Why don't we take your car?" Quill asked, with what she felt was pardonable indignation.

"Because one, if anybody's car gets shot up it's gonna

be yours, not mine, and two, I don't want to be seen leaving the scene of a burglary, if it comes down to it."

"We are not going to get shot up," Quill said crossly, "And I don't want to be seen leaving the scene of a crime, either."

"It's your heist. So we'll use your car." Marge settled herself firmly in the Honda's driver's seat and said, "So who we gonna burgle?"

Quill got in beside her. A faint, very faint, smile lightened her face when Quill told her they were after Ferris Rodman. "And the reason I need you and not Meg, is because you can read a blueprint faster than I can. We'll just get in and get out, right?"

"Right."

"You didn't tell me we had to walk," Marge said some twenty minutes later. They were parked on the shoulder of Route 15. To the south of the road, the land dropped away down to the resort and the river beyond. Below them, a halogen light shone over the graveled parking area, and a state police cruiser was parked beneath it. The office trailer was in shadow about two hundred yards beyond the cruiser.

"We can't just drive into the place," Quill whispered. "We'll have to walk! There's a police guard down there. Come on! We're going to freeze if we just sit here!"

Marge heaved a sigh and got out of the car. She closed the door softly, pulled her knitted cap firmly over her ears and hitched up her pants. "Ready!"

Quill led the way down the access road. The snow-plow had left melting piles along the sides and they tip-toed through the slush as silently as they could. The bulldozers had left little vegetation, and despite the dark and their dark clothing, Quill felt horribly exposed.

Suddenly, the cruiser roared into life and the head-lights clicked on. Quill swallowed a shriek of fright and froze where she stood. Marge poked her in the back and whispered "He's just trying' to keep warm. But we better wait a bit until he turns it off again."

"A bit" turned into twenty minutes, and by that time, Quill's toes were cold and her fingers were numb. The engine coughed, then died, and the headlights went out. The silence was profound.

"Go!" Marge hissed.

They gave the halogen light and the cruiser a wide berth. They skirted the gravel spread around the three wooden steps that led to the front door and stopped.

"Now what?" Marge whispered.

"Wait here." Quill gauged the distance between the gravel and the bottom step, and leaped forward. She teetered, grabbed on to the handrail, and righted herself. She wriggled the doorknob. As she'd expected, the door latch assembly was the type to be found at any Home Depot or Lowe's: a flimsy dead bolt that had been fixed to the door itself with Phillips head screws. She felt for the Philips head screwdriver in her pocket, then removed the four screws keeping the lock assembly in place and gently wriggled the whole affair free of the door. The dead bolt made a loud click as she worked it free, and she stopped cold, motionless, until she could be sure no one—no thing—was moving in the darkness around her. She tucked the lock assembly in the pocket of her pea coat. "We're in!" she whispered. She turned and bent over the railing, her hand extended to help Marge up the steps without stepping in the gravel.

Marge was surprisingly deft. She jumped, Quill steadied her, and she eased the door open.

They *were* in.

Quill shut the door quietly and drew her flashlight from her pocket. The trailer smelled like cigars, boiled coffee, and unwashed floors.

Marge leaned into her shoulder and whispered, "I'll check the curtains."

Quill felt, rather than heard her move through the room. Marge was briefly outlined in the dim light that filtered through the windows as she drew the flimsy drapes to. She tiptoed back, and said quietly. "I think the light's gonna show through."

"We'll keep the flashlight lower than the window ledge. It's one of those laser beam things; it doesn't cast a halo."

"Good thinking."

Quill crouched down, turned the flashlight on and swept the narrow beam around the area. The narrow area was stuffed with equipment: filing cabinets, a fax machine, a Xerox copier, and a gray metal desk piled high with thick, long cylinders of paper. "Okay! You take the filing cabinet. I'll take the desk."

"Okay!" Marge whispered back, then, "Hang on! What are we looking for?"

Quill turned the flashlight off and sat down. "You mean you don't know what we're looking for?"

"Why should I? It's your heist!"

"You were the one that thought something funny might be going on with ROCOR! We'll look for documents related to that. You tell me what we're looking for."

"Jesus Christ," Marge said at her normal volume, which was pretty loud.

"Shh!" Quill hissed, then as an afterthought, "And stop calling it a heist." She thought furiously. "Just give me a minute. Okay. I've got it. We're looking for permits and plans. We're trying to see if what Rodman says he's doing relates to what he's really doing."

"That I can handle."

"Great. So you take the filing cabinet and I'll take the desk. Remember, we go in and we get out. It's faster with the two of us."

Quill's original plan of "get in and get out" was, she admitted, somewhat handicapped by the fact that they only had one flashlight. But she got a pretty efficient system going, nonetheless. They stood shoulder to shoulder at the desk, and ran quickly through the plots and blueprints. Quill took her time over the plan for the Civil War cemetery. To her relief, this blueprint, at least, showed drawings for an eighteen-hole golf course. The only building on the print was a small structure labeled "The

19th Hole" on the J-25 axis, which placed it near the little creek. Quill had some serious doubts that anyone would name an upscale hotel the 19th Hole. And a hotel sized forty by forty feet would only accommodate very tiny guests. Cheered, she completed the survey of the desk contents, and turned to the larger, more painstaking job.

They huddled together over the filing cabinet. Marge held the flashlight. Quill drew out the file folders. If a file title looked relevant, Marge poked her twice, and Quill passed it over. If a file title looked innocuous, Quill carefully reinserted it into the cabinet. They both wore winter gloves, so the work was clumsy, but they managed.

"Well I'll be dipped," Marge said after an eternity of silent perusal. "We've struck gold, Cochise."

"*Shh!* What is it?"

Marge held the flashlight steady on a letter from the New York State Gaming Commission referring to one Ferris Rodman's ("hereinafter to be called PETITIONER") request to open a casino at the Hemlock Falls River Resort.

"Gambling!" Quill said, forgetting to keep her voice down. "Wow!"

Outside, the police cruiser roared into life. Quill shone the flashlight on her watch; they'd been in the site office for more than an hour.

"I feel sorry for the poor guy," Quill muttered. "He has to be freezing to death out there."

She felt Marge tense beside her. "He's not warming himself up, he's headed this way."

"No, he's not."

"He sure as hell it. Listen."

Quill heard the crunch of the tires over snow and gravel. The cruiser's headlights flared in the window and lit the office up. She had time to note that the kitchen at the end of the trailer was an unholy mess of beer bottles, pizza boxes, and used microwave dishes.

Quill hit the floor, turned the flashlight off and dropped it in her pocket, where it clanged against the lock assembly from the front door and her set of screwdrivers. Then she yanked at her hair with both hands in frustration. "We've got to get out of here, Marge. He's going to see the hole in the door. Quick! Out the back door!"

"What back door?!"

"There *has* to be a back door. It's in the building codes. Isn't it?"

"How the hell should I know?"

The cop in the cruiser doused the headlights. The walls of the trailer were thin; they both heard him open the driver's door, then they heard the squall of the squad car microphone.

"He's calling for backup," Marge said. "*Now* what!?"

Wordlessly, Quill pulled her toward the kitchen. The back door had to be near the kitchen, didn't it?

She fumbled along the kitchen walls and yes! There it was. She flung door wide, stumbled forward, and fell out the doorway four feet onto the slushy snow.

Seconds later, Marge landed beside her.

"Stand where you are! This is the police!" The trooper's voice was magnified to a bellow by a bullhorn.

Quill, her knees a little weak, began to stand up. Impatiently, Marge pulled her down. "He can't see us, you fool! He's in front! He's fishing!"

"Drop your weapons and place your hands over your head!"

"What I tell ya! Weapons, my ass! C'mon, this way!" Marge crouched over like a quarterback with a clear fifty yards to the goalposts and ran like the devil. Quill sprinted after her, doing her best to not to breathe until they hit the safety of the access road. Then she sank onto her knees and allowed herself deep, gasping gulps of air.

"Darn fool thinks we're still in there," Marge said. Although her face was red, she didn't have to bend over to breathe. Quill made a mental resolve to start jogging as soon as possible. Marge stared down at the site. "Look at that."

Quill straightened up and looked. Floodlights stationed on the top of the cruiser cast an intense light over the office trailer. The trooper, gun at the ready, was half in and half out of his car. The gun was trained on the trailer door. From here, she couldn't see the hole left by the removal of the lock, but she knew the hole was there.

"Get a move on!" Marge began jogging up the access road to the safety of the Honda. In the distance, Quill heard the scream of sirens. They reached the Honda just as the first streaks of flashing red lights showed up at the east end of Route 15.

Quill was closer to the driver's door than Marge. She tumbled into the car, hoping that (in true Hemlock Falls fashion), the keys were in the ignition. They were. She fired the engine and turned on the headlights as Marge slammed into the passenger seat beside her. She glanced into the rearview mirror and saw two cruisers approaching like bats out of hell.

Marge snatched Quill's hat off. "Looks more innocent!" she puffed, and then, "get out of the coat, too! You look like a burglar!" Then she yelled, "Go-go-go!"

Quill, on the principle that innocent people didn't tear away from police cars at ninety miles an hour, pulled into the westbound lane and proceeded at a decorous forty-five miles an hour.

She pulled over as the cruisers sped past. As soon as the troopers flashed by and screeched into the turn down the access road, she gunned it, and they headed home.

"Jeez," Marge muttered, "that was a close one."

Quill settled into the driver's seat with a relieved sigh. "I think you kept your head pretty well, partner."

"I'll tell ya, when those headlights flashed into that office, I thought it was all over for Marge Elizabeth Schmidt. But you got us out of there, Quill. You're a pretty cool customer yourself."

"You get used to it," Quill said in an offhand way. "I remember breaking into a semi at the QWIKFREEZE a few years ago—that was the case involving the paint factory, you may remember that one—and I . . ."

The sounds of the sirens, rather than fading away, were increasing. Quill glanced in the side view mirror. It was only one cruiser. She glanced automatically at the speedometer. No, for once she was well within the limit, or so close that it didn't matter. It must be some other poor soul up ahead. Obligingly, she pulled onto the shoulder so that the trooper could pass.

The cruiser pulled in behind her.

"Turn off your engine."

Quill switched the engine off. The police lights flashed red-red-red over Marge's grim face. A spotlight switched on and the interior of the Honda became as bright as day.

"Get out of the car slowly. Put your hands over your head."

The rearview mirror showed two troopers out of their car and on the road. Both of their guns drawn. Quill opened her door slowly. Marge muttered, "Shit! I knew I should have been driving!" and wrenched the passenger door open. And they both stood in the garish light of the floodlights with their hands on the tops of their heads.

"Just follow my lead," Quill said to Marge in an undertone.

"If I'd followed my own good sense, I'd be home in front of "Fear Factor" instead being in the middle of it," Marge snarled.

It was hard to see the troopers' faces in the glare of the white light, but from the way both of them walked,

Quill was certain both were male. While believing firmly in the right of each and every woman to make more money than men and split household chores right down the middle, Quill didn't scruple to look helplessly feminine when need dictated. She didn't precisely bat her eyes at the troopers headed toward her, but her voice rose in pitch slightly as she said shyly, "Is there anything wrong, officer?" Then she stiffened. "Oh," she said, her tones glacial, "It's you, Lieutenant Harper."

"Well, well, well." Harper's mean little eyes slid over her in a particularly slimy way. Of all the troopers in all the world, Quill thought bitterly, it had to be Josiah Harper, the first and only sociopath she'd ever had the misfortune to meet. "If it isn't Miss Sarah Quilliam."

"And Marge Elizabeth Schmidt," Marge said at her shoulder. Her voice wasn't so much glacial as out and out surly. "Robbed any Girl Scouts lately, Harper?"

"Shut up." Harper didn't even glance at her. "Keep your hands on your heads, both of you."

"We weren't speeding, the car's licensed, and I want to know why the hell you think you can pull us over," Marge said.

"Police discretion," he said with a smile even nastier than the tone of his voice.

Quill, even more conscious of the current erosion of basic American freedoms than usual, kept her hands on her head.

The second trooper from the car—Quill hadn't met him before—was slightly built, but very tall. He had mild blue eyes and attractively thick brown hair. Quill met his gaze briefly, and he smiled. He also stood well away from Harper—presumably to cover him if Quill and Marge should haul Uzi's out of their jeans and start blasting away.

Harper jerked his head toward Marge. "Pat that one down, Simmons." He slid his pistol into his holster and came so close to Quill she could smell his bad teeth and infected gums. He bent forward and whispered in her ear as his hands slapped at her breasts, her hips and between her thighs. "You like that, little lady?"

She gritted her teeth, cast another principle of independence to the wind and said softly, "Only Myles is allowed to do that, Lieutenant. And he won't be happy to hear about this."

Harper stepped away with a snarl. But Myles' name had worked; he kept his hands off.

Quill glanced at Marge. Her face was stony, and her blue eyes were cold and furious.

"This one's clean, Lieutenant," Simmons said. "I think we can let them go, don't you?" The look on his face was troubled.

"Shut up, Simmons. Check the car."

Harper stood with his eyes on Quill as Simmons flashed his light around the Honda's interior. "Can't find a thing, Lieutenant. Looks like these ladies were just out for a ride." He shook out Quill's coat and began to refold it, "Oops. Sorry ma'am."

The doorknob from the office trailer dropped out of her coat pocket and clanked dully onto the pavement. The flashlight and the screwdriver set clattered after it.

CHAPTER 8

"Well, it could be worse," Quill said cheerfully.

"How?" Marge occupied the cell next to her. She stumped over to the bars separating them and glared at her.

"For one thing, we're home. We're in the Hemlock Falls clink, at least."

"You may be so used to the clink that you think it's home, but I'm not. I've never been in jail in my life!"

"We haven't been arraigned yet, Marge," Quill said patiently, "We're just being held until Davey can get Howie out of the Croh Bar. So we're not 'in jail' as such."

"How could we be any more in jail than we are right now?" Marge rattled the bars. If she'd been a gorilla, Quill thought admiringly, they would have fallen before her like the pillars did before Samson. Marge was a lot stronger than she looked.

"Even if Howie decides to remand us to custody, we'll still only be in jail overnight. And then we can get Howie to represent us in Tompkins County Court in the morning and we'll go home." She sat down on her bunk (a single thin mattress and a scratchy wool blanket) and looked at her feet. The only thing she really didn't like about jail was that they took your boots away. Her feet were cold. She always seemed to end up in jail in the winter; next time she broke in somewhere, she'd have to remember to carry a pair of thick socks.

Marge sighed and sat down, too. "Why the hell I ever agreed to go haring off with you, I'll never know. It seemed a good idea at the time. Musta been the beer."

"I'm not sorry we did it," Quill said a little defiantly, "When do you think Rodman was going to drop the bomb that he's building a casino? A casino! There's going to be all kinds of upset around here, Marge."

"I don't give a rat's ass about any casino," Marge said testily.

"Of course you do. Everybody knows that gambling's riddled with organized crime." She caught her breath. "Oh my goodness, Marge. Melvin Purvis!"

Marge folded her arms, looked up, and addressed the water-stained ceiling. "She's crazy."

Quill stood stock still in amazement. "*That's* why the FBI was here! Marge! Hemlock Falls *is* in the middle of a crime wave, only it's not the kind we thought. And you were right. There is something funny about Ferris Rodman. He's connected!"

"To what?"

"You know. Connected. As in Tony Soprano?"

Marge gave her a long, measuring look. "I've made a ton of mistakes in this life," she said flatly, "But the biggest one by a long shot was getting hooked up with you and your nutty sister. Organized crime. Swell. Wonderful. You know what? I don't want to know anymore. Not a thing, you hear me?"

"But—"

"Quiet! All I wanna do is get back to business. Not another word about—" she struggled for a moment, then finally burst out. "—The Mob. You got it? Not another word."

"Got it," Quill said meekly.

"Now, how long do you suppose it's going to take to get us out of here?"

"Beats me. I'm pretty sure we aren't going to be able to break out." Quill got up and tested the bars. The Hemlock Falls jail—or rather, holding pen, because people weren't actually incarcerated there after sentencing—was very simply built. Two eight by ten stainless steel barred cages sat side by side on the concrete floor. A window placed ten feet off the floor in each cell let in a dim light during the day. A single 100-watt lightbulb suspended from the ceiling lit the cell up at night.

Both cells faced a thick steel door. The door had small mesh window at eye level and led to the sheriff's office. At the moment, it was closed, and Quill couldn't hear a thing that was going on beyond it.

"Actually, I don't think we'll be here much longer. It can't take too long to find Howie. The Croh Bar's just down the street. In the meantime, we can just sit here and chat."

Marge growled like a Rottweiler.

"Did you say something?"

"Nothing I want to repeat," Marge said. "And I'm all out of chat. So don't talk to me." She swung her feet up onto her bunk, lay back, closed her eyes, and started to hum.

Quill was very cold. She tried sitting cross-legged, tucking her feet under her thighs. It helped warm them up a little, but not much.

Marge stopped humming, opened her eyes and demanded, "What time is it?"

"I don't know. Davey took my watch, too."

"I don't know why you just didn't call Meg to get us out of here. She gives more of a hoot about you than Howie."

"Why didn't you call Harland?" Quill demanded heatedly. "He'd bail you out in a second."

"I was embarrassed," Marge shouted.

"I'm not all that happy about it either." Quill admitted.

Marge blew out an exasperated sigh and leaned back against the concrete wall. "Well, we'd better get our stories straight."

"We don't have a story. I talked you into breaking and entering and that's it." Quill took a deep breath. "I am really, really sorry, Marge. If we get into real trouble over this, I don't know how I can make it up to you. Although it's not as bad as it sounds."

"You can make it up to me by keeping us out of jail," Marge said. "What do you mean 'breaking and entering?' isn't as bad as it sounds? What could be worse?"

"Theft," Quill said promptly. "That would be worse."

"Then it's worse," Marge said gloomily. "I took that letter from the gaming commission. I stuck it in my bra. And you took that doorknob. They already got that. We got to think of a defense."

"We don't have a defense. What we have is an excuse. And last time I checked, excuses don't cut it a court of law." Quill was suddenly stricken with remorse. She slumped facedown on the bunk and pulled the thin, smelly pillow over her head. "I'm really sorry, Marge."

"What d'jya say!?"

Quill sat up slowly. "I said I'm really sorry. It's all my fault. Honestly. Oh, dear, I can't believe it. I'm really a criminal. You're really a criminal, too. Here, give me the letter. I'll take the rap."

"Hush!" Marge said. "Somebody's coming. And dammit, Quill, don't you go admitting a thing."

The latch on the steel door rattled, opened, and Davey Kiddermeister walked in, the keys to the cells in his hand. "Okay, ladies. You've been remanded into custody."

"Whose custody?" Marge growled.

"May I have my boots?" Quill asked.

"Who got us out?" Marge yelled.

Davey unlocked the doors and pointed toward his

office. Marge forged ahead. Quill followed. Both of them stopped short at the sight of Ferris Rodman. He'd changed his sports coat and tie for a sweatshirt that read: GO RAIDERS under a pair of crossed hockey sticks. He still wore his ROCOR hat. Quill couldn't read his expression at all.

Davey strolled in behind them and sat down at his desk. "I was kidding about the remand. You're lucky, Quill, Ms. Schmidt. Mr. Rodman's been to his office and says it looks like nothing's been disturbed. He's not going to press charges."

Marge folded her arms. "We didn't do a thing. There's no charges to press."

Davey held his hands up, as if to ward off flying bats. "Ms. Schmidt? Let's just drop it, okay? As I said, you're both pretty lucky."

"We didn't do a thing," Marge said. "And I'll bust anyone who says we did a good one."

"Thank you very much, Mr. Rodman," Quill said diffidently. "I do feel you're owed an explanation, though."

"If there's any explanation coming," Marge frowned. "It's an alleged explanation."

"Oh all *right,* Marge," Quill said. "We did make a visit to your office. At least, I did. Marge went with me to the site, but she stayed in the car."

"Anything Quill allegedly did, I allegedly did with her," Marge snapped. "Jesus, Quill. What kind of person do you think I am? A snitch? Will you just shut up?"

"You see," Quill said earnestly, "There've been rumors floating around town that you weren't going to build a golf course at the cemetery. I heard that you were planning on building a small, elegant hotel that catered to guests interested in fine food, fine wine, and a luxurious country experience. And that you were importing a European chef."

"Which would duplicate your Inn," Rodman said. "I see."

"It might drive us out of business," Quill said. "At least, that's what I thought."

"Why didn't you just ask me?"

"I was going to," Quill said. "That's why I wanted to met you in Ithaca. But I got more and more worried, and I just . . . " She rubbed her cheeks. "I'm very sorry, but I was afraid you wouldn't tell me the truth."

Rodman looked at Marge, who nodded. "That's about the size of it. Allegedly."

Quill took a deep breath. "At any rate, we found the blueprints for the golf course and as soon as I saw that you weren't intending any such thing as a hotel, we left."

"Then you must have seen the old prints," Rodman said.

"The old prints?"

"Yes. I am going to put up a small hotel at the cemetery instead of the golf course, Miss Quilliam. Just as you've described."

Quill took a deep breath. "Oh. I see."

Nobody else said anything.

Davey cleared his throat, frowned importantly, and made furious notes on the file in front of him. (Quill could read upside down. The note said: milk, eggs, toilet paper.)

Marge shook her head sympathetically, turned her back, and pulled on her boots.

Ferris Rodman stared at her with his small gray eyes. Finally, he broke the long, uncomfortable silence. "If that's all, Sheriff, I'll be pushing off. Can I give you ladies a lift?"

Quill and Marge exchanged swift, alarmed glances.

"No!" Marge said.

"We're fine!" Quill said. "But thank you anyway."

"It's not out of my way."

"My car's down the block at my bar," Marge said. "I can walk from here." She scowled at Quill. "But you could give Quill, here, a lift."

"I have the Honda, "Quill said swiftly. "So, thank you very much, Mr. Rodman." (Why was she thanking this man? He was going to run her out of business! And he was a mobster to boot.) "I'll just drive myself home."

"I'm afraid your car's not there anymore, Ms. Schmidt," Davey said. "And the Statie's are still going over the Honda, Quill, so your car isn't here either. Under the circumstances, I think it's very nice of Mr. Rodman to offer to drive you ladies home."

"What do you mean the troopers have my car?!" Quill said.

"What'd'ya mean my Riviera's not there!" Marge roared.

Davey blushed bright red. "I don't know why Harper

took your Honda, Quill. But the state has the discretion—"

"I know, I know," Quill said crossly. "Harper's probably fitting it with a bomb or planting evidence in the trunk. Great. This is great."

"Anyway, you can get in back in the morning."

"Get it back? Where is it?"

"Forensics lab. In Ithaca."

"They took my car, too?" Marge shouted. "How come!? It was right here all the time we were in Rodman's office. Allegedly, I mean."

Davey mumbled something.

"Speak up!" Marge ordered. Quill, admiringly, thought she would make a very good drill sergeant. "I can't hear a word."

"I said the Hemlock Grenadiers impounded it."

The silence this time was respectively menacing (Marge), astounded (Quill), amused (Ferris Rodman), and abashed (Davey). Marge swelled. There was no other word for it. Her face was round with rage. Quill sincerely hoped she didn't have high blood pressure, because her face was so red she looked sunburned. Quill waited for the explosion, but none came. Marge was so mad she couldn't talk.

"Well," Quill said in a diplomatic tone of voice. "I'm sure they had a good reason."

Marge breathed heavily through her nose.

Davey scratched the back of his neck. "There *is* a reason," he admitted. "Carol Ann dug up some parking ordinance. It's illegal to park within ten feet of a Dumpster."

"She's up to the D's already?" Quill said.

Davey nodded and continued doggedly, "The Riviera was parked eight feet from the Dumpster. Carol Ann measured it."

"I see." Marge's voice was a squeak, as if gas were escaping from an overinflated balloon.

"So she had it towed."

Ferris Rodman stirred a little, then subsided into immmobility. Quill was nervously aware that he'd been staring at her throughout Davey's revelations about Marge's Buick.

"We're keeping Mr. Rodman," Quill said. "Mr. Rodman, Marge and I will need to stay here to get this sorted out, so thank you very much for the ride, but we'll be fine."

"I can see why Ms. Schmidt might need to stay, but I'm bound and determined to give you a ride home, Quill." He smiled. Quill didn't trust that smile, even though Davey apparently did.

Davey nodded. "Yeah. You go on ahead, Quill. And if I were you, I'd invite Mr. Rodman here up to the Inn for a nice dinner sometime. You two could have been facing jail time if he hadn't agreed to drop any charges."

"Quill?" Rodman smiled, and gestured toward the door.

Quill glanced desperately at Marge, who seemed, from her indifferent response, to be perfectly willing to let Quill go off into the dark with the mobbed-up owner of a gambling casino. A man, moreover, who was probably very very anxious to discover what they had burgled from his office.

The outside door pushed open, bringing a blast of air that, Quill noted crossly, was warmer than the air in the jail.

Bouncer Muldoon, looking ever bigger than usual in a down coat and stocking cap, walked into the sheriff's office and raised a hand in greeting. "Somebody told me Margie was here."

"You," Marge said.

"Yeah. Good to see ya, Margie. Thing is, I saw that nice Riviera of yours bein' towed down the street a while ago. Thought you might need a ride."

"Ha," Marge said. "Guess maybe I do."

Bouncer swiveled, knocking Ferris Rodman against the wall in the process. "And you, Quill? They told me down to the Croh Bar that's your car got impounded after a high-speed chase by the cops."

Quill could have kissed him. Bouncer was so large, he took up almost all the remaining space in Davey's office. He completely dwarfed Ferris Rodman, who was gazing at the former wrestler in an assessing way.

"Yes! I mean, I'll be happy to go with you guys, if you don't mind," Quill's smile at Rodman was so strained, she thought her cheeks might spasm, "Thank you, but I wouldn't want to take you out of your way."

"Some other time, then," he said politely. "I'd like to take you up on the dinner offer."

"Actually, it was Davey . . . "

"But I'd like it to be my treat. I'll give you a call, shall I?" He nodded to Davey, "Sheriff? Glad I could be of some help? And you, sir." He looked up at Bouncer. "If you're interested in a job, let me know. I can always find work for a guy your size. Marge and Quill know where to find me."

As soon as he was out of the office, Quill sagged against the desk with relief. "Bouncer," she said gratefully, "did I ever tell you that you remind me of John Wayne? All you need is a horse. And a cavalry hat."

"Ignore her," Marge said brusquely. "Davey, you tell that fatheaded mayor and that miserable little snake Carol Ann Spinoza that I'll be looking for them tomorrow. Come on, Quill. Get a move on."

There was more than enough room for the three of them in the front seat of Bouncer's huge truck. Marge shoved Quill into the middle seat, and as she strapped her seat belt on, said, "Drop me off first, Muldoon. It's right on the way."

Bouncer gunned the engine, "You still in that little ranch near Peterson Park?"

Quill thought he sounded wistful. "Is that where you two lived when you were married?"

Bouncer accelerated smoothly. "Naw. We had a nice double-wide out near the paint factory. Three acres and a shed for my workout gear. What ever happened to that trailer, Margie?"

"Sold it," she said briefly. "I stuck a couple of three-bedroom ranches on the acreage. Stop right here."

Bouncer let the truck idle. "You just gonna go in? Thought maybe you had a beer on hand."

"Not tonight, Bouncer."

"Come up to the Inn tomorrow," Quill said. "For breakfast. Both of you. The jurors leave by seven-thirty, Bouncer. You probably don't want to run into Judge Moody. But they'll be gone all day."

"Thought you couldn't have guests," Marge said,

"We're allowed normal operations when the trial people aren't there," Quill said. "Please come."

"Sounds good to me, Margie."

Marge sighed heavily and rubbed her chin. "God. What a day. Okay. Fine. I'll see you there about nine."

Bouncer reached over Quill and put a huge hand on Marge's knee. "I'll be leavin' soon. I just want to say good-bye."

The drive from Marge's place was short, and Bouncer didn't say anything and Quill was suddenly too tired to talk. He dropped her off on the driveway at the front, and Quill stood and watched the red taillights of the monster-sized truck disappear back down the road.

She was, she realized, too tired to sleep. She wandered restlessly around the grounds for a time. The overcast skies of the past few days had cleared, and a bright spring moon flooded the landscape. It was warmer than she'd expected. The snow was melting in earnest now, and she could smell damp earth. The last week of March, she thought, and spring would be here in a few weeks. It was hesitant this far north—there'd be one more snowfall, perhaps, before they could be sure winter had left for another year.

She went down to the lip of the Gorge and listened to the water. The flow was heavier now, with the runoff from the snow, and the air this close to the river humid with spray. There was a rustle in the brush nearby. She stiffened, and then relaxed as Max came loping out of the dark. He nudged her knee and thrust his head under her palm.

"What kind of dog is it, anyway?"

Quill stifled a yelp even as she recognized Corisande's flat, unaccented tones. "You startled me!"

She'd been sitting just below the lip of the Gorge on a rock that Quill had frequently sat on herself. She rose, dusting the damp snow from the seat of her jeans.

"He's just a mutt," Quill said. She ruffled his ears. "You can't sleep?"

"Jet lag, I guess."

"Come on in. We'll make a cup of cocoa."

"I don't drink cocoa," Corisande said. "You know, Quill, that is a really ugly dog." She cocked her head. "You hear that?"

"I do." Quill turned and faced the Inn. Bouncer's pickup truck was coming back up the driveway. "Bouncer's back! I wonder what's wrong. Excuse me, Cory." She jogged up the slight slope and went to the driver's window. Bouncer stuck his head out. "Your purse," he said. "Guess you kind of forgot it in all the excitement."

"Thank you! I can't believe I did that."

He waited a moment, smiling amiably.

"Is there anything else? Would you like to come in for something to eat?"

"Oh, no, Quill. Picked up a couple of burgers at the Croh Bar. I tell ya, it's a dead heat between your sister and Marge's Betty. No, I ain't hungry no more. I was just wondering. Do you think Margie'd mind if I picked her up tomorrow morning? She won't have a way to get up here, with her car being . . . impounded an' all. You two being so close, I thought maybe you could give me a heads up if she wouldn't like it, "

"I should think she'd love it," Quill said, "but I'd call her, first. Just to be sure."

"Good idea." He drew his mammoth head inside, and with a wave, bounced back down the drive again. She looked around, but Corisande had gone.

She went inside, checked her messages, took a long hot shower, and checked her messages again.

Myles still hadn't called.

CHAPTER 9

"It's Claude de Courcy, isn't!" Meg grabbed an eight-inch sauté pan and threw it across the kitchen. It bounced off the fireplace mantel and clattered to the floor. "That little son of a gun's bringing Claude de Courcy to Hemlock Falls!"

"I have no idea who the chef is going to be." Quill had waited until the courthouse crowd had left the Inn for the third day of *ROCOR v. Meecham* before she told her sister about Ferris Rodman's new plans for the cemetery. The kitchen was in its post-breakfast phase, and things were relatively quiet. "For heaven's sake, Meg, the place isn't even built yet. It hasn't even been approved yet."

"That's it, then. I might just as well marry Andy and hang up my toque."

"The marrying Andy part is fine, but why do you think you have to hang up your . . ." Quill broke off, exasperated. "This is ridiculous. I'm not even going to ask why Claude de Courcy seems to be your *bête noir*. We don't have a clue who the chef is going to be, Meg, and it's a small matter beside the fact of the new hotel itself."

Meg sat down in the rocking chair next to the fireplace and began to rock furiously back and forth. "Just give me a minute," she said between gritted teeth. Around her, since everyone was used to Meg's explosions, the work in the kitchen went on as usual. Bjarne, who was supervising one of the under chefs, who in turn was preparing crab for that night's dinner entree, cast a curious glance in their direction. "Claude de Courcy," he offered, "is a horse's patoot. But a brilliant chef. Brilliant. I myself would like to study with him."

Meg glared at Quill; "See!" she hissed. *"He's better than I am!"*

"No one's better than you are," Quill said loyally. "I'm going to track John down and see what he thinks. I didn't sleep very well last night, thinking about all this, and I have to admit I'm a little foggy." She had spent a very restless night: between the Mob, Myles, the new hotel, Corliss Hooker, and wondering how long it was going to be before she clipped Corisande one on the ear, she had hardly slept at all. "What I do know is that this new hotel is a plan, Meg, not a certainty. For one thing, the change from golf course to hotel has to go through the zoning board. And for another, the resort itself's been under construction for donkey's years. That doesn't auguer well for speedy construction of this project. So if this is going to be a problem, it's not going to be a problem for a while—are you even listening to me?"

"Sure I'm listening to you." Meg sprang up from the chair. "Will you call Ferris Rodman for me? And just *ask* him who he's going to hire as a chef? Whatever you do, don't let him know that I'm the one that's asking, okay? Just pretend that it's one little unimportant point of information."

"It *is* one little unimportant point of information." Quill had never been closer to bopping her little sister over the head with the nearest blunt instrument. "I am *not* going to call Ferris Rodman. I'm going to make it a point in life never to be alone in the same room with Ferris Rodman again."

"Why?"

"Why? *Why?*" Quill stopped. She couldn't tell Meg why because if she did, she'd have to tell her she'd broken into the site offices without her. Meg had started the day in a fiery mood, and it was just going to get worse. She'd wait until a more propitious time. Like maybe Christmas.

"Hey!" Dina came into the kitchen, a sheaf of pink While You Were Outs in her hand. "So you're out of jail! Good. Guess what."

"Jail?" Meg said. "What do you mean, jail?"

Quill made a ferocious face at Dina. "Nothing. A little traffic mishap."

"Again? Quill, I thought you learned your lesson about speeding. Did you have an accident? Was anybody hurt? Are *you* hurt?"

"It was nothing."

Meg scowled at Quill. "I can always tell when you're lying to me." Then she turned the scowl on Dina, who promptly backed out of the kitchen and into the dining room. Her voice floated through the closed doors. "Ms. Schmidt is here!"

Quill clapped her hand over her mouth, "Oh migosh, Meg. I forget. Would you have time to do a special sort of breakfast thing?"

"I would not! The kitchen's closed. That was the deal. While the court people are here, we have one sitting at breakfast and that's it. And besides, Cory and I are going to work on some new recipes in the kitchen today."

"Did you have a good time yesterday?" Quill asked casually.

"Yes," Meg said, with suspicious cheer. "We did. Well, we would have, except that she's still suffering from jet lag, Quill. Her sleep schedule's very erratic."

"Well, she's not here yet, so maybe while you're waiting you can make one of your terrific breakfasts for Marge and Bouncer."

"How terrific? You're not talking soufflés, I hope."

"It doesn't have to be really elaborate, there just has to be a lot of it. I talked Bouncer and Marge into having breakfast together. Here."

Meg looked interested despite herself. "Really?

When did you do that? I suppose," she added with a smile, "that you and Marge cooked that up while you were both in jail?"

"Um. Well. As a matter of fact, Meg . . ."

Marge pushed the swinging doors open and looked in at them. " 'Lo Meg, 'lo, Quill. Mind if I come on through?"

"Of course not," Quill pulled a second stool up to the prep table. "Have a seat."

"You seen that bozo Muldoon yet?"

"No, but it's not quite nine o'clock."

Meg got out of the rocker and bounced over to the SubZero. "What would you like for breakfast, Marge? Would Bouncer like some sourdough waffles? Or a frittata? I'm going to cook it myself."

"Just hang on a minute." Marge had a troubled expression. But Quill was touched to see that she had applied a dash of lipstick and curled her hair. She wore her usual chinos, but she'd pulled on a bright red sweater with sequined poinsettias marching across the middle of her chest. "He called on his cell phone after he dropped you off last night, said he'd pick me up this morning at eight. We'd get a bite to eat here, and then he'd drive me over to get my damn car back. I said fine. Bouncer's the kind that looks out for you, you know. Always has been. I waited half an hour and then thought maybe I hadn't heard him right and he wanted to meet me here, early. So I got Betty to drive me up here. Although that don't make any sense either, since he didn't want to run into Judge Moody. He's not here, huh?"

"We haven't seen him," Quill said, "but he may be back in the Tavern Lounge."

"Dina says no." Marge perched on the edge of the stool."

"You're really worried?" Quill said. "He's not that late, Marge."

"You don't know Bouncer. Always been prompt. To the dot. If he isn't where he said he's gonna to be, when he said he's gonna be, something's funny."

Somehow, Quill didn't doubt this at all. "Do you know where he's staying?"

"Yeah. He was bunking in with Dutch Franklin, out on 96. The two of 'em go way back. Dutch was second string quarterback on the team in high school." Marge sighed heavily. "I called Bouncer's cell about eight-fifteen. No answer. I called Dutch about eighty-thirty. Said Bouncer didn't come back last night at all." She darted a sudden glance at Quill. "He say anything to you about where he mighta been headed?"

"No, he didn't." Quill bit her lip. "Did you call Davey? Or the emergency room at the hospital?"

Marge chewed her lower lip. "Little too soon for that. I mean, it's only been what, an hour since he said he'd pick me up. But if he didn't stay to Dutch's last night, where'd he stay? Not here?"

"Not here," Quill said. "He dropped me off at the front door. He wanted to wait until I went inside—he's so nice, Marge! But I said I wanted to stay outside for a bit. I watched him leave. Oh! And then he came back, about half an hour later. Said he'd gotten halfway home and realized my purse was in the truck, so he brought it back. Honestly, Marge, every time I see I like him better and better. He could have waited until today to bring the purse back to me, but he didn't want me to worry. Anyhow, he went straight back into town, as far as I could tell."

"Well, something's up. I don't like it."

Meg, who'd wandered into the office she shared with Doreen, came out again. "Andy said nobody's been admitted to the emergency room within the last twenty-four hours. It was a quiet night in Hemlock Falls."

"If Davey knew anything, he more than likely would have told Dina," Quill said. "But you asked Dina if she'd seen him when you came in."

"Yeah."

"You don't suppose . . . when he called you, Marge, did you tell him anything about last night?"

"Yeah, I did. I mean, he was bound to ask, wasn't he? The two of us locked up like that and my car towed and all. So sure, I told him."

"Locked up?" Meg said. "And your car's been towed?"

Quill had a sudden inspiration. "I know! Maybe he went to get your car back for you!"

"How'd he drive my car and his truck back here? He's big enough for two men, but he can only wear one pair of pants." Marge rubbed her hand over her face, smearing her lipstick. "I figure I better go check things out. Thing is, I don't have a car. So I was thinking maybe you could lend me Meg's car. Betty's got a grocery run this morning, or I'd ask her."

"I'll do better than that. I'll go with you."

Marge didn't say much until they were in Meg's Fiesta and on their way down the drive to the village.

"I never looked for anyone before," she said. "You got any ideas?"

"First, we should just drive the route he would have taken to get back to Dutch's. He may have gone off the road for some reason or stopped at a gas station or pulled over to take a nap—whatever. But I think the best place to look is the place where he's supposed to be. Then we'll stop at Dutch's and see if there's any clue at all in the things he left there. Did you ask Dutch if his suitcase was there?"

"Suitcase," Marge said. "Bouncer'd have a duffle bag. He likes to keep things simple: T-shirts, jeans, boots. That's about it. He always had a hell of a time finding clothes big enough to fit him, so like I said, he likes to keep it simple." She peered out the windshield. "You want to take the road to Dutch's, you take your next left on Maple. Then there's a gravel road about three blocks down. That goes cross lots down to 96."

Quill turned onto Maple, drove three blocks and said, "The gravel road on the right?"

"That's the one."

The Fiesta suspension was tight and stiff, which helped Quill's control of the car, but it made for a bumpy ride. They jounced along the unpaved road, which wound past a few farms, and a lot of woods. Quill drove slowly; Marge scanned the road deliberately, from left to right and back again, like the conning tower on a submarine.

"Shit," Marge said. "There."

Quill pulled the car onto the shoulder. She might have missed it herself. Scrub trees like crabapple and rosa pastura lined the road, and the ground sloped steeply from the shoulder to the brush. One of the willows had a big raw chunk out of the trunk. It listed heavily to one side.

Quill put the car in park. They both got out, Marge trotting slightly ahead. Marge stamped through the rubble of broken branches and stopped suddenly. Quill came up and stood beside her.

The truck was completely overturned. It wasn't damaged, at least as far as Quill could see. But the driver's door had come open, and she could see Bouncer's left shoulder and hip through the open door. The truck itself seemed undamaged. Quill's gaze flickered over the hood, the passenger side.

She froze.

Marge started forward. Quill grabbed her shoulders and, forced Marge around so that they faced each other and said, "No."

"Big jerk's probably unconscious in there."

"He's not unconscious, Marge. He's dead. I can see that from here."

Marge grabbed both Quill's hands and shouted. "Let me go!"

"No. No. I won't let you down there."

Marge stared at her.

"Call 911, Marge. And go sit in the car. Please. Please."

Marge stopped struggling. She looked into Quill's face, her mouth distorted. "What do you see? You gotta tell me, Quill. I gotta know."

Quill swallowed. "Bouncer's body is half out of the driver's door."

"I can see that for myself, dammit!" She started fighting Quill's hands again, but Quill held on.

"I can see his ponytail . . . that nice . . . I always liked men with long hair." Quill knew she was crying because she could barely see through the blur of her tears, but she her voice was steady. "That's all on the other side of the truck, Marge. It's way too far. Even for someone as tall as he was."

"This is just horrible." Meg sat with her arm around Quill. The dingy lobby of the Tompkins County Morgue was quiet. The room was saturated with a horrible gray smell, part disinfectant, and Quill didn't want to think about the other part.

"It was the worst thing I've ever seen," Quill said. She covered her eyes with one hand. "I wish I hadn't. But I did. And it's worse for poor Marge." She looked at her sister. "I can't see how that could have happened. The truck was intact. While we were waiting for emergency crew, I took a good long look at the scene of the accident."

Quill pulled her sketchpad out of her purse. "This is the county line road. It's not paved, as you know, and the shoulders haven't been packed down. It's very rough and sloppy stuff. But that truck is designed to go over pyramids, Meg, much less a sloppy bit of road work. Anyway, I could see the tracks where the truck went off the road. There didn't seem to be any skid marks, and I'll bet you anything that the truck left the road at speed. It crashed through all this brush like this." She was always grateful for her gift, and never more so than now, when she could use it to show Meg what it must have been like. "See how the tire tracks veer back and forth? Each time the truck met an obstacle, it bounced away from it until here, finally." Her pencil flew over the paper, "It slammed up against this boulder. That's what flipped it. He still had his seat belt on, you know."

"No damage to the truck, then."

Quill shook her head. "No glass, no raw metal, nothing."

Meg looked away from her. "You're saying someone sat behind him and what? Swung an axe? A sword? That doesn't seem possible."

"It was a clean cut. A surgical cut. As if a very flexible scalpel had been used as a garrote. And Meg, the man had a neck like an ox. Literally. It must have been someone impossibly strong. Unless . . ." she frowned. "One end of whatever it was could have been hooked to the strap hanger. If the weapon were as sharp as it seemed, a man of ordinary strength could have done it."

"Why would Bouncer sit still for that?" Meg asked quietly. "Don't tell me. There must have been a gun to his head."

"Why? He was such a good man!"

Meg gave Quill's an affectionate pat, then got up and moved restlessly around the patched linoleum floor. "He's been away from home for how long? Marge's divorce was twenty-five years ago. That's a whole other lifetime."

"You're right." Quill looked down at her hands. Then she closed the sketch pad and put it back into her purse. "I can't believe they made Marge identify the body."

"She's next of kin."

"I would have done it, Meg. They wouldn't let me."

There was a clatter of noise in the hall beyond the lobby, and then Marge stumped in. Her face was pale, but she looked much as she always did. "We can go now."

Quill collected the coats, and Meg dug in her purse for her keys. Quill touched her lightly. "Are you okay?"

"Okay as I'll ever be."

She refused to stop for coffee, or for something to eat, even though it was well after three o'clock and she hadn't eaten all day. She didn't start to talk about it until they were well out of Ithaca. And even then, she kept her distance, staring out the window from the backseat as the cold March countryside rolled by.

"It don't take a rocket scientist. Somebody killed Bouncer. That's true, isn't it?"

Meg slowed down, glanced over at Quill, and then brought the car back up to speed. Quill turned around in her seat so that she could see Marge before she answered. "Did the police have anything to say?"

"I wish Davey hadn't turned it over to these boys in

Ithaca. Davey'd tell me straight out." Marge's face was masklike. "Said the 'investigation was ongoing.' Whatever that means. But I know." Her gaze met Quill's, then she looked away again.

"The damn truck didn't have a dent on it. Couple of scratches, is all. They wanted me to tell 'em who was going to pick it up after they were finished with it. How the hell should I know? For all of me, he could have a wife and six kids parked somewhere. I haven't seen him in twenty-five years."

"He would have mentioned them if he had," Quill said gently. "He was such a straightforward man, Marge."

"He was a damn fool."

Neither Meg nor Quill responded to this.

"I was sixteen when we got married. He was eighteen. I never finished high school, didja know that?"

Quill shook her head.

"We moved into that trailer out by the paint factory and the usual stuff happened. I wasn't pregnant, you understand. Just thought Bouncer was the hottest thing since buying on margin." Her mouth quirked in a grin. Not that I knew a margin from a hole in the ground back then. All the money stuff came later, after he left.

"Bouncer liked his beer, back then, and he hung with the guys from the football team. You remember the Croh Bar before I took it over?"

Quill did. It had been a dive with the tables sticky with beer and a pervasive odor of dirt, sweat, and cigarettes.

"Him and Dutch and Corky Gallagher spent most nights there. They worked construction during the day, stop at the Croh Bar right after work and stumble on home drunk as skunks. The times I didn't spend worryin' he was dead in a ditch somewhere, I spent wishin' he *was* in a ditch somewheres. Lookin' back on it, I was bored. Worked at the checkout at the old A&P. I was frustrated as hell. Couldn't see my way out."

Marge's sigh was deep. "So. One night, him and Corky were beered up, like usual, and there was an accident. Gallagher was driving this old rattletrap of a Ford truck. Bouncer was passed out in the truck bed, in back. Truck flipped over, and by the damn fool luck drunks always seem to have they both walked away from it.

"The other people weren't so lucky. It was a family from over to Ithaca, driving back from visiting the guy's sister in Syracuse. The wife was driving. The husband was asleep in the front seat. There was a little kid in the back."

"Was anybody hurt?" Quill asked.

Marge nodded. "Oh, yeah. That car was totaled. Smashed right into the bridge abutment at that ramp down by Route Fifteen. Sheered the top of that sucker right off. Sheered off the wife's head, too."

"The little girl was cut up some. And the husband walked off with a busted arm and a broken spleen. But the wife?" Marge waited a moment. "They said it was instant."

"There was a trial, of course. That damn fool Gallagher claimed it was the other guy's fault that the

208

husband had been driving. The husband's blood alcohol was like, point eighteen or something, I don't remember exactly. Anyhow, Bouncer was the only witness, and he didn't know a damn thing about it. Anyways, Gallagher up and took off before the trial was half over. The jury found for that poor woman and her husband." Marge looked at Quill, her face stern. "It was never the same between Bouncer and me after that. So I threw him out."

Quill reached over and touched her shoulder lightly. "Oh, Marge."

"Thing is, at the time, I thought both Corky and Bouncer were lying their fool heads off. I still think they were lying their fool heads off.

"And that Judge Moody thinks so, too."

"Mitchell Moody presided at the trial?" Quill said, bewildered. "My god, no wonder Bouncer skipped jury duty."

"Mitchell Moody was a hotshot D.A. at the time," Marge said. "Mitchell Moody's wife was driving that car. And now Moody's gone and killed Bouncer."

Meg pulled the car onto the shoulder and stopped.

"It figures, don't it?" Marge glared at both of them. "Why else was the poor bastard's head cut clean off? That was the way that Ellen Moody died. Twenty-five years ago to the day. March 23rd.

"And I got no way to prove it."

"How *is* she going to prove it, Quill?" Meg stared at her stuffed crab, and shoved the plate away. She and Quill sat at their table in the dining room. It was after seven, and the entire contingent of lawyers, jurors, and hangers-on were eating Meg's excellent crab, with the exception of Mrs. Pembroke, who claimed allergies and insisted on pasta.

"It's a horrible story." Quill ate her crab slowly, without really tasting it. She didn't feel like eating, either, but she knew her exhaustion was due in part to hunger. After Bouncer's body had been released and taken to the morgue, Davey had driven the three of them to the Tompkins County Police Pound. Quill reclaimed her Honda, and they in turn had taken Marge to formally identify his body. Even if there had been time to eat then, they couldn't have.

"Do you suppose it's true? That Moody killed Bouncer?"

"Eat something, Meg. You'll feel better. And don't stare at Moody. He'll think something's up."

"Something *is* up. My temper. If Moody did it, I want him to pay for it. We've got to do something."

Quill ignored her own caveat and stared at the justice. He sat hunched over his food, his eyes hooded. His bodyguard sat stolidly beside him, shoveling Meg's crab into his mouth with mechanical regularity.

"Why would he wait all these years?"

Meg shrugged. "Biding his time? Who was it that said 'revenge is a dish best eaten cold'? Maybe he was waiting for the right opportunity. Maybe he saw Bouncer in court, and his rage came flooding back all these years. Who knows?"

"It's a big 'why,' Meg."

"We don't have to prove why, remember? Motive isn't the clincher. Facts provide the clincher. Facts and forensics."

Moody, as if suddenly aware of Quill's stare, raised his head. That black gaze was as fierce and intimidating as ever. Quill lowered her voice, although Moody was too far away for even normal volume to reach him. "He's obviously going to know everything there is to know about physical evidence. He certainly had the opportunity; you can hear Bouncer's truck a mile away. And it 'has that screamer paint on the side—Bouncer's Balls—so that you couldn't mistake it for anyone else's truck. And he came back to give me my purse. So it's possible that Moody heard the truck, got up, came downstairs, and jumped in the back when Bouncer got out to hand me my purse. It's possible."

"And Moody just happened to have a flexible, scalpel-sharp garrote on hand?" Meg took a bit of the crab. The prospect of being able to do something about Bouncer's death had revived her appetite. "It's a stretch. Possible, but a stretch."

Quill smoothed the tablecloth in front of her, and stared at it as if it were a blank slate. The answers would appear if she just had all the facts. "You know, most of what's happened here the last few days has concerned either Moody or Rodman."

Meg nodded. "You're right. Rodman's moving the cemetery and Corliss Hooper is killed there. Rodman's suing Meecham over the deed, and Moody's sitting on the bench to decide the outcome of the case. Bouncer was called as a juror on the case involving Rodman. Someone shoots at Moody when the jurors are out walking the site to help them determine the outcome of the lawsuit. And poor Bouncer—"

"—was involved in the car accident that decapitated Moody's wife twenty-five years ago." Quill tapped the tablecloth with her forefinger. "You know what's missing here? Some connection between Rodman and Bouncer."

Meg blinked a little. "What would that prove?"

"Or between Bouncer and Corliss Hooper. Meg!" Quill sat up with a gasp. "You don't suppose that Corliss Hooper was that guy Gallagher!"

"What guy Gallagher? You mean the guy who was driving the truck when the accident happened all those years ago? Marge said he left town before he could be indicted for reckless driving. And Davey told us that Corliss Hooper worked for Kodak for thirty years. It doesn't seem likely."

"We've got to know more about the accident," Quill mused. Her gaze traveled around the room, and fell on Juror Number Two, Sparky Stillwater. Computer expert extraordinaire. Even if Quill hadn't known he was a computer software engineer, she would have guessed. His hair flowed down his back in a long, dark brown ponytail. His eyes were a vivid blue in a face that was almost a perfect circle. He wore a baggy white shirt and a tie loosely knotted around his neck. Quill would have bet her best camel's hair paintbrush that he'd been forced to abandon his usual baggy T-shirt and jeans as a concession to court decorum. The biggest clue, she decided, was his expression; he looked utterly bewildered at seeing people in front of him rather than a computer screen.

He was sitting with Mrs. Johnson and Brett Coldwell, eating crab with an abstracted expression. "And I know just the person to help us do it. Uh-oh. Watch it, Meg. Moody's headed this way."

Moody loomed over their table like a gaunt bird of prey. "I came to present my compliments to you, Quill, and to your sister. I've rarely had a better meal."

"Thank you," Meg said, "although I wasn't sure about the cheese."

"A Gruyère, I believe. It was delicious. May I join you, Quill? I understand you were a witness at that unfortunate incident today."

"Please sit down." Quill gestured toward the third chair at their table.

Meg rose to her feet. "If you're going to talk about what we saw today, you'll have to excuse me, your Honor. It was awful, I was just wondering, would it be all right with you if I asked Sparky Stillwater to give me a hand with some computer problems we're having? We haven't been able to get our aunt's e-mail from Europe for the past few days."

"That's right!" Quill said a little too loudly. "Her server's down. Good idea, Meg. You can have him help you check up on a couple of things, while you're at it."

Moody's black eyes flickered toward Sparky's table.

"Doesn't bother me, if he's willing. You're not to ask him about the trial, though."

"I don't care about the trial," Meg said frankly, "so what would I ask him? You don't mind if we use your laptop, Quill?"

"Since that's the one with the problem, I don't mind at all." She watched as Meg went to the table and, with a lot of hand waving, described their supposed computer woes to the table. Sparky started to nod almost as soon as she began to speak. He swallowed the last of his dinner and stood up.

"Looks as if that made his day," Moody observed. "These civil matters can be a bit of a bore. I sent the jury out to the site more to keep them awake than anything else."

"They couldn't have been bored there," Quill said with a shudder. "Have the police come up with any theories about who fired those shots?" She had her own. She was positive that Rodman's car horn had provided a signal to the shooter.

"Lieutenant Harper found shotgun shells on the southwest ridge," Moody said. It was clear that he didn't think much of Harper; his face was dark with annoyance and his voice was clipped. "Right now, the supposition is that it was an out-of-season hunter. We'll see about that." He smiled at her. "However, I didn't come over here to talk about that. I came over here to see if I could buy you that drink you've been promising me."

Quill was about to reply, pleasantly, that she hadn't promised any such thing, when his cell phone rang. He held one finger up and drew the cell phone from his pocket.

"Moody," he said brusquely. He listened a moment, his face expressionless. "How did you get this number?" he said abruptly. Then, "I see." He pulled his watch from his pocket and checked it with a frown. "All right. If you insist."

He snapped the phone closed and sat buried in thought for a moment. Then he smiled at her. "I'm afraid I'll have to take another rain check on that drink."

"That wasn't Ferris Rodman, was it?" Quill said anxiously.

Moody's eyes narrowed. "Mr. Rodman's a defendant in this case, Miss Quilliam."

"Of course. Sorry." She smiled apologetically. "None of my business, anyway."

"Precisely."

He left the dining room with long, rapid strides. Seeing him leave, Frank the bodyguard flung down his napkin and followed him out the foyer. Seconds later, Frank came back, a grin on his face, and sat down to the rest of his meal.

Quill bit her lip. Moody hadn't denied that it was Rodman on the phone. And even more tellingly, Moody had obviously told his bodyguard to get lost. If Moody were meeting secretly—and illegally—with a defendant on whom he was sitting in judgment, Moody wouldn't want a witness. On the other hand, Frank had a smile on his face. What was that all about? Quill, torn, debated furiously with herself. She should call someone—but whom? Davey was still furious with both her and Meg. Now, if Myles were here, she could talk to Myles. Or she could call that FBI agent. He'd left her his card. Except that Davey'd as good as admitted that Mrs. Pembroke's foibles about the safety of her former son-in-law were behind the FBI's presence at the Inn. (An anxiety, she suspected, rooted more in Mrs. Pembroke's fear of losing her cushy facilitators' job than any love for the justice.) She glanced around the room until she found Mrs. Pembroke. She sat with Mrs. McAllister, the juror with the expensively-styled hair. Mrs. McAllister nodded politely as Mrs. Pembroke talked with animation. And yes, her day planner was open, ready to receive the hourly totals of Mrs. Pembroke's workday.

Quill sank her head into her hands. She was getting as cynical as Marge. Maybe it was time to give up the Inn and make way for Ferris Rodman and his European chef before she lost all her faith in humankind.

"Quill?"

Quill snapped out of her abstraction. "Dina! What are you doing here?"

"Spring break started today. So I'm staying over with Davey. But he's all tied up with that gruesome thing that happened with poor Bouncer Muldoon, so I came over here. Mind if I sit?" Dina flopped cheerfully into the chair Meg had occupied. "So, what's happening?"

Quill took a deep breath and then let it out. "Not much," she said carefully, "I'm sunk in grim reflection. I'm going to convert. I'm becoming a Hobbesian."

Dina grinned. "Life's nasty brutal and short? We're all condemned to Purgatory by our nasty brutal natures? That Hobbes?"

"The very one." She sighed. "What's happening with you?"

"Oh, the usual." Dina twirled a lock of glossy brown hair around her finger. "The reason I asked what's happening with you is that a *lot* has been happening here."

"Here" Quill looked around vaguely. "You mean the Inn." She looked at her dining room with sudden, sincere affection. The carpeting was a deep blue. The tables were set with cloths the color of creamed butter. The table arrangements were Dutch iris and freesia. The air was alive with the perfume of the freesia, the hum of contented guests, the scent of garlic and herbs. Life may be too short, and for many brutal, but it was neither nasty nor brutish. Not when people could enjoy themselves the way her guests were enjoying themselves.

"Quill?"

"Sorry. You were telling me something."

"I'm sort of a delegation."

Quill raised one eyebrow. "All by yourself?"

"From the staff. You see," Dina hitched herself forward, leaned across the table, and said confidentially, "It's Corisande."

"Oh, dear."

"Or as Doreen puts it, '*that* Corisande.' "

"Oh, dear, oh dear. What exactly is the problem?"

"Well, we all know how excited you and Meg were to have her come here, I mean, everyone else has family, but not you. Doreen," Dina added accusingly, "was under the impression you and Meg were orphans."

"We *are* orphans. Our parents died when I was sixteen and Meg was twelve. So what's the problem with Corisande? I realize," Quill added guiltily, "that Meg and I haven't been around all that much, and we've been neglecting her, but truly, Dina, the last few days have just been wild."

"She's a snot."

"A snot," Quill said.

"Yeah. For one thing, she acts as if we were the peasants and she's like, the Queen of England."

This was true. And it would have to be addressed. Quill loathed pretension. It was a major character issue and she never thought she'd find in a member of her own family. "I'm really sorry about that."

"And she's lazy."

This appeared to be true, too. But it rated high on the MYOB scale, since Dina wasn't responsible for Corisande, and Corisande didn't have any responsibilities that had to do with Dina. So Quill tuned out, as she frequently did with most employee complaints, unless they involved actively criminal acts. Dina recaptured her attention when she said, "not to mention the petty cash."

"The petty cash?" That *was* an actively criminal act. "Oh, no."

"As I live and breathe," Dina said, quaintly. "There was fifty dollars missing from it day before yesterday when I went to get stamp money. So I told Doreen. And

Doreen said of course it was 'that Corisande' so we marked the bills with a little blue dot. And sure enough, another twenty was missing this morning, and this afternoon I asked her—Corisande, I mean—for change for a ten and guess what."

"Little blue dots."

"Yep. I didn't think you wanted me to turn her into Davey . . ."

"Gosh, no. What would I tell Aunt Eleanor?" Maybe Sparky wouldn't be able to find the problem with Aunt Eleanor's server. That would be good. Until she got poor Corisande sorted out.

"So there was nothing for it. We had to tell you. Doreen and I were *both* going to tell you, but Doreen is like, 'I told you so,' and we figured it'd better be me. Plus, I don't mind when you rag on me, but Doreen does."

Quill made an apologetic face. "I'm sorry if I rag on you."

"Oh . . ." Dina waved both hands above her head. "I know you don't mean it. Your job would make anybody squirrelly. I mean, think about it. You're ready to convert to Hobbesism. I ask you, is that a clue that your job's too much for you, or not?"

"My job's a piece of cake," Quill said defensively. "Anything else?"

"Probably. But she's only been here two and a half days. Give her time."

Quill had to laugh at that. Then she said hesitantly, "Dina? Do you think she's into any drugs?"

Dina blinked her big brown eyes at her. "Weren't you listening when I told you about the vodka? Nate's fit to be tied. She doesn't snitch the bar brands you know. She goes for Ketel One and the Grey Goose. The most expensive stuff. Liquor," Dina said with a virtuous air, "is *much* worse than a little marijuana. But if you mean hard drugs, like coke and whatever, no, I don't think so. I can tell when the kids at school get messed up and she's not. Messed up, I mean."

"Thank god for that." Quill put her hands over Dina's. "Thank you for telling me. It must have been hard for you."

"Not a bit," she answered, with the callousness of youth, "Doreen didn't want to tell you. She said you and Meg are lonely for kids and that Corisande was a kind of a surrogate. But if you were lonely for kids, you'd have some, wouldn't you?"

Quill thought of Myles, who did want children, very much, and sighed. "Yes. I would. I will."

Dina took a breath. "Okay. So that's over."

"There's more?"

"Bjarne asked me to type out his C.V. for him. And a cover letter. I did it, of course, because we're friends, but I felt badly about it."

"You mean, he's quitting?" This, too, was bad news. Quill made a face. This happened every time she made even the teensiest foray into the detective business. Everything at the Inn went promptly to hell.

"I told him he should talk to Meg, but he said he was very fond of his . . . ummm . . ."

"I get the picture. He didn't want to risk his masculinity."

"Right. He would have talked to you, but you just weren't around. So I said I'd mention it, casually, the next time I saw you."

"He can't be applying to the Marriott," Quill said with a frown. "He'd hate it there. It's all banquets and rubber chicken."

"He wants to study with this Claude person."

"Claude de Courcy? But . . ." Quill gritted her teeth. That damn Ferris Rodman had a lot to answer for.

"So *that's* over," Dina muttered to herself. "What else?" She rummaged in her jeans pocket and pulled out a crumpled piece of paper. "Hang on a second."

"Is that a list?" Quill asked, dismayed.

"Yep. I didn't want to forget anything so I wrote it down. Oh! Right. We got a kitchen ticket. A couple of kitchen tickets, as a matter of fact."

"Tickets? What do you mean, tickets? Did the Board of Health do an inspection? They usually let us know they're coming. Rats."

"It wasn't the Board of Health. It was Carol Ann Spinoza. Did you know—"

Quill jumped out of the chair and shouted, "Carol Ann Spinoza's been in Meg's kitchen?!" which made all the jurors who were still eating stop and stare at her. She heard Mrs. Pembroke's disapproving, "Drugs! I thought so!" all the way across the room.

"She's there now," Dina said. "I thought you knew."

Quill slammed into the kitchen, leaving the doors

swinging wildly. Carol Ann was there, all right, and so was Donald Dunleavy.

"Out!" Quill said flatly.

Carol Ann had a pair of handcuffs clipped to her belt and a nightstick stuck in her pocket. She was wearing a dark blue hat with a bill. So was Donald Dunleavy. Donald Dunleavy looked uncomfortable. Carol Ann looked smug. Most of the staff was giggling nervously.

The hats had printing on them. Computer-generated labels with a gummed back had been glued right in the center of the peaks. The label read HEMLOCK FALLS VPD. Underneath in a curly font was the legend: The Hemlock Grenadiers. Carol Ann had wasted no time in assuming the uniform of a volunteer policewoman.

She hadn't wasted any time in taking on volunteer police duties, either. Bright red HVPD Violation stickers were plastered on Meg's SubZero, her Aga, one leg of the prep table, and the cobblestone fireplace. Carol Ann had a fifth one in one hand, apparently ready to stick it somewhere else. The other held a tape measure. Quill had a very good idea where she would like to stick the both label and the tape measure, but she remembered that she was, essentially, a nonviolent person.

"What are you doing?" she asked coldly.

"This kitchen is in violation of many, many restaurant codes," Carol Ann said. "All of these appliances have to be moved or I'm going to shut this place down."

"I beg your pardon?"

"As Assistant to the Chief of the Volunteer Police

Force, I am making sure that you are forced into compliance. For the safety of those poor guests out there, if nothing else." She walked over to the pans dishwasher and stuck the red label on the front.

Meg kept her sauté pans on an overhead rack at the prep table. Quill unhooked the ten-inch one and brandished it in the air. "See this?" she said, quietly. "I am going to mash that little hat of yours flatter than a crepe, Carol Ann. With your head still in it."

She flushed with rage. "You can't do that. It's assault."

"I'm committing assault at the moment. If I mash that hat flat, it's battery. I'm cheerfully committing the first, as you see." Quill smiled, to prove her good humor. Carol Ann jumped nervously back. Quill smiled wider still. "I will happily commit the second."

"Help me, Donald. Handcuff her!"

Donald shifted the toothpick in his mouth from the right side to the left. Then he shifted it back again. "I'm going to count to ten. One." (Quill took a step forward.) "Two." (She took a second step forward.) "Three."

Donald Dunleavy turned and walked out the back door. "Four."

Carol Ann shoved Donald out of the way and jumped past him.

Quill hung the sauté pan back on the rack.

Bjarne shouted, "Hurray!" The under chefs applauded.

"Everybody back to work," Quill said, and walked out the doors to the dining room. Dina was still sitting at the table, frowning over her list. Quill sat down in her accustomed place. She smiled at Kathleen Kiddermeister, who was clearing the tables of the remains of the jurors' meals. She smiled at Dina, who smiled back. "Carol Ann's not in the kitchen anymore."

"You asked her to leave?"

"I did."

"And she went? Gosh, Quill. That assertiveness course you're taking at the Cornell Hotel School of Management is really working. Did you do the body language thing?"

"I did. I don't like to waste my tuition money," Quill said modestly. "Okay, give me the rest of it."

"Well, there isn't too much more. I told Sheriff McHale about you and Marge breaking into—"

"Myles called?"

"He practically dragged it out of me, Quill, honest."

"You didn't tell me Myles called!"

"I didn't have time to tell you."

"Did he say when he'd call again?"

"Tonight, I think."

"You think!?"

"I couldn't hear him all that well, Quill! There was a lot of background noise! Yes, tonight, but I couldn't tell if it was ten o'clock our time or his time. He's six hours ahead. Or is it behind? I can never remember."

"It's ahead. But he sounded well?"

"He sounded just fine. And you look happy."

"I am very happy."

"Good. You remember that I tried to give you your

phone calls this morning, but you and Marge rushed right out of here."

"I remember. You did try, yes."

"Is Marge okay?" Dina's round face was troubled. "That must have been so horrible."

"It was. But she's tough, Dina. She's very practical and she's not at all sentimental. I admire her a lot. She has a lot of resilience. Meg and I left her with Betty, you know. They've known each other a long time. She'll take care of Marge."

"That's good. Davey says Bouncer was murdered."

"He was," Quill said tightly. "And in a particularly vicious way."

"I'm sorry. I thought he was great."

"He was." The rush of adrenaline subsided, and Quill felt suddenly depressed. "I hope that's everything on your list. If there's more, I'd rather hear it tomorrow."

"Poor Quill," Dina's eyes were warm with sympathy.

"Nope. You're in luck. That's all I wanted to tell you." Dina began to gather her duffle bag and her coat. "I'll be in at ten, like usual, but I'm going to leave at twelve, if that's okay with you. I'm collecting samples from the duck pond."

Quill roused herself with an effort. Dina was in the last stages of a Ph.D. in freshwater pond ecology, and Quill knew that she had been monitoring the life cycle of something or other in the duck pond in Peterson Park.

"Are they doing well, your copepods?" she asked politely.

Dina grinned. "As if you'd know a copepod from a liver fluke! They're doing nicely, thank you. I'm comparing the samples from G-54 with the samples from M-42 at the moment, and it's really fascinating what the slightest difference in temp . . . what?"

Quill stared at her. "From G-54? What G-54?"

"When you're studying copepods the first thing you do is make a map-grid so that you can identify the populations. I made a map-grid of the pond so that I could tell where my little guys are. You know, I lettered A through Z at the top of the grid and then I numbered down along the sides."

"A map-grid! And the copo-whatsis are at G-54? Is there a K on your map, Dina?"

"Nope. I ran out of squares."

"But there are K's on other map-grids, right?"

"Well, sure, I guess. It depends on how may squares you need."

"It wasn't the Horn Concerti! It was a map-grid!"

Dina nodded. "Right," she said encouragingly. "Whatever. But you look at lot more cheerful. So that's good."

Quill took the stairs to her rooms two at a time. When she burst into her room, Meg and Sparky were hunched over her laptop. Printouts littered the floor.

"We haven't had much luck," Meg said glumly. "Although Spark's been terrific."

Sparky, his fingers clattering on the keyboard said, "Hey. I got us into the Kodak Human Resources files, didn't I?"

Meg patted him on the arm. "Yes you did, Sparky,

and I can't tell you how much I appreciate it." She looked over her shoulder at Quill. "He seems to be who Davey thinks he was."

"Corliss Hooker?"

"Yep." Meg sat back and stretched. "And we got into the newspaper files, too. We didn't find a whole lot about the accident, but there's enough. The Syracuse *Herald* and the Rochester *Democrat and Chronicle* don't have those records on line. But Spark Googled the date and the name, and we came up with a few facts. Not much more than Marge told us, though."

"Hey, too bad about Judge Moody," Sparky said. "Heck of a thing, losing your wife like that."

"We Googled Moody, too," Meg said in a lowered tone of voice. "He certainly likes the spotlight. There was a ton of stuff on him. We got his vita from the American Bar Association, too. He never remarried."

"Sparky," Quill said urgently. "Can you find maps on that thing?"

Sparky blinked at her. "Maps? Like geographic maps? Sure."

"You don't think there'd be a map of the Civil War cemetery, do you?"

"The one they're relocating? Sure. MapQuest'll have it. Why? You want me to bring it up?"

"Please."

Quill stood behind him, watching the screen intently. Sparky clattered away and within seconds, a map of Hemlock Falls appeared on the screen. Sparky clattered away some more, and the cemetery itself showed up.

Claudia Bishop

"Can you place a map-grid over that?"

"It's already got one," Sparky said patiently.

"Then can you pinpoint K-47 for me?"

Sparky tapped, tapped, tapped, and said, "There. Upper northwest corner."

"Let's print it out."

"So it *wasn't* Mozart," Meg said. "Omigosh! How did you figure that out? I thought it was Mozart, too."

"No, it wasn't Mozart."

"It's making sense, Quill! Are you thinking what I'm thinking?" Meg gestured at the printouts littering the floor. "You should read this stuff. Gallagher's defense was that Moody had been driving, not his wife. And Moody's blood-alcohol level was high. He was drunk. Gallagher's was high, too, but he claimed that Moody blew that stop sign where Route 15 feeds into the county line road. And if Bouncer and Gallagher were coming back from the Croh Bar, it's the only story that makes sense. So the accident was Moody's fault."

"And Gallagher 'disappeared' before he could testify." Quill glanced at Sparky, who, oblivious, was staring at lines of squares and boxes on the screen.

"What?," he said, his voice abstracted. "Ho! Is this game cool, or what?" He attacked the keyboard with renewed force.

Quill collected the printouts, and then laid her hands on Sparky's shoulders. "We owe you one, Sparky. Anytime you'd like to spend a week here, it's on us. And bring a friend."

He didn't take his eyes from the game. "You've got what you want, then?"

"We do. And I mean it about the vacation here."

"I'll cook for you myself," Meg said,

"Thanks, guys, but you don't have RoadRunner out here." He paused, turned, and his blue eyes lit up. "Soon as you do, give me a call, though. And let me know anytime you have a real problem. It's a lot better than sitting in that courtroom, let me tell you." He frowned. "They took away my iPod, you know."

Quill made commiserating sounds.

Refusing all other offers of bed or board, he clumped out of Quill's rooms and disappeared down the hall.

"RoadRunner?" Quill asked. "Like the cartoon?"

"It's speedy access to the Net," Meg said knowledgeably.

"As if you knew anything about it."

"What I know is, we're about to make a trip to the cemetery, right?"

"Right. Just to check that there's a grave there. That's what Hooker's note was about, Meg. Gallagher's grave is there, Meg. I'm sure of it. And Moody found out that Corliss Hooker'd found out—"

"And Moody killed him." Meg's face was set. " 'Time for Justice.' Right."

Quill's dark clothes were in the wash, so she settled for ski pants and a down jacket.

"You're going to be hot," Meg said. She was driving her battered Ford Escort. Quill's Honda, she pointed out, was on the hit list of every trooper from here to Buffalo.

"We aren't even committing a misdemeanor," Quill said. "It's a public place and anybody can walk through it. We'll just say we're looking for some relatives."

"Everyone in Hemlock Falls knows we're from Connecticut. And look." Meg pulled into the small area that served as the cemetery's parking lot. "It says, 'Hours From Sunrise to Sunset'. It's way after sunset, in case you haven't noticed. So you'll be able to add a misdemeanor to your rap sheet if we get caught."

"I told you, Rodman isn't going to press charges. I don't have a rap sheet."

Meg, unbuckling her seat belt, paused for a moment. "I'm so glad you and Marge didn't get in his car last night, Quill. You said he just stood there last time, looking at you? He was probably measuring you for a pair of cement overshoes."

Quill didn't bother to respond to this. She got out of the car. The cemetery was located on a side street, not far from Main, and the streetlights were on. She stood under the one closest to the wrought-iron gates and unfolded the map from the computer. "It looks like we take a left after we go into the gate and walk up to the back fence. K-47 should be on the right. The note said 'Quill' so I think we should either look for a name on the gravestone or a feather, or—Meg! Why do you have a shovel?"

"We came to find out what's in K-47, didn't we?"

"Yes, but we can't dig up a grave!"

Meg stuck the point of the shovel into the ground and leaned on it. "Let me ask you this. How long is Moody going to be here?"

"Another few days, I suppose. I talked to one of the defense lawyers briefly tonight. She said they were about to go into deliberations. And she confirmed what Moody said: it's a pretty straightforward case that depends on the interpretation of the language of a deed."

"So we're looking at what, seventy-two hours while he's still around and arrestable? And how long do you think it's going to take to get a court order to dig up a grave?"

"Longer than that," Quill said.

Meg waved her arms and the shovel fell over with a thud. "Weeks!"

Quill thought about digging into a grave. She shuddered.

"Come on, sis. Dead is dead. And we only have to dig a little bit of him up."

"Honestly, Meg. You have the sensitivity of a medicine ball. Aren't you at least reluctant? It seems so disrespectful."

"I'm feel very respectful," Meg said, surprised. "Don't you? This is a respectful place."

Perhaps Meg was right. The wrought-iron fence surrounding the cemetery was no more than knee high. It had been designed to set this land apart—not keep people out. And Quill thought of the journey that she and Meg took once a year, back to Connecticut, to visit the place where their parents were buried. That cemetery was a peaceful place, as well, where all the storms and violence that human beings were heir to had been laid to rest.

Quill took a very deep breath. "If, and I say *if* we decide to do this, how will we know it's Gallagher?"

Meg jabbed the point of the shovel into the ground in a thoughtful way. "How will we know it's Gallagher?"

"You're stalling," Quill pointed out.

"Let me ask you this: who else could it be but Gallagher?"

"But . . ."

"Look, if we find some poor soul with a Civil War uniform in tatters around a pile of bones . . . we'll know *that's* not Gallagher."

"True, but . . ."

"And if we find a coffin, we'll be pretty sure Gallagher isn't in it, because what murderer would find the time to do a proper burial?"

"I suppose . . ."

"And how many murderers do you think are running around Hemlock Falls dumping bodies anyway? Who *else* could it be but Gallagher? Logic, Quill, logic." Meg tapped her temple with her forefinger. "You are not using the little gray cells, *mon ami*."

Quill regretted, not for the first time, that she was too old to pull Meg's hair.

"Okay?" Meg said. "We can do this. Do you have a flashlight?"

Quill pulled it out of her pocket and switched it on.

"You brought the big one," Meg said. "Good. Let's go."

The cemetery hadn't been kept up very well. Hemlock Falls only had three employees in the Parks department and two of them subbed as snowplow drivers in the winter months. Last year's weeds poked up out of the melting snow. Several of the headstones had tipped to one side. The acreage was divided by narrow paths covered with a thin skin of gravel, and the paths were filled with holes. Meg trotted along determinedly, and Quill followed her, seeping the broad beam of the flashlight from side to side.

"Here's the fence," Meg stopped, pivoted, and picked her way through the short line of gravestones that comprised the last row.

Quill was hot in her down jacket and ski pants after the mild exercise. The air had a definite touch of spring and this cheered her. She tucked the flashlight under one arm and unzipped her jacket.

Meg's voice floated out of the darkness. "Shine the light over here."

The name on the gravestone read: WILLIAM QUILL 1848-TO 1862. MAY ANGELS SPEED THY REST.

"Okay," Meg said. "Dig away."

Quill balked. "I thought you were going to dig."

"You start."

Quill shook her head. "I don't think I can. This is a real person."

"Then he'll have a real coffin."

"It'll be six feet deep!"

"We won't dig that far. If Gallagher is here, Moody wouldn't have buried him six feet deep."

"You think it's Gallagher, too?" Quill desperate for reassurance, peered at her sister in the dark.

"I do," Meg said grimly. "I'll bet you my best sauté pan that Moody killed him twenty-five years ago to keep him from testifying. And I'll bet you Moody killed Bouncer to keep him from accusing Moody of murder."

"Oh, ugh." Quill sat down on the ground, "I don't think I can do this."

"We came all the way here, and I'm not going to chicken out now." Meg sat down beside her and said, "Look. What if you weren't an artist and I weren't a chef and we'd joined the forensics unit of the Tompkins County Police Force? And suppose we were assigned to the detail to dig up the possible grave of a possible murder victim? Would your principles force you to refuse? You'd lose your job!"

"True," Quill admitted.

"Give me the shovel. Now, where do you think I should start?"

Quill stood up, pulled Meg to her feet, and swept the flashlight over the mound of dirt. "Let's just start scraping, sort of. In the middle."

Meg took a firm grip on the shovel. She made a sound like *gguuuuaaagh* and scraped lightly at the mound of dirt.

"Oh, for heaven's sake! We'll be here til next Sunday if you do it like that." Quill took the shovel from her and scraped away the snow mounded on top.

"Good grief," Meg leaned over and moved the flashlight up and down. "This is fresh dirt."

"Are you surprised?"

"You aren't?"

"No, I think that Corliss did what we're doing. Maybe he discovered that William Quill lived to be ninety-three and didn't die in the Civil War after all. Maybe he found out William Quill was reburied somewhere else by his family. That happened, you know. I think Moody discovered Corliss digging this grave up and killed him. You remember how much he wanted to talk to the judge? He got Moody out here to see for himself and whack! Moody hit him with a rock, or something. Corliss was found here, you know. Stoke was walking that little dog they adopted and—"

"I know," Meg said. "Well, poor Mr. Hooker made it easier for us, I guess."

Quill took small shovelfuls, testing the ground beneath with the point before she dug in and lifted. The ground was packed down, but not tightly, as if someone had tamped it down with their feet. In a matter of five minutes, she'd cleared a hole about eighteen inches wide and eight inches deep. She pushed the shovel gently down and struck something. She swallowed hard.

"Shall I take a turn?"

"No. Just shine the light down there." She shut her eyes. "Oh dear, I hope it's not a skull."

"After all those anatomy classes in art school? Phut! Here. Give me the shovel."

Meg scraped carefully away, then leaped back.

"What?!" Quill grabbed Meg by the arm. "What do you see?"

"Sorry. I just didn't expect it." Meg took several deep breaths, calming herself. "Look for yourself."

Quill crouched down and directed the light into the hole. She sat back, suddenly. She recognized that thick, distinctive graying hair.

Meg knelt by her anxiously. "Are you okay?" she put her arm around Quill, supporting her neck with one cold hand. "It's Gallagher, isn't it? We were right!"

"The body's warm, and ugh-ugh-ugh-Meg. It's fresh. It's not Gallagher. It's Moody!"

Davey Kiddermeister's chief asset as deputy sheriff was that he was an even-tempered man. His sister Kathleen had been head waitress at the Inn for nine years, and she was even-tempered, too. The Kiddermeister clan, as a whole, rarely lost its cool. Quill was taken aback to discover that Davey's unflappability had its limits.

"I just don't *get* it, Quill! What the hell were you doing out here?!"

Quill and Meg sat in the back of the police cruiser. The back door was open. Davey leaned over them. He shouted, "Aaagh!" and then "Jeez!"

He was in a swivet.

Quill opened her mouth to protest.

"And don't tell me you two were just out for a walk. Jeez. Jeeez!" He backed away, straightened up, looked up at the heavens, and jammed both hands in his pockets.

Quill cleared her throat. "We were pretty sure that Moody had something to do with Bouncer's death."

"So you swanked on down here to dig up a hundred-and-forty-five-year-old grave? *Why?* How did you know it was Moody?"

"That will take a little explanation. We didn't know it was—"

"Be quiet." He took a deep breath. "Please, be quiet, I mean. Just tell me one thing. I mean it, Quill. I want to the truth. You didn't put him there, did you?"

"Us?" Meg said. "You think we sliced off Moody's head and buried him on top of Gallagher? If we'd done that, David Kiddermeister, why would we have called you to tell you we'd discovered the body?"

"Who knows why you two do what you do. I sure as hell don't. And who the hell is Gallagher?!"

"That's part of the explanation," Meg said crossly. "Can we go home now?"

"You gave your statements to Harper?"

Quill shuddered. "Yes."

"Then sure. Go on. Beat it. Get out of here."

Quill waited until Davey stamped off to the gravesite, then she and Meg both got out of the cruiser and headed for the Escort. The reporters hadn't started to arrive yet, but that was only a matter of time. Yellow police tape cordoned off the whole cemetery and there were six black-and-whites parked at all angles in front of the wrought-iron gates. People were standing outside their homes, some wrapped in blankets, some in their winter coats. Quill looked at her watch. "Gosh, it's only nine-thirty. Can we make it back to the Inn by ten? Dina thinks Myles might call."

"Might or will?"

"She wasn't sure if it was ten our time or ten his time. She said there was a lot of interference."

Meg turned the ignition on and pulled carefully onto the street. "Andy's back tomorrow, thank god. I'm going to be glad to see him. This is getting to be too much for me, Quill."

"Mm."

Meg glanced over at her. "What now?"

"What now? Isn't it obvious? Our theories have been blown sky high. Our most likely suspect is dead. Now we have to figure out who killed Moody."

Quill parted with Meg at the door to her rooms and let herself in. It was after eleven o'clock. The light at the computer desk was on, and the clutter of printouts had been tidied and stacked on the oak chest she used as a coffee table.

Quill stripped down to her T-shirt and jeans and flung her coat into her small hall closet. A familiar duffle bag sat on the floor next to her boots. She whirled. Myles stood at her bedroom door, his face lit in a welcoming smile.

Quill ran to him, her heart alive with surprise and joy.

"Well," she said, her voice muffled against his chest. "It's about time you showed up."

CHAPTER 10

"The jurors want to pack up and leave right now, Sheriff," Davey said. "I told 'em 'no.' You think that's the right thing to do?"

Myles looked up from the plate of eggs Benedict Quill had prepared for him. Davey had called her rooms at eight that morning, apologizing for the early hour, but urgent with distress. Quill had gotten less than five hours sleep, but she felt wonderful. She'd showered, pulled on jeans and a bronze sweater that matched her hair, and flung the French doors open to the first warm day they'd had in months. She fielded a somewhat anxious call from Meg at eight-thirty and then made breakfast. When the deputy had arrived at nine, she had settled both of them at her small breakfast table and told Myles everything she could about the discovery of the two bodies in the cemetery,

She smiled at Davey now, and gestured toward the third chair at the table. "Would you like some coffee? If you have a few minutes, I can make you breakfast, as well."

"Thank you, Quill, but I should really get back down to the lobby." He shifted his gaze back to Myles, and he said again, "So what do you think?" He sat down at Quill's small dining room table in a very tentative way. "I've already written up a preliminary report. You might want to take a look at it."

Myles shook his head slightly. "I'm only back for a few days, David. I don't know that I can be of much help."

Quill looked at him anxiously. He was thinner. The gray at his temples had increased. And the lines around his gray eyes seemed deeper. There was a scar on his left hand that hadn't been there before. She reached over and ran her thumb lightly over it. Myles clasped her hand in his, pushed his chair back, and extended his long legs.

"As far as the jurors are concerned, I think you can take their statements and let them go on home. My guess is a mistrial will be declared some time today and the whole case will have to be heard over again."

"But what if one of them killed the judge?"

"Are any of them flight risks? Do you have enough evidence to hold any of them for questioning? Did any of them witness the murder itself?"

"Harper's taking statements from them now. That's another thing, Sheriff. The staties are trying to take the case over. Something about the location of the cemetery . . ."

"Harper's a problem," Myles said.

"Do you mean he's a problem because of the jurisdiction issue or a problem because he's a son-of-a—sorry, Quill.

Quill waved his apology away. "You don't have to worry about the jurors, Davey. I mean, you do, of course. But what about Ferris Rodman?"

"Quill," Myles said patiently, "there isn't any evidence linking Rodman to illegal activities. And as far as I know there's no reason to link him to Moody. I think we can forget Rodman for the moment."

"But . . ."

Myles squeezed her hand briefly, then rose from his chair. "I'll be with you in a moment, David. I'll see you in the foyer."

Davey settled his hat on his head, nodded good-bye to Quill and left. Myles drew Quill close to him and stroked her cheek. "Why don't you take the morning and start those preliminary drawings you told me about? The ones of the resort site. I liked that idea, Quill. It's a good one."

"Draw when the Inn's set on its ears?" She pushed her self away from him. "I don't think I could."

"Then why don't you and Meg take what's her name, Corisande, out for a drive. From what you've told me, she hasn't had much of a chance to see Hemlock Falls."

Quill studied him. He was in his early fifties. His life as a homicide detective at the NYPD had left its mark—not just the physical scars on his chest and back—but in the way he viewed their life together. She'd fought his refusal to let her into the feelings that drove his life in law enforcement, and she'd go on fighting it. Probably, she thought ruefully, until they were both too old to do much more than bang their walkers against the floor.

"I do need to talk to Corisande this morning, but there's a couple of more important things to do first."

His voice hardened. "This is a police matter, Quill."

"I know enough not to interfere with an ongoing investigation . . ."

"Which is why you and Marge spent the evening as a guest of the county two nights ago?"

"I don't know why Dina had to blabber on about that," Quill said crossly. "Besides, I discovered that Rodman is very likely connected to—"

"Quill."

"I did! And that's a vital piece of evidence!"

"It might be," he said cautiously. "Although Purvis, for one, has known about the application to the gaming commission for months."

"You knew about it, too" Quill said. "Why didn't you tell me?"

Myles hesitated. "I'd rather not go into that right now."

Quill put her hands on her hips. "Oh. You wouldn't? Well, what about poor Bouncer Muldoon and that whole traffic ac . . ." Quill stopped in mid-sentence. "Oh my, somebody has to see to poor Mrs. Pembroke. I forgot all about her. I feel just awful. She lost her daughter and now this. And Meg seemed to need some help in the kitchen." She took a deep breath, determined not to fall prey to distractions. "I have a full morning."

"That's a good. And after you've settled the kitchen, take Corisande for a drive."

His tone of voice was maddening. Quill bit her lip. She absolutely refused to get into an argument with Myles the minute he came back to her.

Myles shrugged himself into his sports coat, gathered his keys, and picked up the raincoat he wore every season of the year except summer. He smiled and kissed her "The information about the accident that killed Ellen Moody? That was good detective work," he said. "And, my darling, it is an important piece of information. But it's time for you and Meg to let the process take over. Agreed?"

Quill picked up her coffee mug. "Would you like to take this with you?"

He shook his head. "I'll see you at seven or so, if not before."

Quill walked up and folded her arms around his neck. "I love you. I don't know why, but I do." She kissed him twice and watched as he let himself out the door. "Stay out of the line of fire, Myles!"

She recombed her hair and went to discover how much havoc the discovery of a second corpse had wreaked in the kitchen.

"I am not happy," Bjarne said. He folded his arms across and looked at her mournfully.

Meg wasn't in the kitchen, but Bjarne was. In a reassuring fit of pragmatism, (he was, after all, a chef, and as prone to displays of temperament as her sister) he had set up a breakfast buffet in the dining room. The people in line for pickled herring, sour cream scrambled eggs, and freshly-baked brioche included the lawyers, the jurors, several state troopers, and several reporters. Doreen had set up a cash box at the head of the line and collected cash with satisfied air.

"I'm sorry you're not happy," Quill said. "Nobody could be happy at this turn of events, Bjarne. But you've coped beautifully. Did Meg—"

"Bodies?" Bjarne snapped his fingers in the air. "I care this for bodies. Working here I am used to bodies, although I must tell you, Quill, that in Finland, the murder rate is not so high."

"I'm sorry about that, too. Not that Finland has fewer murders—I'm glad about that." She stopped. How had she gotten onto the murder rate in Finland? "Did Meg step out for a minute? I thought I'd—"

"I am not happy with my life."

Quill didn't clutch her head with both hands, although she wanted to. "Bjarne, this isn't quite the time."

"Yes," he said bitterly. "You don't have the time. Meg does not have the time. Claude de Courcy? He has the time."

"Claude de Courcy is not coming to Hemlock Falls," Quill said loudly.

"He is not?"

"He is not."

"Do you swear that this is true?"

Quill decided she could swear to a lot of things—*at* a lot of things, one of them being her Finnish cook—but she couldn't swear to the lie direct.

"I don't know," she confessed. "He may be. But it won't be for a long, long time yet. Not for months, at least."

"You will tell me if he comes?"

"I will, Bjarne, I promise. And if you want to leave to cook with someone else, then you certainly can."

"You will write me a good recommendation?"

"I will. But before you make any decisions, Bjarne, you should know that you do a wonderful job for us here. You'd be missed, if you left, of course, but I want what's best for you, always "

"Then perhaps I will not go." He smiled at her. "It is good that we talk now and then, isn't it? That's all we need. A few words of encouragement. So. You are wishing to find Meg. She is with that Mrs. Pembroke, I believe. In the Provençal suite."

Quill left the kitchen feeling guilty. Bjarne was right. She didn't take the time to tell the employees how important they were and what a good job they were doing and what happened when she failed in that most basic of all managerial responsibilities? Bjarne went and got Dina to type up his C.V. She went into the dining room. There was Doreen, collecting money for the breakfast buffet. Money that they would have lost if Doreen hadn't taken it upon herself to pitch in.

Quill stopped and put an affectionate hand on her housekeeper's shoulder. "Everything going all right?"

Doreen glared up at her, "That Corisande . . ." she began.

"I've neglected her, too. I know. Doreen I don't tell you enough how much we appreciate you around here. But we do. I just wanted you to know that. I know Corisande's been difficult. After I go up and see poor Mrs. Pembroke and Meg, I'll find Corisande and we'll start all over again."

"That'll be a trick and half. She's gone."

"Who's gone?"

"That Corisande. Packed up her bags and skedaddled. Left her rooms a mess, too."

"She's gone!?" Quill said. "Oh, no! What am I going to tell Aunt Eleanor? This is awful! Did you see her go?"

"Nope. Just went to do her room like always and all the stuff was outa there."

Despite her best efforts, the morning was getting away from her. Quill counted backward from ten, which sometimes helped, but didn't this time. Then she took several deep breaths. This made her dizzy. Then she decided that if Meg had been with Mrs. Pembroke, why hadn't she said so? And that most of this was Meg's fault. She wasn't sure why, but at least she could yell at her sister, and her sister at least, wouldn't threaten to quit or pack up all her bags and march out the door without a word to anybody.

Quill stepped out of the way of the brunch line and spent several minutes feeling awful about Corisande.

"Quill?" Dina tapped her on the shoulder.

"Not now, Dina, honestly. I can't stand it. Did I tell you you're doing a really good job, by the way? You are. You're terrific. And if you're standing there to tell me you're about to quit and go work at the Marriott or something—what is it?" She really looked at Dina. Dina had a very strange expression on her face. "What?!"

"There's someone here. In the lobby."

"It's not Melvin Purvis, is it? I don't have any time for Melvin Purvis."

Dina wheeled and marched toward the foyer without a word. Quill followed her, saw who was in the lobby, and stopped as if she'd been struck down in stone.

The girl in the lobby was in her mid to late twenties. She was about Meg's height. A wealth of red gold hair tumbled over her shoulders. Her eyes were the color of sherry. She was slender, with a hopeful, eager expression that was very very familiar.

Quill's mother had looked like that.

"This," Dina said, "is Corisande Quilliam."

"Hi!" She had an attractive, low-pitched voice. "Mom was getting a little worried that her e-mails weren't getting through. Did you know that I got stuck in Amsterdam? Somebody stole my ticket!"

The in-house line rang at the desk. Dina picked it up and said, "Yeah, she's here, but Meg, you'll never guess what."

Quill enveloped Corisande in a hug. "We'll figure this out," she said happily, "but I can't tell you how glad I am to see you."

"*Quill!*" Dina's voice was sharp. "Sorry, sorry, I didn't mean to yell. But Meg's upset. Can you go on up to Mrs. Pembroke's room right now?"

Quill released the real, genuine, Corisande and said, "I have to make a quick run upstairs to get Meg. Don't go anywhere, okay? Dina. Can you see if she needs any food or something to drink . . . I'll be right back."

Quill took the stairs two at a time and arrived at the Provençal suite a little out of breath. The door was slightly ajar, so she tapped on the frame and pushed it open.

There was something behind it. Frowning, Quill, called out and pushed harder. A trickle of blood came out from the bottom of the frame. Quill threw her shoulder against the door and pushed. She stumbled into the room.

The first thing she saw was Max. The dog lay with his broad back to the door and his muzzle pointing toward the French doors that led to the balcony over the Falls. There was blood on his neck. His flanks moved rapidly in and out.

The second thing she saw was her sister, paler than she had ever seen her before. She sat curled up in one of the fake Louis XVIII chairs that sat at either end of the round breakfast table in front of the windows.

Mrs. Pembroke sat in the other. There was a gun in her hand and the gun was pointed at Meg. Mitchell Moody's pocket watch was strung on a gold chain around her neck.

"There you are," Mrs. Pembroke said. "We couldn't finish until you got here. I need two witnesses, you see."

She lifted the gun to her temple and fired.

"Every other time in my life that I've needed you, you've come at a gallop," Meg complained. "Even when I *don't* need you, you come at a gallop. And the one time I really, really need you, you take your own sweet time about it. I was up in that damn suite for hours."

Meg sat with her back the French doors overlooking the terrace of the Tavern Bar. The rest of them—Quill, Myles, Andy, and Corisande—were gathered in a circle around her.

"Stop," Quill said. "I'm sorry. Plus, I am sorry that I'm tired of saying I'm sorry, but I am." She looked over at Corisande and smiled. The real Corisande preferred Cory, just as the fake one had. And the real one loved Max. The dog sat with his head on her knees. He had a cone around his neck, to prevent him from pulling out his own stitches.

"I think," Cory said, "that this is the most exciting place I've ever been in my life." She fondled Max's ears. He looked at her adoringly.

Andy Bishop, back from his seminar, sat next to Meg. His eyes never left her face. Quill sat next to Myles, her hip touching his thigh in a comfortable way.

Cory sipped at her wine and cradled it thoughtfully in one slender hand. "I'm not sure I completely understand what happened, though. I know that Mrs. Pembroke," she bit her lip, "that is, she killed herself because she'd hired this woman who stole my airline ticket to kill her son-in-law and Bouncer? Was that his name? But didn't you say that the car accident happened twenty-five years ago? I can understand that she wanted revenge. But why did she wait so long?"

Meg rubbed fiercely at her temples, as if to get rid of something none of the others saw. Let me back track a minute. I went up to see that Mrs. Pembroke was okay about eight-fifteen that morning. She didn't come down to breakfast with the rest of the jurors, and I was worried about her. So I took a breakfast tray with me. I thought that Moody's death would be a real blow. I mean, she never got over her own daughter's death, and she and Moody seemed to be close. Anyhow, Max came along with me, you know, the way he pokes his nose into everything. I set the tray down. She pulled the gun on me as soon as put it on the table. Max growled and lunged at her. She grabbed the knife from the bread basket and stabbed him in the neck. He staggered over to the door and fell down. Then she told me to get you, Quill, because she had something to say to the both of us. I tried to get up to help Max and she pulled the safety off the gun and cocked it. So I sat. And while I sat, she told me everything.

"She started the set-up work on the ROCOR trial months ago. She came to see you, Quill, and I guess you told her about Aunt Eleanor."

"I did," Quill said, remembering. "She was talking

about how hard it was to lose her daughter, and she asked if we had any family."

"Yeah. That started it. At the beginning, she was after Bouncer, you know. She was the one who killed Corky Gallagher—or rather had him killed. And believe it or not, she was the one who smacked Corliss Hooker over the head when he discovered Gallagher's body in that grave. You were right, Quill. There was something funny about William Quill. He was supposed to be buried K-34. What Corliss discovered is that the headstone had been moved to K-47. And then when he dug down to see if there was a coffin there, bingo. He comes on Corky's twenty-five-year-old bones. He tries to reach Moody to get him to authorize an investigation and, of course, tells his loyal F.O.D buddy Mrs. Pembroke all about it.

"Anyway, Mrs. Pembroke knew four weeks ago that Bouncer Muldoon was in the jury pool. So she went online and brought an assassin to Hemlock Falls."

Quill held her hand up. "Hold it right there. I have a really hard time believing that Louise Pembroke could find an assassin online. What did she do, Google 'gun for hire'?"

Meg smiled faintly. "I asked her that. She was a trusted employee attached to a federal courthouse for more than thirty years, you know. She talked her way into getting access to closed federal cases involving terrorists and assassins-for-hire. And she spent a lot of nights online. She even adopted a cyber-persona. She called herself Jason."

Quill drew back in distaste. "After the horror film character? That doesn't sound like Mrs. Pembroke."

"I should think she was referring to Medea," John offered.

Meg nodded. "Medea murdered Jason's children. Mrs. Pembroke said it seemed an apt name for a mother bent on revenge. Anyway . . . because she didn't know when and where she could get access to Bouncer, she wanted someone who could hang around a town this small and not be noticed. So she picked on us.

"And Mrs. Pembroke's a pretty good hacker. She Googled you, Quill, and you have that bio your gallery posts for you. Mrs. Pembroke just picked through the whole thing until she found Aunt Eleanor. Aunt Eleanor's a well-known journalist. She has a bio, too, which lists Corisande as her daughter. And, of course, Aunt Eleanor can be reached through the *New York Times*. So Mrs. Pembroke hacked into the Inn website, wrote an e-mail from you to Eleanor asking her if Corisande could come and visit. Eleanor responded, you got the e-mail, and Mrs. Pembroke kept intercepting the correspondence. She knew Cory's flight schedule, for example, so Ms. Tomb Raider or whatever her real name is could swipe her ticket and strand her in Amsterdam. Mrs. Pembroke sent you the picture of Ms. Tomb Raider, too. The internet," Meg brooded, "has a lot to answer for."

"Wow," Quill said. "And all this time, you thought it was Ferris Rodman."

Meg's cheeks grew pink. "*You* thought it was Ferris Rodman!"

"Okay, so we both thought it was Ferris Rodman. I still think there's something funny about him." She glanced at Myles. "There is, isn't there?"

"I don't think we want to talk about that, just yet."

Quill sighed, "There's something going on there, Myles. I can feel it."

"I think this is the most exciting place," Corisande said. "It's funny. I was almost positive that . . ." she broke off and blushed an attractive shade of pink. "Do you know? I thought I was going to be bored in Hemlock Falls."

THE WORLD'S BEST OMELET

Meg ended up serving this omelet at the April meeting of the Hemlock Grenadiers Volunteer Police Department Brunch. In return, they tore up all her kitchen violations, and she didn't have to move her refrigerator after all.

(Serving for two)

4 oz. cream cheese, softened
1/2 c. chopped smoked salmon
4 tablespoons chopped chives
1 tablespoon very good mustard
Mix well.
4 eggs
1 tablespoon cream
1 tablespoon flour
Beat until frothy.

Melt two tablespoons butter and a dash of olive oil into an eight-inch sauté pan. Heat on medium high until butter is melted and slightly brown. Pour egg mixture into pan and cook, running the tip of a spatula around the edges so that the mixture cooks evenly.

When the omelet is cooked, remove from pan, spread with mixture, fold over, and return to pan. Cook about fifteen seconds on one side; flip and warm the other side.

Serves two.

CLAUDIA BISHOP is the author of twelve Hemlock Falls mysteries and is at work on the next. She divides her time between a cattle ranch in upstate New York and a home in West Palm Beach. She can be reached at www.claudiabishop.com.

Hungry for another
Hemlock Falls Mystery?

CLAUDIA BISHOP

A Puree of Poison	0-425-19331-4
Fried by Jury	0-425-18994-5
Just Desserts	0-425-18431-5
Marinade for Murder	0-425-17611-8
A Touch of the Grape	0-425-16397-0
Death Dines Out	0-425-16111-0
A Pinch of Poison	0-425-15104-2
A Dash of Death	0-425-14638-3
A Taste for Murder	0-425-14350-3

Available wherever books are sold or at
www.penguin.com

B026

*Get cozy with a cup of coffee and
a delicious mystery.*

The Coffeehouse Mystery series
by Cleo Coyle

On What Grounds

Clare Cosi is the manager of the historic
Village Blend in Greenwich Village in
New York City. Life is looking pretty good until
one of her employees is attacked in the shop.
Could Clare be the next target?

"CLEO COYLE IS A BRIGHT NEW LIGHT
ON THE MYSTERY HORIZON."
—BEST REVIEWS

0-425-19213-X

The Coffeehouse Mystery series continues with
Through the Grinder
0-425-19714-X

Available wherever books are sold or at
www.penguin.com

NANCY FAIRBANKS

The Culinary Mystery series with recipes

Crime Brûlée   0-425-17918-4

Carolyn accompanies her husband to an academic conference
in New Orleans. But just as she gets a taste of Creole, she gets a
bite of crime when her friend Julienne disappears at a dinner
party.

Truffled Feathers   0-425-18272-X

The CEO of a large pharmaceutical company has invited
Carolyn and her husband to the Big Apple for some serious
wining and dining. But before she gets a chance to get a true
taste of New York, the CEO is dead. Was it high cholesterol or
high crime?

Death à l'Orange   0-425-18524-9

It's a culinary tour de France for Carolyn Blue and her family
as they travel through Normandy and the Loire valley with a
group of academics. But when murder shows up on the menu,
Carolyn is once again investigating crime as well as cuisine.

Chocolate Quake   0-425-18946-5

Carolyn's trip to San Francisco includes a visit to her mother-in-
law, a few earthquake tremors, and a stint in prison as a murder
suspect. A column about prison food might be a change of pace.

The Perils of Paella   0-425-19390-X

Carolyn is excited to be in Barcelona visiting her friend Roberta,
who is the resident scholar at the modern art museum. When an
actor is killed during a performance art exhibit, Carolyn must
get to the bottom of the unsavory crime.

B415

The Tea Shop Mystery Series by

LAURA CHILDS

DEATH BY DARJEELING

0-425-17945-1

Meet Theodosia Browning, owner of Charleston's
beloved Indigo Tea Shop. Theo enjoys the full-
bodied flavor of a town steeped in history—
and mystery.

GUNPOWDER GREEN

0-425-18405-6

Shop owner Theodosia Browning knows that
something's brewing in the high society
of Charleston—murder.

SHADES OF EARL GREY

0-425-18821-3

Theo is finally invited to a social event that she
doesn't have to cater—but trouble is brewing at the
engagement soiree of the season.

Available wherever books are sold or to order call at
www.penguin.com